CASINO QADDAFI

GRAHAM TEMPEST

BRIGHTWAY PRESS

CASINO QADDAFI
Brightway Press, 522 Hunt Club Blvd., Apopka, Florida 32703
ISBN (print) 978-0-9996727-5-4, bp#260515

"I am a Bedouin warrior who brought glory to Libya and will die a martyr."

Muammar al Qaddafi

Colonel Qaddafi was killed in October, 2011. These events occurred just after his death.

PROLOGUE – TRIPOLI

NOVEMBER, 2011

Staccato gunfire crackled; a vivid flash lit up the night sky. The driver of the limousine carrying Kathy Smith cursed and changed course, turning onto a narrow side street and accelerating away from the fighting.

Damn, thought Kathy.

She leaned back against the cushioned leather, her shoulders tense, trying to control her breathing as the vehicle sped on towards Tripoli's five-star Corinthia Hotel.

'What the hell have I got myself into?' she muttered, half aloud.

She had a hollow feeling in her stomach, a physical sign that she was heading for the edge. It would not be the first time. She was academically bright, with a postgraduate degree in finance from USC, but she was also accident prone and here she was again, heading smack into danger. It showed real attitude to keep taking such risks with her own safety.

She was still determined to track down Muammar Qaddafi's natural son and the young man's rumoured fortune. So far, that had involved only some desk research and a lively meeting with Carlton Tisch at his villa on Tortola. Her Lufthansa flight from Miami to Frankfurt had been routine and the onward trip via Vienna uneventful, but now she had a dreadful sense that life was about to get real.

The driver heard her speak, but he said nothing. He spoke passable English – he often chatted with passengers from abroad – but he had trained himself to be discreet and, when in doubt, to say as little as possible. Who was this girl? A journalist perhaps? Libya was not the sort of place where a young woman should be travelling alone, but the Americans were different.

She leaned forward.

'What's your name?'

'Faroukh.'

'What do you think of all this? You must be delighted that Qaddafi's gone, right?'

He shrugged. Fortyish, shaven-headed, white shirt straining to contain an incipient paunch, he was not cut from revolutionary cloth. He had a wife and family. The Qaddafi state had raised him. It provided a house and schooling for his children. He could not see how the recent overthrow and lynching of Muammar Qaddafi would help him personally.

'These are dangerous times,' he said.

'But the new government is better, isn't it?'

How could he explain? There was no government.

There was something called the Transitional Council but it had no real power. It certainly did not control the militias, some of which were no more than ragged bands of youngsters led by petty despots with incoherent agendas. They roamed the streets at will, looting and bullying.

He mustered a smile. 'Dangerous times,' he repeated.

'How long before we get to the hotel?' she asked.

'Five minutes.'

She was not reassured. She had asked the same question a quarter of an hour ago and got the same answer.

She felt in her purse for her new phone. In the store, the salesman had assured her that it would work anywhere in the world. What about Libya? she had asked.

'Anywhere,' he smiled. He looked about sixteen.

She would soon find out. She pressed the speed-dial key for her friend Mimi on Tortola.

'Hi, Kathy.' The response was scratchy but audible. Kathy almost wept with relief.

Mimi was Carlton Tisch's young third wife and, by the look of things, his last – a retired Playboy Bunny from Liverpool with a level head on her shoulders. She and Kathy were both 25. Carlton was 60.

'What's happening?' asked Kathy. She made herself speak as though nothing out of the ordinary was going on.

'Not much. Lower down!' The last words clearly meant for Carlton. 'Carl's giving me a back rub. Where are you?'

'I'm in a taxi in Tripoli.'

A long pause. 'Did you say Tripoli?'

She bit her tongue. She had not told Mimi or Carlton that she was going to Libya. They had discussed it but Carlton had just looked thoughtful and counselled caution.

Mimi said, 'He wants to talk to you.'

The next voice was Carlton's; New York, sharp-edged.

'I hope I misheard my wife. Tell me you're in Tripoli, Iowa, not Tripoli, Libya.'

'I had to come here. It's where he is.'

'He?'

'Hassan.'

'Allegedly,' Carlton snapped.

'Certainly.'

'It's very dangerous.'

An almost pleading note had entered his voice. She could picture him, thin and intense, relaxing with Mimi at their Caribbean villa. His manner was gruff but underneath, she knew, he cared deeply for his wife and her friend.

'Don't believe the TV,' she said. 'You know how they exaggerate.'

'That's not what I heard. There is no law and order, the militias are everywhere.'

'It's okay, really.' She spoke with a confidence she was far from feeling.

'Well I think you are very foolish. You should have waited.'

'Waited for what?'

'I could have sent someone with you – Kon, or Oliver.'

'If I know Oliver, he'll be here himself soon. He must realise he can achieve nothing without Hassan.'

Carlton was silent. She had presented a *fait accompli* and they both knew it.

'What are your plans?' he asked.

'I'm meeting Victor Berg at the hotel.'

'Well, be careful.'

The line went dead.

The limousine approached a multi-storey glass and steel building with a Moorish-style façade.

The Corinthia Hotel looked a bit like a fortress which, in a sense, it was. Amid the turmoil, it provided a refuge for expatriates. Maltese owned, it was a haven where the wi-fi worked, the beer was cold, and the service, considering the chaos swirling around outside, was still good.

'Is this it?'

'Yes, ma'am.'

A commissionaire stepped forward and opened the car door. She climbed out of the vehicle and marched into the hotel.

Already she felt better.

Berg sat on a sofa in the hotel lounge with an untouched glass of Perrier in front of him.

He was Swiss, a lawyer in his country's foreign ministry, his job being to identify the assets of former dictators around the world – 'potentate funds' – and return them to their rightful owners.

The lounge was almost empty. Two middle-aged men in suits were having an intense conversation over what looked like martinis but were probably mineral water – per Libyan law, no alcohol was served. They were too well dressed for journalists, he thought; they must be bankers, or oil executives.

Across the room, a couple of young Arabs sipped

coffee nervously; their keffiyehs looked out of place in the Western décor.

There was an early-evening trickle of guests arriving, but he had not seen a young woman of Western appearance. Then the glass doors swung open. The woman who came in could only be Kathy Smith. Blonde, with an aura of Midwest cheerleader, her skirt uncompromisingly short, her smile a mile wide.

Victor stood up and waved. Kathy saw him and waved back. He looked neat and personable. She was encouraged. In a strange culture, a reassuring presence was welcome.

They sipped Turkish coffee.

'Well, I must say you have strong nerves, coming here,' said Berg. He did not sound pleased.

She smiled. 'So have you.'

'Things are very unstable, after Qaddafi's death.'

'I read that he was pulled from a culvert, shot and his body dragged through the streets,' she said.

'Yes, it happened.'

'But that was a month ago. The war is over. Surely things have calmed down by now?'

'Not really. The problem is that there is nobody to take his place.'

'What about the Transitional Council?'

Berg shook his head. 'Ineffective. The militias do whatever they want.'

'That's anarchy.'

'Yes, it is. Nobody is safe. A few days ago, a Libyan former diplomat was called in for questioning by militiamen. The next day, his family found his dead body at a local hospital. His nose was broken and so were his ribs. There were cigarette burns all over his body.'

There was sudden movement from the two Arabs. They leaped to their feet and sprinted across the marble floor. Producing pistols, they shoved Berg aside and grabbed Kathy by the arms. They frog-marched her over to the main entrance and out into the street and pushed her into the back seat of a waiting car.

The car disappeared into the night.

Victor Berg's intelligent face sagged with horror.

It had all happened in seconds.

1

SEVERAL WEEKS EARLIER

I was roundly cursing Carlton Tisch as I sprinted through San Juan airport, briefcase in hand and passports – both the US and the UK versions – in pocket.

I am a forensic accountant. I trace people's money that has gone missing. Since nine out of ten people only vaguely know what 'forensic' means, I carry business cards that say 'Oliver Steele, Financial Sleuth'. I know it's a Mickey Mouse sort of thing to do but they are meant to be amusing and put people at their ease.

I was racing to catch a flight to Tortola BVI that was leaving in ten minutes. I dislike last-minute panics but Carlton had summoned me and he can't bear to be kept waiting. He is my biggest client and he writes the cheques. Annoyingly, his phone call had cut short a weekend's fishing with my buddy Kon, a grizzled Israeli who lives on Coquina Key and usually knows where the marlin are biting.

After all that, the plane was late – island airlines tend to run on island time. I collapsed on a bench to collect my thoughts.

This was my new life. Three years ago I was a confident young accountant with a squeaky clean résumé – expensive boarding school followed by Oxford, junior partner in a respected firm. But then came disaster. I was tricked by my boss into signing off on a phony balance sheet. Lawsuits followed. He went to prison; I went bankrupt, owing a million pounds. I was obviously finished in London so, being American on my mother's side, I left England for Florida where I met Carlton, a pushy New York financier who keeps me supplied with investigative work. I am still bankrupt but hopeful that, sooner or later, earnings from people like him will bail me out. Regularly in the small hours I wake up wondering if that will ever happen.

The tiny Cessna, bucking and shaking in the heat, got me to Tortola's Terrance B. Lettsome International Airport. There, I rented a jeep – Tortola is a paradise but it has some truly dreadful

roads – and drove the 12 miles to Spring Point, Carlton's cliff-top eyrie on the far west tip of the island.

He was sitting in the sunshine, flip-flops kicked
off, clipping his toenails and reading a dog-eared
copy of *Vanity Fair*. His pale blue eyes were watery
from long days of sailing and his hollow cheeks were
dusted with salt. A gold Star of David nestled in the
grey curls on his skinny chest. His sun-dried face
showed a few creases at 60 but they were not worry
lines, more the result of wind and weather. Carlton
never smiles, but once you know him you don't
expect that.

'About time.'

I ignored him. You can't let Carlton get the upper
hand.

His modus is simple. He hangs out on his
terrace, shirtless, in underpants and Yankees base-
ball cap, hatching up schemes on the back of an
envelope with seven zeros attached, making it look
easy. The villa, designed by him and Mimi, makes
me sick with envy whenever I go there. It consists of
a series of interconnected island-style cabins that
cascade down the slope of the rocky extreme
western end of the island, looking out over blue
water towards St Thomas. With a year-round
temperature in the low eighties, fanned by the
gentlest of sailing breezes, if there's a better place to

sit in the sun and enjoy one's ill-gotten leisure I can't imagine where it would be.

He is of course very clever. The son of Prussian immigrants who ran a small deli on New York's Lower East Side, he has manoeuvred his way to a position of extreme wealth. But he is lazy. What he sees in me is someone, not brilliant but smart enough, who can do his legwork for him. So that is what I do. No false pride, just glad to be working.

'I see another car,' I said. 'Who's your guest?'

He nodded. 'Someone you know.'

From the house strolled a figure from the recent past, carrying an open can of Budweiser. An ultra-brief dark blue Speedo emphasized his muscular chest and bulging thighs.

Searching brown eyes gazed deep into mine as he gripped my hand and pumped it. 'Oliver, how are you? Boy, oh boy, long time no see.'

When your hand has been shaken by Michael Kalestian, it really knows it's been shaken. Luckily I knew the drill and was braced ready for him. It was a Las Vegas kind of greeting, but then Michael is a Las Vegas creature. The son of the legendary Armenian mogul Ara Kalestian, his deep voice and bushy black moustache make him seem much older than his 28 years.

He was a person of interest in a case last year. When his father was gunned down in Los Angeles, Michael inherited the Excelsior Casino, one of the biggest in Las Vegas. His loud and insensitive manner briefly led me to suspect him of killing his own father but, as it turned out, he was just not very emotionally attached to the man.

'How long has it been, buddy?' he gushed.

'Only six months,' I said. 'How's business?'

'Fantastic!'

'I've been reading that some of the Vegas casinos are in trouble,' I said.

There was an awkward pause.

'Michael wants to talk to you about that,' said Carlton.

Michael nodded earnestly. He took a deep breath as if gearing up for a major sales pitch.

'Let me ask you a couple of questions. First, does the name Hassan Qaddafi mean anything to you?'

'Qaddafi? Yes, obviously; Libya.'

'What about Hassan?'

I shook my head. 'Hassan – no, doesn't ring a bell.'

Michael smiled knowingly.

'Next question: How much do you know about Macau?' he asked.

I had to think. 'Isn't it a Portuguese colony on the coast of China, a sort of Portuguese Hong Kong?'

He shook his head. 'You are a decade out of date. I see I shall have to educate you.'

2

S tu Goldberg sat behind an expensive desk in an office high above Wall Street, looking for money.

It was something he spent a lot of his time doing. He was a banker, or at least called himself a banker because he was the president and largest individual shareholder of a bank, Goldberg Freilich Inc., of which he was the same Goldberg.

In actual fact, he knew very little about banking. What he *did* know was how to buy businesses. He was a takeover specialist who had chosen money as his target area. In his mind that included as broad a definition as possible – banking, stock broking, insurance, fund management, hard money lending, just about anything that remotely involved dollar signs.

He looked like a melancholy spaniel. Physically he was tall and narrow-shouldered, in his forties, with a large head topped with a heavy thatch of straight black hair. His pale face, lugubrious expression and sunken brown eyes made him look soft but appearances were deceptive, as anyone who had bid against him for a company knew; when necessary, he could move very fast with cheerful disregard for what was generally accepted as proper behaviour. Disgruntled rivals sniped that he had rewritten the ethical rule book in a way that shortened the text considerably.

From his 60th-floor office in the bank's headquarters on Wall Street, he could look down on the Statue of Liberty. On the desk was an extra sweet latte with a double shot of espresso. It came not from Starbucks but from the machine operated by his South African intern, Hansi. He slept with Hansi off and on, not because she was lovely, which she was, but to gratify his sense of ownership. She was like the Bentley, the yacht and the ski lodge in Davos, all of which he – or, to be precise, the bank – owned. It never ended, the pursuit of expensive toys to set him above and apart from his peers.

The bank made money by investing money, sometimes its own but more often – which for Stu was the real fun – other people's. The pursuit of money was crucial; it was a bank's life blood. That was one fact about banking that he did understand.

Next to the coffee cup on his desk was a list of so-called Sovereign Wealth funds, representing the money of a select group of unusually well-endowed countries:

Abu Dhabi

$627 billion

Kuwait

$260 billion

Qatar

$85 billion

Libya

$53 billion

Iran

$23 billion

Bahrain

$9 billion

Across the desk sat Jim Gelson, one of his junior vice presidents.

'Where did you get this list?'

'It was in last week's *Journal*.'

Gelson was a pallid young man with a beaky nose, John Lennon glasses and a humorous mouth. He was smiling a tad nervously in the presence of the big boss.

'Is it accurate?'

'Only at a point in time. Obviously the numbers will go up and down.'

The 'obviously' was mildly impertinent, but word around the office was that you had to stand up to Stu or else be quickly discounted to zero.

'It's not correct,' Goldberg barked.

'Why do you say that?'

He tapped the sheet. 'Are you trying to tell me that Abu Dhabi is twelve times as wealthy as Libya? Can't be right.'

Gelson adjusted the specs on his bony nose and peered at the list. 'I see what you mean.'

'So?'

'Maybe it's because of how some countries' wealth is owned,' Gelson ventured.

'Meaning?'

'Sometimes the wealth is, ah, distributed differently . . .'

Goldberg laughed shortly. 'Looted, you mean?'

'In a word.'

Goldberg seemed okay with that. He thought for a minute and lit a Cuban cigar. He was breaking various laws both state and federal, but this was his bank and, if anyone didn't like it, they could go whistle.

'How much money have these funds placed with us?'

Gelson coughed discreetly. 'Not much.'

'Why not?'

Gelson paused.

'We're a young bank.'

Goldberg frowned.

'Relatively speaking,' said Gelson quickly. 'We're growing fast of course, but investors like these are conservative; they tend to stay with the more established groups.'

'Such as?'

'J P Morgan Chase, Société Générale, Goldman Sachs – household names.'

Goldberg drew on his cigar. Gelson, who was asthmatic, coughed and leaned away.

'What about their rulers? Maybe we should approach them as individuals.'

Gelson was pretty sure that the big banks had thought of that already but he nodded brightly. 'Excellent thinking.'

Goldberg looked pleased. 'Do another list. Focus on the rulers' families; some of those dictators really like to spread it around.'

Gelson nodded.

'Make it detailed, something I can use. Take all the time you need.'

'Yes, sir.'

'Tomorrow morning will be fine.' Goldberg stood

up. He selected a squash racquet from the umbrella stand in the corner.

'I must go, I have a meeting.'

A few days later, Goldberg was studying the new list.

Gelson sat opposite.

After their first meeting, he had been up most of the night working feverishly to have the new list ready, only to get a call at nine am from the mini-skirted Hansi.

Stu had taken the Bentley and left for the week-end. Something about a French squash champion who had agreed to play an exhibition match on the private court at Stu's place in the Hamptons.

Hansi was charmingly apologetic. 'It was just too good a chance to miss,' she explained.

Gelson, who did not play squash, said nothing.

It was now Tuesday. Gelson had welcomed the extra time, to be truthful. He had found something he thought would intrigue the chairman.

'What am I looking at?' asked Goldberg. 'I see a lot of names, most of them Arabs. Arabs here, Arabs there, Arabs everywhere. I guess those sovereign wealth funds all belong to Arabs?'

'Except Iran,' Gelson pointed out.

'Aren't they Arabs?'

'Not really.'

Goldberg sniffed. 'Same difference.'

He pointed to a paragraph about Libya.

'Qaddafi had so many children. Who knew?'

The list of names, with birthdates, read:

Muhammad (1970)

Saif al-Islam (1972)

al-Saadi (1973)

Moatassem (1974)

Hannibal (1975)

Ayesha (1976)

Saif al-Arab (1982)

Khamis (1983)

Other (1986?)

'al-Saadi. Isn't he the soccer player?'

'That's right,' said Gelson.

'Some of this lot must have banking connections already.'

'That is true. Saif al-Islam has been seen palling around with a Rothschild; it might be tough to lure him away.'

'Who is this "Other"?'

Gelson smirked. 'I thought you might ask.'

'What's the story?' Goldberg was impatient.

'It concerns Colonel Qaddafi's marital fidelity, about which reports differ widely.'

'Meaning?'

'Some people loved him, others hated him. He is dead now, of course.'

'Didn't he blow up a Pan Am airliner? That would make him a murderer.'

'You are talking about the Lockerbie disaster over Scotland in 1988. Two hundred and seventy people died. Fifteen years later, under pressure, Libya acknowledged responsibility for the deaths and paid compensation to the families.'

'So?'

'On the other hand, his supporters remember him as a good Muslim who improved the lot of his subjects.'

'Is that true?'

'Well, he was one of the less tight-fisted in a region of dictators. He provided average Libyans with education, housing and medical care.'

'How was his personal life?'

'Again according to supporters, he was a good family man. After a brief first marriage resulting in one son, he met his wife Safiya by whom he had seven more children and they remained married for forty years.'

'Is there another side to that story?'

'Yes, and very different. A rampant egotist and unspeakable libertine who travelled with an all-female bodyguard, his so-called Amazonian Guard. The girls were sworn to celibacy, but some claim to have been raped by Qaddafi. Others were passed around among his associates. He's also alleged to have had sex with young men.'

'Which version do you believe?'

Gelson shrugged. 'It depends who you listen to. But it brings me to the "Other" reference.'

'Go on.'

'It is rumoured that the Brother Leader fathered a son by one of his Amazons.'

Goldberg raised his eyebrows. Gelson nodded

'My source for that titbit is a cousin of mine who knew the son, Hassan al-Manwani, as a fellow student at Columbia, where the Libyan was studying for an MBA.'

'The boy is not stupid, then.'

'Not at all. A shrewd young man who likes to invest. Word on campus was that he managed a large portfolio, courtesy of his dad.'

'Surprising that Qaddafi would favour a child from the wrong side of the blanket.'

'But true, apparently.'

'Let me see if I understand,' said Goldberg. 'Other banks may not know about this Hassan, since he only mentioned his investing activity to his fellow students casually, just guys chatting, so to speak, right?'

'That is correct.'

'So we may have an inside track. Something the

other banks don't know about.' A Cheshire cat smile was spreading across Goldberg's face.

Gelson looked doubtful. 'We don't know how much money he controls. It may not be very much.'

Goldberg shook his head stubbornly.

'It's worth a try. I want you to get on a plane to Tripoli or wherever he hangs out and make a pitch.'

Gelson blinked. The worry lines on his pale brow deepened. Something was clearly bothering him.

'You do know that I'm Jewish?'

'So am I, so what?'

'How will that play in Libya? Safety-wise, I mean.'

Goldberg waved the idea off.

'If you're nervous, we'll find some Arabs to go with you. Check with the London office. A bunch of them hang out there; they like the gambling and the easy women.'

'If you say so.'

'I do say so. I want you in Libya within a week.'

Gelson nodded.

But he did not look happy.

A week later, Jim Gelson was on a plane en route for Tripoli, via London. Such was the power of a direct order from the boss.

With him was a surprised 25-year-old Arab employee of Goldberg Freilich called Samir.

On the way from New York, Gelson had stopped off in London to visit Goldberg Freilich's UK office, located in the distinctive building at 30 St Mary Axe, known as the Gherkin. There, he had made contact with Samir.

Samir had joined the firm as an analyst a couple of months before. He was actually only half Arab, on his father's side. His parents met when his father, a young Lebanese from an affluent family in Beirut, was sent to England to acquire polish. His English mother, who at the time was learning to type at Mrs

Foster's Secretarial College in South Kensington, had been swept off her feet.

Samir followed in his father's footsteps, first to school at Eton and then to read law at Cambridge. As a result, he felt more British than Arab, but he did speak some Arabic. He also looked the part – slim and dark, with wavy black hair, brown eyes and an Omar Sharif smile.

They sipped coffee in a conference room on the 34th floor. When Stu Goldberg was told that the Gherkin was the most valuable building in London – it was sold in 2007 for a billion dollars – he knew immediately that he had to have an office there. Besides, the view towards St Paul's Cathedral was spectacular.

Gelson explained to Samir that he was now Goldberg Freilich's top Arab investment specialist and he must do his best to stay in character. He was promoted on the spot to the fine-sounding position of Senior Manager, Middle East, with a small increase in pay and some handsome business cards, printed overnight.

Gelson explained what he needed from Samir.

'We have to show these guys in Tripoli that we can grow their money faster than they could do for themselves.'

'How large is their portfolio?'

'I don't know.'

'What are they invested in?'

'Beats me.'

'What return are they earning?'

'I've no idea.'

Samir felt like asking, 'Then why the heck are we interested in this guy?' but he was a tactful young man and Gelson was obviously obeying orders from above, so he just nodded seriously.

Hurrying home to pack, he tossed a couple of books into his briefcase for the trip. One was *The Intelligent Investor* by Benjamin Graham. The other was called *How I used the Power of Positive Thinking to Make a Million Bucks Overnight*, by someone called Tex Finkelbaum.

On the plane, Gelson saw what Samir had brought. 'That book by Finkelbaum is all right, but lose the Ben Graham stuff, okay?'

Samir looked surprised.

'I mean it,' said Gelson. 'Hassan has an MBA, I'm sure he knows about Graham already.'

'Graham's strategy was to buy stocks in good businesses and hold them.'

'That's exactly the problem,' said Gelson.

'Many authorities think that is a good idea,' said Samir, surprised. 'Graham is highly respected.'

Gelson sighed. 'He may be respected by your professors, but not by Stu Goldberg. Stu likes to see a hefty rate of return, say thirty percent a year. If that isn't working, we have orders to sell and get into something else. Repeat as often as necessary until you find a winner. Charge the client a hefty commission each time.'

'I see,' said Samir.

But he did not.

4

OCTOBER 20TH, 2010

The meeting with Hassan al-Manwani started out like the blind date from hell.

Each of the younger men was chaperoned – Samir by Jim Gelson, his boss from New York, and Hassan by a man who introduced himself as Laith Saad, from the Libyan Ministry of Finance.

The meeting took place at Laith Saad's spacious beach house outside Tripoli. They perched awkwardly on little-used brocade sofas in Saad's air-conditioned living room, separated from the glittering ocean outside by huge picture windows.

Samir, acting under orders, greeted the Libyans in careful Arabic but they smiled slightly impatiently and replied in perfect English. The meeting continued in that language.

At first, neither principal took to the other. There

was an awkward silence while a young Arab, who Gelson suspected was Saad's catamite, served them mint tea.

Saad, who appeared to be a veteran of such meetings, was the most self-possessed. He smiled urbanely. 'You gentlemen are most welcome to my house. However, we are not sure what we can do for you?'

Gelson launched into a standard paean about Goldberg Freilich, pointing to the presence of Samir as proof of the bank's total dedication to their Arab clients. He indicated that the bank would be honoured to manage some of Hassan's money, and could promise sensational returns.

Saad nodded politely and turned to Hassan as if to ask, 'What do you think?'

Hassan asked bluntly, 'What are your investment principles?'

It was a sneaky question because it was like asking a politician what he believes in. He desperately wants to first find out what *you* want, so that he can promise to give it to you. Gelson rabbited on for a while about combining sky-high returns and rock-solid safety.

Hassan interrupted him. 'Would you say you are value investors, or momentum investors?'

Before Gelson could stop him, Samir smiled and flourished his copy of *The Intelligent Investor*.

At that point, the ice melted. Hassan and Samir conversed easily, to Saad's amusement and Gelson's discomfort. Even to Gelson, though, it was clear that a rapport existed that could be very valuable.

He took advantage of a break in the conversation to ask, 'If you don't mind my enquiring, how large is your portfolio?'

Hassan was about to answer but Laith Saad interrupted. 'Beside his own portfolio, Hassan consults regularly with the Brother Leader on such matters.'

This was a bit of a reach. Hassan only spoke to Muammar Qaddafi once or twice a year and, in recent meetings, the Brother Leader had been far too wasted to focus on return on investment. But mention of the dictator's name was enough to snap the Goldberg Freilich people to attention. They nodded respectfully.

Laith Saad knew when to quit while he was ahead. He stood up and looked at his watch. 'Well, this has been a pleasure, gentlemen, but we have a meeting in town with the Société Générale people. Let me see you out.'

On the way out, he drew Gelson aside. Gelson motioned Samir to walk ahead to the car while he and Saad exchanged a few words.

'Do you have a business card?' asked Saad.

Gelson produced one.

Saad wrote something on the back. He gave it back to Gelson, who studied it. It was a ten-digit number.

'Where?' Gelson asked.

'Julius Wolff Privatbank. The Basel branch.'

Gelson nodded and tucked the card away in his wallet.

After their guests had left, Hassan turned to Saad and asked, 'Well, what do you think?'

Saad shrugged. 'It's a very successful firm.'

'Should we give them some money to handle?'

Saad rubbed his blue chin. He thought about the card he had just given Gelson. 'Maybe. Let's see what SocGen have to say first.'

Gelson had booked a flight home to New York. Samir was returning to London. At the airport, they sat in the cafeteria drinking iced tea out of cans.

Samir said, 'I'm guessing they'll give us fifty million.'

'Could be,' said Gelson absently. He was considering how to slant what he would tell Stu Goldberg.

But Samir was fired up. 'We should keep the funds offshore, maybe in the BVI. I can make the investment decisions in London and execute trades by e-mail.'

Gelson stared at him.

'With copy to you, of course,' said Samir hastily.

'Right,' said Gelson. One thing he did know was that he was not going to let this jumped-up kid usurp decisions that belonged to him. But there was no point in discouraging the lad, not yet anyway.

Two days later, Saad contacted Gelson to let him know Hassan's decision.

The young Libyan had decided to appoint Goldberg Freilich to manage a billion dollars.

5

NOVEMBER 1ST, 2011

I listened politely while Michael Kalestian educated me on Portuguese colonial history, with a gusto I found mildly irritating.

'Macau isn't Portuguese any more. It reverted to Chinese rule in 1999. Since then, it has become the biggest gambling destination in the world.'

'Bigger than Las Vegas?'

'Much bigger.'

The comparison was thought provoking. I had been to Las Vegas a few times and, like many people, had been overwhelmed by the opulence of the huge casinos on the Strip. It was hard to imagine somewhere even bigger.

Michael warmed to his story.

'You are right that business in Vegas has been a little slow,' he said. 'But the Macau Excelsior will more than make up for that. Boy is that market growing!'

'I didn't know there was a Macau Excelsior.'

'Oh yes. It will be coming on stream very soon. I've been living in Macau, getting it ready.'

'Will it be as big as the Las Vegas Excelsior?' I asked.

'Double the size!'

I was not sure whether to take him literally. 'Really?'

'Sure. Four thousand rooms. It will be the biggest place of its kind. Even the Macau Venetian only has twenty-eight hundred.'

'Will you be able to fill them all?'

He looked at me pityingly. 'Macau is right on the doorstep of more than a billion Chinese, the biggest gamblers in the world. It can't fail!'

That kind of vague logic has been a feature of more failed projects than I can count. It is usually much too optimistic. I glanced at Tisch; he is not someone who is impressed by vagueness. He shrugged.

'Got to build it first,' he said.

'It is built. It just needs some finishing touches,' said Michael.

'What it needs is another fifty million dollars.'

'Less than that,' said Michael defensively.

There was a longish silence.

'So why exactly am I here?' I asked.

Michael drained his beer and looked around for another. I suspected he had already had a couple.

'Here's the story: I inherited the project from my dad. At the same time, I inherited a Japanese partner called Naguchi who makes slot machines. Naguchi was going to put up half the cash.'

'Sounds like a good partner to have.'

'I thought so too, until I discovered he was screwing me.'

'Screwing?'

'The deal was that he would supply all the slots for the casino. But he was cheating. He was inflating the price of the machines with all kinds of phony costs.'

'That's dreadful,' I said. I tried to look sympathetic. Michael was not stupid by any means, but he was a salesman. His grasp of numbers was limited to the odds at blackjack.

As an accountant, I knew that one man's 'phony costs' were another man's legitimate overhead. In a business relationship, it was something you had to define very precisely. I guessed that Kalestian *père* had not done that; he had been brilliant at initiating a project but, when it came to the small print, less so.

'What happened?'

'I fired him before I got in too deep.'

'And you found a new partner?'

Tisch cleared his throat. He seemed to be having trouble keeping a straight face.

'It's not funny,' said Michael.

'Who is your partner?' I asked.

Michael examined the sky. 'It is Middle Eastern money.'

'Nothing wrong with that,' I said.

'It's Qaddafi,' said Tisch, almost grinning.

'Oh,' I said. The Libyan dictator had been assassinated a few weeks ago.

'His son, actually.'

'Which son?' I asked.

'Hassan.'

I raised my eyebrows. I was not an expert on Libya but I read the newspapers. Qaddafi had sired a number of children, but I had never heard of Hassan.

'Illegitimate,' said Michael.

'Ah.'

'He is a fine young man.' Michael sounded a bit defensive.

'Where did you meet him?'

'Las Vegas.'

A light went on.

'Was he one of your Invited Guests?' It was the trade term for high rollers, the gamblers who received free hospitality because they bet so heavily.

Michael nodded.

'Isn't a casino rather a frivolous investment for a Muslim ruling family?' I asked.

'Not really,' said Michael. 'Hassan is, I would say, quite secular. We had a deal where I kept him supplied with female company – he is partial to oriental women. When I offered him the opportunity to take over Naguchi's position in Macau, that may just possibly have been a factor in his decision.'

'A bit of a risky bedfellow, though?'

'In hindsight, perhaps. But a year ago, before the Arab Spring, nobody knew all that stuff was going to happen. And he came up with the money when I needed it. Until now, that is.'

'Let me guess. His funds have been frozen?'

'Possibly. But I don't know for sure, because he has disappeared.'

I began to get the picture. I could not blame a son of Qaddafi for wanting to disappear from view. Even if he was as pure as the driven snow, to the rebels he would be a target for revenge, like any other Qaddafi still in town.

'What has happened to the rest of the Qaddafis?' I asked.

Tisch said, 'I saw on CNN that Qaddafi's wife and several of his children escaped from Libya. They put together a convoy of Mercedes and made it to the Algerian border.'

'I saw that too,' I said. 'If this Hassan is still in

Libya, there must be a hefty price on his head. He will be lying low.'

'And there is your challenge,' said Tisch.

'Exactly,' said Kalestian.

They both grinned at me.

'Let me summarise,' I said. 'You dumped your Japanese partner and brought in the bastard son of Muammar Qaddafi. How old, by the way?'

Michael frowned. 'Hassan is 27. And it was not as dumb a move as it sounds; I did not have many options at the time. Naguchi was getting ready to screw me. I just beat him to the draw.'

'What do you want me to do?'

'Find the source of Hassan's funds and get them flowing, so that I can finish the Excelsior and open on time.'

'Is that all?' I asked.

Michael's bushy moustache twitched. He may have noticed the sarcasm. 'Yes,' he said.

'Would you like me to make sure Hassan is safe, too?'

'Oh. Yes, of course.' He had the grace to look embarrassed.

I turned to Tisch. 'What is our business arrangement?'

'You'll be working for me,' he said. 'I will pay you a commission.'

'How much?'

He looked momentarily flustered. 'Five percent of all the funds you recover.'

That meant that Carlton already had an understanding with Michael, probably for fifteen percent. After paying me five, he would keep ten. In other words, he would make twice as much as me, just for sitting at home and supervising. Did I mention that he was smart?

'I think I need a beer,' I said.

I went indoors and helped myself to a Red Stripe from the massive steel fridge in Carlton's designer kitchen. When I came out, they were talking quietly but they fell silent as I appeared. I wondered what it was they did not want me to hear.

'How were the construction funds paid to you?' I asked Michael.

'They were wired to the bank in Macau where the casino has its account.'

'Where did they come from?'

Michael shook his head. 'I don't know.'

'Somebody must know.'

He looked blank. 'The bank would have that information, I suppose.'

'I shall need to talk to your bank manager.'

'No problem. I'll arrange a conference call.'

I shook my head. 'A conference call won't do, I'm afraid; I need to meet him in person.'

'Why?'

'That's how I work.'

It was true. Call me old-fashioned, but there are subtleties that come out only in a face-to-face meeting between two human beings.

And, to be honest, I love to travel and I had never been to Macau.

I was comparing travel schedules with Michael when there was the sound of another car arriving and two handsome young women appeared on the terrace, one brunette and one blonde.

Their arrival was good news and bad news. The brunette was Carlton's 25-year-old wife Mimi. Mimi is delightful, I must say. She was the good news. About blonde Kathy I was not so sure.

Kathy Smith is my nemesis. A nemesis is the implacable agent of someone's downfall. That may be a bit strong; she may not exactly have caused my downfall, but she is certainly implacable. She is an intelligent woman who acts naïve to conceal the fact that she has a master's degree in international taxation from USC. Calculating and devious underneath, she looks thoroughly wholesome and attractive with corn-blonde hair and a nice figure. Her smile can melt icebergs. She and Mimi are friends. They spend a lot of time together.

Carlton has a weakness for girls young enough

to be his granddaughter and, in his eyes, Kathy walks on water. He consults her repeatedly on projects where he has clearly led me to believe I am his primary advisor.

So I was outnumbered. The Caribbean sun had slipped behind a cloud.

The girls had been shopping. They shed carrier bags, kissed Carlton, hugged me and, after a brief hesitation, shook hands gingerly with the Speedo-clad Michael.

'Such serious faces,' said Kathy.

'Council of War?' asked Mimi.

'Sort of,' said Carlton. 'Oliver and Michael are off to Macau to look for money for Michael's new casino.'

'Oh, the Qaddafi billions?' asked Kathy.

That meant she and Carlton had been talking already. Things were worse than I thought.

'Why don't you fill Oliver in on what you've learned?' said Tisch.

'Yes, why don't you?' I said.

She nodded. 'I've been doing some research.'

'And?' I asked, maybe a bit sourly.

She smiled. 'The first question people ask is how much money did Qaddafi salt away?'

'Well, how much?' I asked.

'Nobody knows.'

'Nobody?'

'I suppose Qaddafi knew, but he's dead. Libyan officials are saying $200 billion, but that may be just a guess.'

'Well it's a start,' I said. Does anybody know *where* it is?'

She shook her head. 'We can see some of it, but not the stuff you are looking for.'

'Where is the part you can see?'

'There is about $100 billion in the name of institutions like the Central Bank of Libya, the Libyan Investment Authority and the Libya African Investment Portfolio. The situation is confusing because Qaddafi did not distinguish between his own and the country's assets; he seemed to consider them one and the same.'

'Is that money frozen?' I asked.

'Yes. Until recently, Qaddafi or his family could access many of those accounts at will. Western governments have put a stop to that; they've shut off the spigot.'

'How did Libyan officials come up with a figure of $200 billion?'

'That's a good question. Maybe they just took the $100 billion figure and doubled it.'

I nodded agreement. If I had to guess, they just assumed that there was a lot more money out there. And that, like other dictators before him, Qaddafi had squirrelled away large chunks of it in secret accounts. Were there also discreetly hidden safe deposit boxes, full of currency, precious metals or marketable art and collectibles? Was there real estate held under assumed names, or controlled by trusted associates?

Probably all of the above.

Well I had to start somewhere. I was not too happy about jetting off to Asia and leaving Kathy behind to cause trouble by dripping smart-aleck criticism in Carlton's ear, but I couldn't see any alternative.

I turned to Michael.

'How do we get to Macau?'

Michael said, 'I'll make the travel arrangements. Do you have a business card, so that I can get in touch with you?'

I fished in my wallet and produced one. He studied it.

A broad grin spread over his face. 'What's this?'

I felt my cheeks getting warm; I may even have blushed. 'What?'

'Oliver Steele, Financial Sleuth?'

'So?'

'Sleuth?'

'What about it?'

'You use to be a forensic accountant.'

'It's the same thing.'

'Really?'

'More or less.'

The others were looking at me.

Tisch sniffed. 'I hired a forensic accountant,' he said.

'I told you, it's the same.'

Mimi Tisch fetched a dictionary and made a great business of paging through it.

'Sleuth. Verb. "To carry out a search or investigation in the manner of a detective".'

'That's what I said.'

Tisch said, 'The hourly rate for a sleuth is much lower than for a forensic accountant. We should renegotiate our contract.'

'What contract? We don't have one.'

'The origin is the old Norse word *slóth*,' said Mimi.

Tisch was as near to smiling as he gets. I think I have as good a sense of humour as the next man, but I was starting to get a tiny bit irritated.

I looked at my watch.

'Well, you can all sit around in the sun having your little jokes; I have work to do.'

6

NOVEMBER 4TH, 2011

Michael had his own Gulfstream, which he had left at San Juan airport. Commercial jet aircraft do not land on Tortola – the runway is rather short. It is something the island's wealthier residents are probably not unhappy about – people with names like Branson, Brocklebank and Rockefeller value their privacy. So, to get from Tortola to San Juan, we had to catch a tiny propellor-engined Cessna operated by Cape Air.

Michael's Gulfstream did not have enough range to get us from San Juan all the way to Macau, but it did get us as far as Los Angeles. From there, we flew first class to Hong Kong on my favourite airline, Cathay Pacific. It took a long fifteen hours. Between naps, I watched a series of forgettable movies.

Finally we caught a helicopter from Hong Kong to Macau – a short twenty-minute ride.

We arrived somewhat wrung out at our hotel, the Pousada de Sao Tiago, a charming old converted fort set in the rocks overlooking the channel between Macau and mainland China.

Kalestian had rented an entire floor as the working headquarters of Excelsior Macau.

'I'm pleasantly surprised at your choice of hotel,' I said.

He missed the mild insult. 'I could have set up shop in a high-rise on the Cotai Strip but that would have meant staying in a place owned by the competition and they would probably have bugged my room. Besides, it's more relaxed here.'

'The Cotai Strip? Is that like the Las Vegas Strip?'

'Sort of. There are a bunch of new hotels there – the Wynn, the MGM, the Venetian. It's still a bit of a construction site, though; several other places are not fully built.'

'Including yours?'

'Including mine. Want to take a look?'

'Sure.'

We waited in the lobby for a taxi.

'What should I use for money?' I asked.

'You will need some patacas.'

'Patacas?'

He handed me a banknote. It was for fifty patacas. It was issued by 'Banco Nacional Ultramarino'
and was printed in both Chinese and Portuguese.

'Here, keep it!'

'Are you sure? That's a lot of patacas.'

He laughed. 'A pataca is worth the same as a
Hong Kong dollar and there are eight of those to the
US dollar. So that note is only worth about six
bucks.'

'What about US dollars? Are they accepted
here?'

'In some of the big hotels, but not on the street.
The Chinese currency, Renminbi, will work. But the
best thing to carry is the Hong Kong dollar – it is still
used for most everyday transactions.'

'How come?'

He shrugged. 'I guess it's a holdover from the
time before Hong Kong and Macau came under
Chinese control in the nineties.'

Our taxi arrived, a brand new black and yellow
Korean vehicle. A placard on the side said, 'Catch
the Show at City Of Dreams. Get Tickets Now.'
That made me feel at ease, it was reassuringly
American.

We sped down the road, driving, to my surprise,
on the left-hand side, and swerved onto a long
causeway, narrowly missing two startled tourists in a
tricycle-powered rickshaw.

Michael kept up a running commentary, with gestures.

'We are now leaving Old Macau. Over there is where the sixteenth-century Portuguese trading post used to be.

'Now we are on the Sai Van Bridge; it is almost two miles long. Across the bay is mainland China.'

He grinned. 'That is our market. A communist country with an endless supply of well-heeled Chinese gamblers.'

He sounded a bit crass but I nodded encouragingly. 'What's coming up ahead?'

'The rest of Macau. There used to be two separate islands, Coloane and Taipa. Coloane is mostly forest. Taipa is where the airport is. The two islands are joined together with landfill, now. The connecting part, combining the *Co* of Coloane and the *Tai* of Taipa, is known as the *Cotai* Strip.'

'It must be very valuable land.'

'It sure is. The infilling began in 1912, long before Macau became a gambling haven, but the developers must have had second sight, it is so suitable for the casinos.'

After driving through Taipa, we approached a large flat area.

'This is Cotai,' said Michael.

He pointed out a series of obviously new hotels. 'Over there is the MGM, four hundred and fifty rooms. It is a partnership between MGM and Pansy Ho, a member of the Ho family who are well connected around here.'

'Very nice.'

'Steve Wynn is also in Macau. His place is built in the form of two towers, the Wynn and the Encore. Altogether, a thousand rooms.'

He waved. 'Here, the Venetian. Two thousand eight hundred rooms.'

'Is that the biggest?'

'For now. The Excelsior will be bigger.'

'I'm impressed. Where next?'

He grinned. 'Now for the highlight of our tour.'

We drove a short distance, then stopped in front of a huge white structure that looked slightly sinister in its inertness.

There was no name on the front. Unlike its brilliant neighbours, it was lit only by a few construction floodlights.

It was certainly big. We could not get really close because of the metal-railed barriers but, from the front, it looked much the way I remembered its sister resort, the Las Vegas Excelsior. I recognised the same pretentious front courtyard and entrance façade. I could envisage the huge glass atrium behind it, filled with a riot of tropical flowers and jungle that customers had to stroll admiringly through in order to reach the gambling casino and the living areas.

Looking down the side street marking one edge of the property, I could see that it extended a very long way back. The resort occupied a whole city block; in fact it was a mini-city in its own right, consistent with Michael's claim that, when it opened, it would be Macau's biggest yet.

The place was silent now, but with the aid of a bit more money it would all spring to life, accompanied by the jangling chorus from massed ranks of gaudy slot machines.

And that was partly up to me. As I stared up at the ominous bulk, the prospect was exciting and also a bit daunting.

I thought of a question.

'Who really runs Macau? Is it the Chinese Government, or the people from the old Portuguese era?'

'In a sense, both. Officially it is China but some say that if you really want to get something done here, you need to talk to Stanley Ho.'

'Any relation to Pansy, part owner of the MGM Grand?'

'Very much so; he is her father. He is over 90 now and in a wheelchair, but he wields great influence. He has led a colourful life – four wives and seventeen children. For many years, he had an exclusive licence to run gambling here on Macau. Through STDM, his *Sociedade de Turismo e Diversões de Macau*, he controlled hotels and property development. He had stakes in the airport, the airline, the Jockey Club, the lottery, dog races and the TV stations that promoted them.'

'That's quite an empire.'

He nodded. 'Visitors from Hong Kong still travel on high-speed ferries run by Shun Tak Holdings, a company controlled by Ho. There is no gambling in Hong Kong or mainland China, by the way, so Macau is literally the only game around.'

'How were *you* able to get your foot in the door?'

He shrugged. 'It was my dad rather than me who broke in. After the colony reverted to Chinese rule, Stanley Ho's monopoly was ended. The Government split Macau's gambling operations into three parts. The casinos in Macau remained under STDM, whose biggest shareholder is still Stanley Ho, but licences were opened for bidding in Coloane and Taipa.

'So at last, other casino operators had a chance to get into the business. That led to the arrival of the Sands Macau, the Venetian Macau, the Wynn Macau and others. My father was able to join the bidding and make a hefty down payment to back it up. Money talks, he was successful and here we are!'

Michael leaned forward and spoke to the driver. 'Back to the hotel!'

The driver frowned blankly.

'Pousada de Sao Tiago.'

'Ah, Pousada!' A thin smile.

'He's acting dumb,' muttered Michael. 'They understand English just fine when they want to.'

Back on the main peninsula, we passed through Old Macau's jumbled streets and squares with open-air cafes and Catholic churches; the look and feel was European once again.

By now I was fading fast, after the journey. 'What about the bank?' I asked.

'I haven't forgotten. Tomorrow we shall meet Henry Chu of the Hongkong Macau Bank. He's the guy who handles our account. He can get you everything you need.'

'Let's hope so.'

I was less sure than Michael. It would depend how many layers of secrecy surrounded the Hassan Qaddafi funds.

I breakfasted on coffee and fresh fruit – star fruit, jackfruit and other Asian delicacies, unfamiliar but delicious, before we took a taxi to the bank.

The Hongkong Macau Bank was in the Old Town; it looked picturesque rather than businesslike. Two gold painted lions knelt outside, one on each side of the steps, which were crowned by an elaborate portal of gold screens and finials. The décor inside was consistent. We were shown into a conference room.

Moments later, in came a man of medium height, dapper in a well-cut grey suit, white shirt and crested navy tie. His straight black hair was slicked down in a widow's peak above his smooth brow; he might have been fifty. He was carrying a manila file folder stuffed with papers.

He shook hands, bowing slightly and smiled showing perfect teeth.

'I'm Henry Chu. Welcome to Macau. I hope your journey was not too tiring. Lots to discuss. But first, how about a cup of tea?'

His manner was relaxed, with a trace of humour. An encouraging start. He turned to Michael. 'I drove past the Excelsior yesterday. It looks nearly finished. You must be very excited.'

'It's going well,' said Michael, beaming.

That was not quite what I had heard, I thought. But that was business – everyone lying cheerfully to one another.

Henry Chu turned to me. 'I understand you have some questions?'

Michael looked at his watch. 'I'll leave you bean counters to get on with it. I have to meet the guys installing the surveillance cameras in the casino.'

After he left, Chu smiled and sipped his tea. 'Everything is so high-tech now. I remember when Macau only had two casinos. One was Stanley Ho's

Lisboa Hotel. The other was on a junk moored down by the jetty. There was a handwritten sign on the wall to tell gamblers the level of typhoon alert outside.'

'Was that when everything was controlled by Mr Ho?'

Henry Chu smiled. He could have said 'yes' or 'no' or 'things have changed in that regard,' or 'things have not really changed much at all,' but he said nothing. A discreet banker.

'How much do you know about the source of the funds used to build the Excelsior?' I asked.

It's not easy to raise one eyebrow without the other, but Henry Chu had the knack.

'I knew the previous partner, Mr Naguchi. I also knew Ara Kalestian, Michael's father.'

I nodded. 'I never met Ara,' I said. I did not mention that my interest in him only began on the day he was murdered.

'A very talented businessman,' said Chu.

Another wordless smile.

We sipped our tea.

'What do you know about Michael's new partner?' I asked.

'Hassan al-Manwani? Only what everyone knows about him, which is to say not much.'

'But you do know that the funds from Hassan have stopped flowing?'

Chu nodded. 'Of course, and that is a concern. Something needs to be done immediately.'

'Immediately?'

'Here's the problem,' said Chu. He tapped the manila folder. 'In here is a pile of unpaid bills. One of my staff at the bank is acting as Michael's financial controller – it is a service we provide – and we are supposed to pay these but frankly, right now we don't have the money.'

'How much do they add up to?'

'About three million dollars.'

'American or Hong Kong dollars?'

'American.'

I whistled.

Henry Chu said, 'It sounds a lot, but for a major project like the Excelsior it is not that unusual.'

'Does Michael know this?'

Chu nodded.

'What does he say?'

'He says don't worry, things will work out.'

Our eyes met and Chu smiled sadly. 'He is a likeable young man, but . . .'

'I see you know him,' I said.

I shuffled through the pile of bills.

'How much will it take to pay these bills and any others, finish the project and open the casino for business?'

'Somewhere between forty and fifty million dollars.'

'What if I could get you three million to pay off the urgent bills, the stuff in this folder?'

'That would help but there is also a time problem. If I don't pay them very soon, word will start to get round. People will say the Excelsior is in trouble.'

'Then what happens?'

'Bad things. When suppliers hear that sort of rumour, they get very nervous. They insist on payment in advance for any further work. So, effectively, it means the whole forty million or so will be required before work can proceed – any of it.'

'How much time do I have?'

He thought for a minute. 'Maybe a week. Two at the most.'

'Oh thanks,' I said drily.

He shrugged. 'I've been in this business for quite a few years. There are a number of cultural differences between you Westerners and us here in the Orient but I can assure you that the way business creditors can sniff out a customer's lack of money is not one of them; that is something universal. Trust me, I'm not exaggerating the urgency.'

'Well, I am trying to get the money flowing again,' I said.

'That is the bank's hope, too.'

'What will happen if he just can't find the funds?'

I asked. 'Will the Excelsior become an empty eyesore, a vacant shell in the middle of the Strip?'

He shook his head. 'No, someone else would step in. It is a very desirable property; there are plenty of competitors who would love to snap it up.'

'But Michael would lose control?'

'Yes, and Hongkong Macau Bank would probably lose a customer. So we want to help.'

I produced a recent bank statement of the Excelsior. 'One thing you can do is to tell me the source where Hassan's funds came from.'

Chu looked at the document. 'I am not sure of the original source but I can take you some of the way, at least. This shows funds being sent via SWIFT from New York.'

'Perfect,' I said. 'I can use the SWIFT code to identify the sender.'

Cho shook his head doubtfully. 'As you know, the Society for Worldwide Interbank Financial Telecommunication, based in Brussels, provides a way of transferring money confidentially. The information is encrypted so that only the sending and receiving parties know each other's identities.'

I pointed to the most recent entry, dated a month ago. It was for five million dollars and had a string of characters next to it.

'But the code identifies the sender, and that's what I want. That's where the funds came from.'

Henry Chu shook his sleek head. 'It's not that easy, I'm afraid.'

'Why not?'

'The SWIFT code identifies the sending bank, but that is just the final link in the chain. There may be a string of a dozen banks before you get back to the original source.'

'Any of which could refuse to help me, arguing the need for confidentiality?'

'Exactly.'

Deflated, I asked 'Can you at least check and see who that code number belongs to?'

He smiled. 'I don't need to check. It belongs to Goldberg Freilich, the New York investment bank.'

I knew them by reputation. They were a major firm on Wall Street, a household name and not for the best of reasons. They had expanded very rapidly and had a reputation for ruthlessness.

It looked as if I might have to continue my search in New York. I thanked Henry Chu and left, making my way back to the hotel by taxi.

On the way, I remembered something about Goldberg Freilich – they were also the 'marriage brokers' who put together the deal for Michael's father Ara when he bought the Las Vegas Excelsior, years ago. They still owned five percent of the Excelsior.

This was not necessarily significant – they were a

big financial conglomerate with fingers in many pies.

But you never knew.

At dinner that evening, I asked Michael if there was any connection between the Goldberg Freilich bank and his young Libyan investor Hassan.

He shook his head.

'I don't know. I never asked Hassan what channel his funds came through. I was not aware that they came via Goldberg Freilich.'

'Who have you dealt with at Goldbergs in the past?'

'A guy called Jim Gelson. He's a vice president, so he is quite high up; he would know all about Hassan's dealings with the bank.'

I did not want to disappoint Michael but 'vice president' does not mean much in a bank like Goldberg Freilich. They probably had several hundred vice presidents. But it was a point of contact. Besides, their five percent stake should dispose them to be helpful.

I had Michael call the bank and arrange for me to meet Jim Gelson.

The next morning, leaving Michael to play with his casino, I boarded a plane for New York.

Carlton Tisch maintains a big, expensive house in Manhattan. It is a four-storey brownstone on East 62nd Street, between Second and Third Avenues.

Personally I like the West Side better – it's funkier and the restaurants are more interesting – but Carlton is still a bit obsessed with appearances and status, so he's an Upper East Side person. Maybe it's because of his impoverished childhood. Anyway, the house is in a pretty swanky neighbourhood. Legally, it belongs to his master company, Eastern Debt Factors but, if you take a peep inside, it looks suspiciously like a very comfortable – and very valuable – family home.

The decorating was done by Mimi; she has a gift for that kind of thing. However, Carlton always keeps one eye on the Income Tax Code. There is a gleaming mahogany table in the living room suitable either for dining or for board meetings, according to need. At the top of the house is a suite with its own elevator. This is Carlton and Mimi's private domain, but it can be reintegrated swiftly with the rest of the house by unlocking sliding doors in the event of a visit from the IRS. In matters of tax, Carlton's first commandment is 'Do not get caught'.

I was greeted by Lori, Carlton's Austrian housekeeper. The house was comfortably warm, in sharp contrast to the chilly autumn weather outside. I tossed my bag on the floor and checked my e-mail.

There was a message from Michael Kalestian:

'A sad thing. Henry Chu, the bank manager, died last night. Auto accident. Single car affair, drove off the road into the Pearl River Delta. The presence of alcohol suggests he was drunk. Nice guy, who would have thought it?'

I stared at the e-mail for several minutes. At our meeting, Chu had appeared to be relaxed, intelligent, very much under control. Did he seem like someone who would get drunk and kill himself?

Not for my money.

7

NOVEMBER 2ND, 2011

Kathy Smith was not a girl to sit and do nothing.

After Oliver and Michael had left the villa, Carlton went indoors to work while Kathy and Mimi put on bikinis and stretched out by the pool.

'What do you make of Michael?' Kathy asked.

Mimi wrinkled her nose. 'His swimsuit is a bit on the brief side.'

'Still, with muscles like that . . .'

'Muscles don't do much for me,' said Mimi.

'He can't be stupid. He went to Harvard, runs a big casino.'

Mimi said, 'He was always overshadowed by his father Ara while Ara was alive.'

'Tell me about the father.'

'Ara Kalestian was the son of immigrant farmers

in California. As a young man, he bought land in Silicon Valley and developed it. He made a lot of money and bought the Las Vegas Excelsior, which caters to high rollers. It made billions. When Ara was murdered, Michael inherited the casino. They say it is struggling now, though.'

'So Michael is trying to maintain his father's success by expanding in Macau?'

'Exactly.'

'Sounds as if he's got a lot to live up to,' said Kathy.

'It's not the hand you're dealt; it's how you play it,' said Mimi.

'Very profound,' said Kathy.

With one arm, Mimi reached for her plastic beaker of iced water and upended it over the small of Kathy's back.

'Pig,' Kathy gasped.

After a few minutes of silence, Kathy said, 'What about this character Hassan?'

'Don't know much. I think his mother was a member of Qaddafi's female bodyguard.'

'I wonder how I could track him down.'

'That wouldn't be easy.'

'I'd like to try.'

'Isn't Oliver supposed to be handling that?'

'Yes, but . . .'

'But?'

Kathy thought about how to say it. 'Oliver is clever and he works hard, but . . .'

'What?'

'He's a numbers guy.'

'Is that bad?'

'Sometimes; it can blind you to non-numerical solutions.'

'What non-numerical solution did you have in mind?'

'I don't know,' said Kathy.

Then, almost to herself: 'If I could track down the mother, I bet I could find her darling son.'

8

NOVEMBER 7TH, 2011

Next morning, I took the subway downtown to the Goldberg Freilich building, a sixty-storey stainless steel fortress on Wall Street.

I had to wait ten minutes in an intimidating lobby. Finally a thirtyish Woody Allen lookalike, with his receding hair and horn-rimmed specs, appeared wearing a pinstripe suit.

He stuck out a hand. 'Jim Gelson.'

The high forehead made him look thoughtful. His smile was friendly enough, if a bit preoccupied.

He surprised me by whisking me straight out of the door.

'Coffee time,' he explained. 'The office brew sucks; we'll go down the road.'

He walked fast and I had to hurry to keep up. I thought he looked nervous.

In a bustling hole-in-the-wall coffee shop a block away, we settled into a booth.

'I recommend the jelly doughnuts,' he said, unsmiling.

As Steele and Gelson were leaving the bank, neither of them noticed another man, dressed like Gelson in Brooks Brothers suit and club tie, who followed them outside and down the street. When they entered the coffee shop he waited a minute and then followed them in. He slipped into a seat a few tables away. From there he only had a view of Gelson's back, but he could see Steele's face and watch his lips move.

Our order arrived; apple fritter for me, jelly doughnut for him.

We ate in silence. I waited for him to speak; maybe he was waiting for me, I don't know.

'Pastry and coffee both excellent,' I said finally.

Gelson nodded. 'Look I'm sorry,' he said.

'For what?'

'The cloak and dagger stuff.'

'I hadn't noticed,' I said.

He looked embarrassed. 'The bottom line is that I can't help you.'

'But you don't know what I want yet.'

He shook his head. 'Sorry. The word has come down from on high.'

'What word?'

'For reasons of customer confidentiality, the bank is not in a position to help with your research.'

I was starting to feel irritated. 'You sound like a recording,' I said.

He blinked. I pressed on. 'I'm not doing research, as you call it. My mission is simple. I just want to free up the flow of funds so that Michael Kalestian can finish his casino and open it for business.'

'I know that.'

There were a couple of beads of sweat on his brow, which he brushed away with a paper napkin. He smiled at me apologetically.

'You've got powdered sugar on your forehead,' I said.

He brushed again. 'Is that better?'

'Much.'

We sipped our coffee in silence for a minute.

'I must say I'm a bit surprised at the bank's position, considering that Goldberg Freilich is a shareholder in Excelsior,' I said.

'It doesn't matter,' he said. 'There are other factors.'

'Oh really? What other factors?'

He took an unnecessary minute finishing his donut. He wiped more sugar from his chin with a pinstriped sleeve. His hand shook slightly.

'Look, I'm just trying to follow the money trail,' I said. 'Hassan's funds used to arrive in Macau via Goldberg Freilich. I know that because of the SWIFT code. Now I want to know how they reached Goldberg.'

He gave me a strange look. 'They didn't.'

'What do you mean?'

He said nothing.

The truth started to dawn on me. 'Do you mean that the money was already *at* Goldberg?'

He nodded.

'Well good,' I said. 'At least we've established that Goldberg Freilich are looking after Hassan's money. If I can speak to whichever of your colleagues deals with it, we can sort things out in no time.'

'They won't meet with you.'

'Why?' I asked. 'Are the funds frozen? If Goldberg Freilich's hands are tied by some government edict. I would understand, it's no disgrace. At least I could eliminate them as a source and move on, look for money elsewhere.'

He shrugged. 'Listen, I want to help. I like Michael. When his father was killed, some people here wanted to dump the stock, they felt the son would not measure up as a businessman. I persuaded them to hold off.'

'Well, bully for you. Maybe Goldberg would like

to invest some of their own funds?' I ventured. 'It's a great investment, from what I hear.'

Gelson still looked uneasy. There was something more.

I tried the silent treatment. It sometimes works. If it doesn't, you just move on, the subject may not even notice you were doing it.

I stirred my coffee and waited.

'The real problem is that it's so embarrassingly profitable,' he finally muttered.

'Embarrassingly?'

He nodded. 'You didn't hear that from me, it's just chatter round the water cooler.'

'Go on.'

'Hassan put in a billion dollars and, frankly, we've doubled it!'

'You're kidding!'

He shrugged. 'It sometimes happens. We made some bets on interest rate futures when everyone thought PIGS were going down the drain.'

'PIGS?'

'Portugal, Ireland, Greece and Spain. It looked at one point as if Greece would default and the euro would go into the toilet. Fortunately, we got the timing just right. But the bank is afraid that, if word gets out, it will become a major news story. The Hassan connection would be all over the media. Then the authorities would freeze the funds for sure.

So, even though we are delighted about the profit, we are keeping quiet about it. We're pulling down the shutters.'

He blinked at me, half apologetic, his humorous mouth twitching slightly.

I could see his point of view, even if I disagreed with it.

'I'm curious,' I said. 'How exactly does Goldberg Freilich make money out of this?'

'We get paid a percentage of the funds under management.'

'What sort of percentage?'

'Two percent.'

'Per year?'

'Yes.'

'So on a billion dollar portfolio, you would have earned twenty million a year, probably more.'

'Sounds about right.'

'Which you probably extract promptly on the first of every month?'

'Of course.'

'Quite a lot to charge, just for watching your clients' dough.'

He shrugged. 'We have expenses. Rents are high around here.'

The Brooks Brothers man was a fresh-faced young fellow, not long out of business school. He could not hear what was being said but he could see the surprise on

Oliver's face and draw his own conclusions. When he sensed the conversation was winding down, he left hurriedly.

Back at Goldberg Freilich he took the elevator to the sixtieth floor, which was the partners' floor, and stepped out onto deep pile carpet. An imposing female receptionist was seated at a desk in the mini-lobby but he just nodded at her and walked straight down the wood panelled corridor. He looked both earnest and excited. He knocked at a door and entered.

Inside, two middle-aged men in expensive suits with a certain gravitas about them were sitting, chatting. 'Ah, Jeremy,' said one. 'Come in. Tell us what's going on.'

Gelson finished his coffee and stood up, obviously feeling he had said enough. He made for the door, forgetting to pay the bill, so I left some notes on the table.

As we walked back, I said, 'Well I'm glad you folk made a little money.'

'We always do,' he said unguardedly.

We reached the bank's steps.

'Sorry I couldn't help,' said Gelson. We shook hands.

A thought struck me.

'Besides your two percent a year, do you take a share of the profits?'

'Of course. Twenty percent.'

He walked away, a spring in his step.

As soon as I got back to East 62nd Street, I phoned Carlton. I described my meeting with Gelson.

'I seem to be getting nowhere.' I said. 'Do you have a contact at Goldberg Freilich?'

'No. I actually don't like them very much. They are wannabes, expanding in a hurry, trying to become another Goldman Sachs.'

'Are they succeeding?'

'Nah. They don't have that outfit's obsessively customer-friendly attitude.'

He waited for me to say something. 'That was a joke,' he said.

'Okay,' I said.

'Give me a few hours. I'll make some calls.'

'Thanks,' I said.

He grunted. 'We can talk when you get to Tortola.'

'Tortola? Must I?'

'Yes.'

'Why?'

'Mimi misses your cultured conversation.'

'Oh sure.'

Manhattan always used to be a town where you triple-locked your front door and looked over your shoulder when you walked down the street, but after a couple of law-and-order mayors, things are safer nowadays – or supposed to be. So I was surprised when, as I walked out of the brownstone and looked around for a taxi, another vehicle zoomed out of nowhere, mounted the kerb and clipped me from behind. I was knocked violently to the concrete pavement.

I must have lost consciousness briefly because, the next thing I knew, I was being sniffed by two well-groomed poodles on a spring-loaded leash.

'Come along girls, don't bite the tourist,' said the young man holding the leash. He was pretty well groomed himself, with blond curls, paisley-patterned silk shirt open to the waist and low-rider jeans. He held a pooper-scooper at the ready.

'I am not a tourist,' I said.

'Well, you're certainly not from here, dear.'

'What's the giveaway?'

'You didn't look both ways for traffic.'

'But I was still on the sidewalk.'

'This is Manhattan,' he smirked.

I tested my limbs gingerly. My right hip was quite badly bruised. I hauled myself upright.

'Did you see the car that hit me?'

'Yes, it was exciting.'

'What sort of car was it?'

'A big black car.'

I tried to be patient. 'What make?'

He sniffed. 'Do I look like a car expert? It was trying to hit you head-on, though.'

'Are you sure?'

He nodded.

It was also the second suspicious accident in two days, Henry Chu being the first.

I did not bother to ask poodle walker if he remembered the number plate. At least I was not at the bottom of the East River.

9

NOVEMBER 7TH, 2011

S everal aeroplanes later, I got to Tortola.

It was dark, and too late to get anything done so I checked into Myetts Hotel in Cane Garden Bay. For dinner I ordered their cracked conch, which I washed down with a couple of Red Stripes. I was fully mellowed out by the time I finished eating. Tortola will do that to you.

I joined Carlton for breakfast at the villa.

He built the house after sailing past the cape with Mimi one day. It looked like a nice spot to build on, so they bought it, all nine acres. You can do that when you have that sort of money. I grit my teeth with envy each time I visit.

To get there, you have to drive for several miles

along a deeply rutted path, avoiding sundry resentful chickens and indifferent goats. It's not a house exactly, more a series of connected island-style cabins that cascade spectacularly down the side of the rocky cliff. Although it was hellaciously expensive to build, it is basically simple, which suits Carlton and Mimi just fine. The cabins are wood, with copper roofs, the walls are mostly window to let the breeze waft through. Carlton's minimalist sculptures are dotted around the house and patio – abstract but with breasts, sort of Maillol meets Henry Moore. At the bottom level is a private jetty.

Carlton was sitting on the main terrace, which faces south across the sound. He was dressed formally, for him, in scuffed Yankees cap and unpressed khaki shorts.

We munched croissants with our coffee. The coffee grows on the nearby island of St John. Carlton has the beans rushed home in airtight jars. He stores them in the freezer, then roasts and grinds them just before brewing. The noise of the grinder hurts your ears but the taste is sublime.

'What's new?' he asked.

'I was nearly killed outside your New York house.'

He sniffed. 'And that is my fault how?'

I changed the subject.

'Where is Hassan now?' I asked.

'Nobody seems to know.'

'Do you think he is in Libya?'

Carlton laughed. 'If he is, he's in trouble.'

'Why?'

'Why do you think? He is a Qaddafi; there's a price on his head.'

'Maybe there's a price on mine,' I said.

Carlton didn't seem too concerned.

'Someone doesn't want us nosing around,' I said. 'First the bank manager drives into the sea, then I get knocked down in Manhattan.'

'Coincidence. You are hearing horses and assuming zebras.'

'It's a heck of a big coincidence,' I said.

But his interest was waning. He has a notoriously short attention span.

'Tell me a bit about Goldberg Freilich,' I asked.

He waved dismissively. 'Bunch of second-raters.'

'How so?'

'It was cobbled together in a series of mergers.'

'Is that bad?'

'When it's done badly, yes. In this case the cobbler was Stu Goldberg, a man I despise.'

'Despise is a strong word.'

Carlton shrugged his skinny brown shoulders. 'His guiding motivation is self-aggrandisement – that and making money.'

'That's shocking,' I said. 'How do you really feel about him?'

Perhaps I was overdoing it because he scowled.

'You can wipe that smirk off your face. Stu Goldberg is shallow and Goldberg Freilich is a mess, an incoherent collection of units – stockbrokers, insurance companies, shaky banks – stuffed into a rented building with their name in letters six feet high.'

'None of which is illegal,' I said.

He ignored me. 'The image may be impressive from the outside, but it is superficial. With Stu Goldberg, as soon as one acquisition is complete it's on to the next. He has no idea about making the pieces work well together.'

He sniffed. 'Besides, the man's a jerk. He wants to be the first Jewish president.'

'Is that bad? We've tried most other kinds.'

'He's a poor advertisement for the brand.'

He warmed to his subject. 'He also has a massive inferiority complex. You can see this in his attitude to his competitor, the celebrated Goldman Sachs. He has watched many of Goldman's senior people getting top jobs in Washington, so now he is angling for a cabinet appointment himself.'

'What are his chances?'

'Good. The present Commerce Secretary is retiring, so there is a vacancy. Goldberg is being vetted for the spot.'

'The job requires congressional approval, presumably?'

'Yes it does. However, Stu donates heavily to both political parties. He can buy his way into office, so to speak.'

I began to get an inkling of why Goldberg Freilich wanted so badly to keep their raffish Libyan connection away from the spotlight. That kind of spicy revelation could easily tip the balance against a candidate in Stu Goldberg's position – not only being linked to Qaddafi, but making a handsome profit from the relationship.

I thought about the mishaps that had befallen first the luckless Henry Chu, and then me. I started to get angry.

With me that is a slow process. When something bad happens, I don't get all agitated and raise my voice but, over time, I build up a powerful resentment and in the end I am liable to do something rash.

Right now, I wanted to do something about Stu Goldberg. It might or might not be a distraction from my main job, which was to track down Hassan and get access to his money, but it was certainly connected. It can be hard to concentrate on the task at hand when someone is trying to kill you.

'Well?' asked Carlton.

He was eyeing me expectantly. I felt I should say something intelligent.

'I'm working on a plan,' I said importantly.

But the truth was I had no idea where to begin.

A forensic accountant is paid to investigate, to follow the evidence until he triumphantly leads his client to the place where the money is hidden, whether it is in a bank account, in someone's pocket, or under a rock – I've known all those to happen. Only then has he earned his reward, hopefully a fat cheque.

But even the smartest detective needs a clue, a place to start. Carlton expects me to generate my own leads, which is the toughest part of the job, and I was at a dead end.

'I think I need to get face to face with Stu Gold-berg,' I said.

I paused.

'Don't look at me,' Carlton said impatiently. 'He's no pal of mine.'

'You're no help.'

His eyes narrowed.

'Help is what I pay *you* for,' he said quietly.

I had crossed a line. Carlton has mellowed with age but occasionally you get a glimpse of the scrabbler from the streets. The message was, 'You and I are friends, sort of – but that is because you provide a useful service – we are fine, but only as long as you perform.'

I had to perform.

As soon as I decently could, I made my excuses and went home.

Home is in Coconut Grove, a jungly quarter of Miami. I've been living there for a while. I used to live on Tortola but after a bit I moved to the mainland, mainly to get away from Carlton who kept wanting to talk business all hours of the day and night.

So now I'm renting a small house on Kumquat Avenue in the South Grove. I love it there. The trees in my garden include mango, avocado, lime and grapefruit. There is even a lychee tree, although that one overhangs the property line and the neighbourhood kids steal most of the fruit.

It's quiet, apart from occasional flocks of colourful parrots. I can think there.

10

NOVEMBER 11TH, 2011

The question was how to meet Stu
Goldberg.

For my first attempt, I simply called
the head office of Goldberg Freilich and asked to
speak to him.

No dice. I was passed up the chain by a series of
charming secretaries who asked my business. I did
not want to mention the name Qaddafi so I said I
wished to discuss 'an investment matter'. When I
was asked who I represented, I dropped Carlton
Tisch's name.

That went down like the proverbial lead balloon.
Well, Carlton had warned me that he and Stu Goldberg weren't bosom pals.

For my next effort, I phoned again, posing as a
freelance financial journalist doing a series on bank

presidents. I got shunted off again, this time to the secretary of a vice president, one Verdon P Schermerhorn. He was not just any old vice president, she told me in hushed tones, but Senior Vice President for Public Affairs.

I was invited back to the Wall Street headquarters and this time, instead of ten minutes in a cheap coffee shop, I was shown up to the sixtieth floor. I got to wade through the deep-pile carpet.

Verdon Schermerhorn was fiftyish, round faced and round bodied but energetic and fit looking, with a twinkling smile and a whiff of aftershave. Gold-rimmed specs, pale grey suit and waistcoat, a shirt that looked handmade in a tiny blue check and the crested navy tie of a presumably good club. He bounded out of his chair, pink face beaming, met my eye sincerely, and shook my hand.

He had a corner office with picture windows, looking out across the water at the Statue of Liberty. Any executive given these digs would think he was in heaven or at least at the top of the tree. But the rules might be different when it came to PR, I reminded myself. Image was all. Mr Schermerhorn's empire might not extend very far beyond these richly decorated walls.

'Amazing view,' I said.

'Not bad, eh?' He grinned complicitly. He seemed to really like me. Him and me, buddies.

'So you're doing a piece on Stu?'

I had to think, then got it. Stu Goldberg. Of course Verdon, being a *senior* vice president, would be on first name terms with Stu.

'Have you known him long?' I asked.

'Oh, you know. Yalies together.' His pale blue eyes narrowed slightly. 'And you were at...?'

'Oxford.'

He nodded. My first test. I guess I passed that one.

But I was surprised. I had somehow not expected the hard charging Stu Goldberg to have an Ivy League background.

Verdon Schermerhorn pushed a sheet of good quality paper towards me. It was a biography of Stuart Goldberg. It went into great detail. I scanned it, and smiled at Verdon.

'When can I meet him?'

Schermerhorn looked deeply apologetic.

'Ah. Thing is, Stu is funny about meeting the gentlemen of the press. He's happy to answer questions but the way it works is this: you submit your questions in writing. Stu answers them the same way and presto, there's your interview.'

Artfully written by you, I thought.

I looked again at the bio. In the part about leisure activities it mentioned an interest in sports, including squash and golf.

'He sounds quite an athlete.'

Schermerhorn nodded. 'Captain of squash at Yale. Three handicap at golf.'

'Three?'

'Not bad, eh.'

I was reluctantly impressed. Low single figures was a lot better than I can manage.

'Which sport does he play the most?'

'Squash. The trouble with golf is that it takes all day, by the time you've driven to the course and so on.'

Poor Stu, I thought, burdened with such a crushing schedule.

'I heard Mayor Bloomberg jets off to Bermuda on Friday afternoon, plays three rounds in two days and is back at his desk on Monday,' I said.

'Stu does a bit of that. But most days during the week he pops round to the Racquet Club for a lunchtime squash game.'

'Who does he play with?'

'Oh, pickup games. They have a challenge court system.'

Verdon was starting to look bored. He was too polite to be really obvious, but I caught him looking at his watch. My fifteen minutes of fame were winding down.

But it didn't matter, I had what I wanted and, it's

safe to say, Verdon Schermerhorn had absolutely no idea how helpful he had been.

I stood up and held out a hand. 'Thanks for the bio, I'll send you my questions.'

He beamed. 'E-mail would be good.' A card appeared. 'My private address.'

A final sincere handshake and I was out of there, trying hard to suppress the spring in my step.

I knew my next move.

The Racquet and Tennis Club is a dignified institution situated on Park Avenue. I have played squash there a couple of times as a guest of my friend Freddie Parrott. Freddie is an accomplished player, a former Rhodes scholar who makes an indecent amount of money as a partner in a Wall Street firm of lawyers, advising greedy corporations on mega-mergers.

I telephoned him.

'Hi,' he said. 'Want a game some time?'

'Actually, yes. I'm in New York and need some exercise. I also have an ulterior motive.'

'Sounds intriguing. How are you playing these days?'

'Not well. Haven't played for a month.'

'Sounds like a rare chance to beat you.'

Freddie was being unduly modest. As an undergraduate, he played No.1 for Princeton. We met when a Princeton team visited Oxford a few years ago and surprised the senior university, that's us, by almost winning.

'We'll see,' I said.

He laughed. 'Where and when?'

'Can we play at the Racquet Club?'

'Sure. When?'

'What about tomorrow?'

Freddie was a man of few words. 'You're on. Twelve noon?'

'See you there.'

I marched up the steps of the Racquet and Tennis Club. Its 200-foot-long, five-storey grey stone Italian Renaissance facade, *circa* 1918, dominates that stretch of Park Avenue with aplomb.

I said the club was dignified. The unenlightened might describe it as just a tiny bit old-fashioned. The tennis in its name is real tennis, as played by Henry VIII – the club is one of only four facilities in the world that can boast not one but two real tennis courts.

A commissionaire stared coolly at me. 'Yes, sir?'

'Here to play squash, a guest of Mr Parrott.'

He paged Freddie who came and signed me in.

In the locker room, I explained.

'I really want to play Stu Goldberg.'

Freddie wrinkled his nose. 'Good luck with that.'

'Meaning?'

'He's a tricky bugger. I don't like playing him.'

'Is he any good?'

'Okay for his age, I suppose.'

'Which is?'

'Fortyish.'

Age makes a big difference in squash. As the years slip by, it's the legs that start to go. If you play with people your own age you don't realise it is happening, but get in there with a kid half your age and it's watch out!

We went off to the squash courts and wrote our names on a list pinned to the wall.

The way a challenge court works is that, when your name gets to the top of the list, you step on court. You play one game against the player already there; then he leaves the court and you play another game against his successor. Then you leave. If there is enough time, your turn may come round again.

Stu Goldberg's name was on the list. Two players were on court already and several others were sitting behind the glass back wall, watching the play. Not having met Goldberg, I couldn't tell whether he was one of them.

A few minutes later it was my turn to go on court. A shortish but fit-looking character with a genial face and manner was already there. He nodded.

'I'm Bill. And you are?'

'Oliver.'

'Hi!'

'You a New Yorker?' I asked.

He shook his head. 'Bangor, Maine. I'm in town visiting my son Will.'

We played. I reckoned I was about ten years younger than him, but I was a bit rusty. And he knew his way round a squash court. He beat me 11-9. Should I have won? Maybe.

Bill duly left the court and his successor arrived. He smiled and shook my hand.

'Stu,' he said.

The door to the court closed and I was alone with Stu Goldberg.

So was this the man who had ordered my intimidation and possible murder on a Manhattan sidewalk?

He looked pleasant enough – high forehead, big chin, wry, humorous mouth. Deep-set dark eyes gave him the look of a mournful dog, a Great Dane or bloodhound. Not the out and out monster I expected. After Carlton's unflattering preview, I had envisaged a brash, fast-talking hustler with a blue chin and a flashing smile. The blue chin was there, certainly, along with those sunken eyes, giving him a haggard, sleep-deprived look, but the smile was understated and the face thoughtful. His head was very large, under shiny, oiled black hair. He did not look like a murderer. More like a mild-mannered intellectual with a dash of melancholy.

You can be melancholy and still be a corporate takeover king, I suppose. I had met a few financial movers and shakers – appearances don't count for much in that line of work. What matters is what you actually do.

We stood in a court 21 feet by 32 feet. Each of us clutched a tautly strung racquet. No other weapons.

But the handshake should have warned me. Terry Eagle in Santa Barbara always shakes your hand before a match and smiles politely. He then devotes the next half hour to knocking the socks off you. As I would learn, Goldberg had a spot of that.

Too late for second thoughts. All I could do was give it my best shot.

We spun a racquet to see who would serve, and he lost.

I served.

I like to vary my service. I favour a hard serve at eye level but, if my opponent has good reflexes and can obviously handle that, I will try a slow lob which gives him time to think and, possibly, overthink. Sometimes he will get nervous and make a poor return.

Goldberg was not bothered by my fast serve. He dug it out of the corner with a strong backhand. Luckily I got a racquet on his return for a boast that died in the front court, leaving him stranded.

Point to me. But his reactions had been quick.

Clearly he had played plenty of squash. I would have to keep up the pressure.

Which I did. But so did Goldberg. He was ultra-competitive. We were brothers under the skin as far as that went.

He mixed drop shots with wily cross-courts. Some of them worked, others did not. For a man of forty he was not bad. Not a superstar, but useful.

The game was close. Soon I was serving at 10-all. At that stage, you must get ahead by two points to win the game.

He won the next point. The score: 11 points to 10, game ball in his favour.

The next point went on for three minutes which, at our level, is a long time. We were both gasping by the end.

His final shot was a desperate lunge, after I had pinned him in the back of the court with some good length drives. He got a racquet on the ball. It shot towards the side wall, hitting me hard on the right knee on its way. He turned on his heel and walked off court.

I had not been expecting that. Since the ball had not been travelling directly to the front wall, we should have replayed the point. But Goldberg seemed to have other ideas, since he was claiming victory.

Confusion reigned. For one thing, it was my turn

to leave the court, not his. For another, he had fudged the score to get the win. It's called cheating.

I sat on the bleachers, annoyed. Although there was nothing at stake, I was still cross. Actually, I was furious.

One of the many reasons I shall never be a billionaire is my respect for rules. Not the law, necessarily – that is something different – but rules. At my boarding school, I was considered pretty competitive but I was taught always to play by the rules. If you broke the rules at Bunnington, you were tossed off court in disgrace. It made life simple. I suppose I carried that respect into adult life.

But for tycoons, apparently, the rules were different. Or non-existent.

Maybe Goldberg had not been to boarding school.

To my surprise, he came and sat beside me.

'You played well,' he said.

'Not well enough,' I responded mechanically. Apparently I could not conceal my pique because he turned and looked at me with a faint, but sympathetic smile.

'It's just a game, dear.' He patted my leg. It may have been my imagination but I thought his hand lingered slightly on my upper thigh. I moved my leg away.

He laughed and stood up.

'Nice meeting you,' he said and walked away.

That was my introduction to Stu Goldberg.

What did I take away from it? Well, that he was a devious character. Charming; amusing if you appreciate that kind of wit. An egotist for sure.

But a murderer?

Freddie found me in the locker room.

'Lunch?'

'Sure.'

'We could go up to the dining room.'

'Can we go somewhere else?' I asked. Goldberg had creeped me out. I didn't feel like meeting him again.

He raised an eyebrow. 'Whatever. There's a sushi bar round the corner.'

'Perfect.'

We sat at the counter, a pitcher of hot saké in front of each of us.

'I'm chasing a pile of money,' I said.

'Nice.'

'It's not for me.'

I explained.

Freddie listened in silence. He is the sort of guy you just feel like sharing your innermost thoughts with. It helps him greatly in his work.

Finally he spoke.

'So you want to get close to Stu Goldberg and

pump him for information about Hassan and his money?'

'Exactly.'

'He's no fool, you know.'

'I'm well aware of that.'

'Good because for a moment I thought you might have overlooked the fact.'

I dipped the corner of a tuna roll in soy sauce and then wasabi and munched it appreciatively.

'I can tell you a couple of things about Goldberg,' said Freddie. He topped up my glass.

'Fire away.'

'First, the bad news. If you want to get closer to him, you're on the right track with the squash thing. But you're going to have to let him beat you.'

'He just did.'

'Not really. He knows he cheated. He won't be able to relax until he beats you, as he believes, fair and square.'

'So what should I do next?'

'Come back tomorrow.'

'Will he be there?'

'Sure, he seldom misses when he's in town.'

After Freddie had left, I looked in on David Palmer, the former world squash champion, who was at the club that day. I knew him from when I had helped with the admin at a tournament he ran in Florida. A thoughtful, super-fit Australian with an awesome winning streak in his makeup, he won the British Open four times and the World Open twice. He also happens to be one of the best coaches around.

'I need help,' I said. I explained.

He listened carefully, then nodded. 'No worries, mate.'

That afternoon we spent an hour doing some drills that he suggested.

Next day, with Freddie Parrott watching, I stepped on court again with Stu Goldberg.

The first point lasted four minutes. I did nothing particularly clever, not trying for winners; in fact I deliberately refrained from putting the ball away a couple of times when I had an open court. I just hit the ball solidly down the side wall, over and over again.

Seeing what I was up to, Goldberg did the same thing; it was pretty monotonous to watch. Finally it was the older man who mishit a drive. It clanged into the tin; point to me.

The next point was more of the same. Eventually I hoisted a lob that floated high over his head, out of reach. Again, point to me.

We made eye contact. He was breathing hard. I smiled. I wasn't feeling too wonderful myself but I wasn't going to let him see it.

I won the third and fourth points. We were both sweating freely. A patch of sweat formed on the floor at the back of the court. Glad of an excuse to rest, Goldberg called for a mop. There was a brief delay while we left the court.

Freddie pulled me aside. 'You are supposed to lose,' he hissed.

I nodded. 'I understand. Just trust me.'

When we resumed, things continued the same way. When I won the fifth point, Goldberg said 'good shot' through gritted teeth. After the sixth point, which he also lost, he muttered inaudibly.

He had nothing left, and I won the next five points. Game to me, 11-0. He scowled and walked off court without a word.

'You did the exact opposite of what I said,' said Freddie.

'I know. It's a gamble.'

'Well at least you got his attention.'

'That was the plan. Now we wait and see.'

I did not have long to wait.

I was enjoying scrambled eggs and devilled kidneys at the brownstone next morning when my mobile rang.

'Mr Steele?'

'Speaking.'

'This is Jean, Stu Goldberg's secretary.'

She sounded really nice – cheerful and intelligent, somewhat motherly. That's a lot to infer from just a few words, but sometimes you get a feeling.

'Hi!'

'He says do you have plans for the weekend?'

It was like when you are fishing, you have a line out and suddenly there is a tug on it. The game was afoot. Don't act too eager, said a warning voice.

'I was planning on heading back to Florida.'

'Oh, that's too bad. Stu wanted you to come out to his cottage in the Hamptons.'

I was briefly lost for words. I don't know quite what I had been expecting but it wasn't this. It sounded a bit intimate. I couldn't help remembering his hand on my leg.

She may have been partly reading my mind because she said, 'It isn't really a cottage, you understand.'

'Figure of speech, eh?'

She giggled. 'Not unless you call a thirty-room mansion on five acres overlooking Southampton Sound a cottage.'

I was going to accept the invitation no matter what, but I still hesitated.

'It has a squash court,' she said.

That was my opening. 'Oh, really?

'Brand new a year ago. Air-conditioned, with separate locker room and gym.'

'I'm impressed.'

'He likes to do things right.'

'We played at the Racquet Club yesterday,' I said.

'So I heard. He mentioned the score.'

'Did he now?'

'Yes, he did.'

I called Freddie Parrott. 'Guess where I'm spending the weekend.'

'The Hamptons?'

'You guessed!'

'Well I heard about his new court out there. Have fun! But next time, you really *do* need to lose or it's goodbye to a beautiful friendship.'

'Of course.'

'By the way, I promised you two pieces of advice about Goldberg.'

'I remember. What is the second?'

'He can't hold his drink.'

I wasn't sure what that had to do with anything. But not much Freddie said was inconsequential.

'I'll keep it in mind.'

11

NOVEMBER 12TH, 2011

When I drove through the white gates of Goldberg's Southampton estate on Saturday morning, there were already several cars parked on the smoothly raked gravel. A bright yellow Ferrari and a green Jaguar XJ, the long wheelbase version, made me salivate; my rented Camry looked pretty humble in comparison.

'He usually has a houseful of people,' Jean had said. Not poor people, apparently.

The house was pseudo-*Gone-with-the-Wind*, complete with white antebellum pillars, set in wooded grounds that stretched down to the seashore.

Goldberg himself came down the front steps to meet me. He looked studiedly casual in navy polo shirt and dazzlingly white jodhpurs. Sun tanned, with every black hair in place, he could have stepped straight out of the pages of *Vogue*. When I looked closer, I saw that the polo look was not just for show. He was dressed for the game, his legs stuffed into tight, calf-high boots of chestnut leather, buffed to a mirror finish. There was a large white figure 3 on the back of his shirt. The word 'ROLEX' appeared in large capitals across his chest, presumably as a sponsor, and sure enough he wore a massive gold Rolex wristwatch on a chain-link band that he had not had on when we met at the Racquet Club. I could understand why – the folk at the Racquet Club generally have pretty good BS meters and a sharp eye for the vulgar; he wouldn't have had the nerve to wear it there.

On his left breast was some kind of oversized insignia involving crossed polo mallets. Overall, he was either the complete polo player or way over the top, depending on your point of view.

'Got to pop round to the club for a practice chukka,' he laughed, pumping my hand. He showed no sign of annoyance about his recent annihilation on the squash court.

'Make yourself at home. There's a few people here already.'

He climbed into the Ferrari and was gone.

I grabbed my bag from the Camry and entered

the house, where I was met by a slim, well-muscled youth in tennis gear.

'I'm Rick. I'm Stu's personal trainer.'

He took my bag and led me upstairs.

My large bedroom faced the ocean. It had a king-size bed, its own bathroom and a general air of extreme comfort. The view of the sound from the window dominated the room, with white-sailed yachts wheeling in the bright sunshine.

I wondered when Stu and I were going to get our squash game. I knew it had to happen.

I strolled round the downstairs rooms. The first people I bumped into were an older couple, who were sitting on the terrace having afternoon tea. They introduced themselves as Sam and Rhoda Ofrichter. They seemed nice enough; Sam reminded me of my grandfather. He told me that he played bridge with Stu Goldberg.

With them was a dark-haired girl in her twenties, introduced as Hansi van Rensburg. Shoulder-length hair, pale oval face, nice figure.

'Hello,' she said. Just one word but the accent came through.

'Cape Town?' I asked.

She laughed.

'Johannesburg. And you? London?'

'Born there, raised in rural Oxfordshire.'

'Good for you.'

'What brings you here?' I asked.

'Study.'

'How so?'

'I'm going for a Masters in Business Administration at Columbia. I'm also an intern at Goldberg Freilich. I work for Stu.'

'Paid work?'

'Expenses only.'

'What was your BA in?'

'Mining Engineering. I was at Wits.'

I knew that Wits was short for the University of Witwatersrand in Johannesburg. It was one of the two leading South African universities along with the University of Cape Town, and a world leader in mining studies. The name was Afrikaans for 'Ridge of White Water,' the mineral-rich heart of South Africa's mining belt and one of the biggest gold producing areas in the world.

'You don't look like an engineer,' I said.

She just laughed.

Later, Rick the personal trainer caught up with me again.

'He wants to play squash tomorrow morning at ten,' he said.

'Fine,' I said. 'Seeing as you're here, could you show me the court?'

'Sure, this way. It's courts, plural. There is a full-size North American doubles court as well.'

'Do you play?'

'Squash? No, I'm more of a tennis guy.'

'I bet you're pretty good,' I said.

He inclined his head, smiling. 'Let's just say I've been playing a long time.'

The courts, needless to say, were in perfect condition. Walking back to the main house, I saw that the Ofrichters had left, but Hansi was sitting there alone, sipping some kind of iced drink through a straw.

She patted the deckchair next to her. 'Come and sit.'

'Rick was showing me the squash courts,' I said. 'I was going to suggest we have a hit, but he doesn't play; apparently tennis is his game.'

'He's not much of a tennis player either,' she said.

'Really?'

'Well, I can beat him, and the best I ever did was the second team at boarding school.'

I digested that.

'Well, if Rick doesn't play squash or tennis, what *does* he play?'

'Polo?' she suggested.

'He doesn't look rich enough.'

There was a companionable silence.

Finally she giggled.

'Oh,' I said. 'Sorry to be slow. Actually, I assumed the reason that you yourself were here was as Stu's partner, so to speak.'

She laughed. 'At cards, maybe.'

'So what is the connection between you and him?'

'It's complicated.'

I waited for her to go on, but she did not seem inclined to expand on the topic so after a moment I changed the subject.

We were chatting when my mobile phone rang. I saw from the screen that it was Carlton.

'Any progress?' he snapped. No 'Hi, there' or 'Hope you're well'.

'Hi, Carlton. how's the sailing?' I asked mildly.

'Fine. Where are you?'

'In the Hamptons, staying at Stu Goldberg's place.'

'Are you any closer to finding our man?'

'Hassan, you mean? No, but I'm working on it. Somewhere in Libya is my best guess at present.'

'Well, snap to it. Kalestian's getting anxious.'

'Sure, Carlton. Good night!' I hung up. His call had helped the cause not one whit. My irritation must have shown, because Hansi smiled sympathetically.

'Problems?'

'Not really. Sometimes work just follows you around.'

She laughed. 'I know the feeling.'

Next morning, punctually at ten am, I strolled downstairs, dressed for squash, racquet in hand.

As I left the house to walk to the courts, Goldberg appeared, also in squash kit. Waving, he caught up and we strolled across the grass together.

'When are you playing polo?' I asked, to make conversation.

'Two-thirty.'

'Hope this won't wear you out, playing squash!'

'Won't be a problem,' he smiled. 'Different muscles.'

'Fairly rough game, polo?'

'It can be,' he said lightly. 'Well, here we are.'

We played. Wouldn't you know, he got ahead by two games to one and 10-3 in the fourth game. Just couldn't find my form, I guess. Some days are like that.

He had a look of fierce concentration as he served what could be the final point.

I meant to hit it into the tin and lose the point, but some subconscious reluctance made me direct the ball an inch too high, resulting in a clean but unintentional winner for me. 10-4.

Still match point to him. This time I was more

careful and my shot clanged into the bottom of the tin. Gritting my teeth, I turned and shook his hand.

The smile on his face said it all; I've never seen a man who wanted to win so badly.

For a moment I almost liked him because I knew how he felt.

After lunch, we all went to watch Stu Goldberg play polo. Everyone was there – there was a feeling among the house guests that it would have been rude not to.

I sat next to Hansi on a hard wooden bench.

We watched the players cantering to and fro. They were swinging their mallets at the ball with mixed success – some of them seemed to miss the ball as often as they made contact. We watched for twenty minutes without saying much.

Finally, Hansi turned to me. 'Is this stirring your blood?'

'Not really.'

'Me neither.'

'It's like watching the ballet,' I said. 'If we were polo players ourselves, it might help because we would understand how difficult it is.'

'Maybe these players are just not very good?' she said.

'That too is possible.'

She stretched her arms over her head and

sighed. 'How would you like to drive us back to the house?'

I looked round. None of the other guests were looking.

'Okay.'

We got back to the estate.

It was a hot day.

'Want to go for a swim?' she asked.

'Sure.'

The temperature was a pleasant 78 degrees, with bright sunshine. Surrounding the immaculate pool, perfectly mown and watered lawns sloped down to the seashore. I had to hand it to Goldberg, every last detail about his expensive 'cottage' was perfect.

Hansi looked the picture of health in a white one-piece as she swam a couple of lengths using a proficient crawl, golden arms slicing through the surface, before stopping next to me, tossing her head and spraying me with water. We looked each other in the eye, laughing. It was an exhilarating moment.

'Tell me about "It's complicated",' I said.

She looked blank for a moment, then laughed, remembering.

'Well, I shouldn't say too much, but it has to do with my thesis on potentate capital and also with Stu's interest in money; he's pretty obsessive when it comes to the stuff.'

I had a flash of inspiration. 'Let me guess. Could it involve Hassan Qaddafi?'

Her jaw dropped. 'How in the world did you know that?'

'Oh, a lucky guess,' I said modestly.

She gave me an odd look.

'Well, it sounds as if you already know that Hassan was in the MBA programme at Columbia, partly at the same time as me; also with a guy called Sid Gelson who just happens to be the cousin of Jim Gelson, a vice president at Stu's bank.'

Actually, I had not known that at all. It helped explain how Goldberg had come to have control of Hassan's money, but it did not explain why the bank were so paranoid about giving me information, or about releasing some of the funds. It connected a few dots, sort of, but it was at best another thread in a pretty tangled ball of string.

'Very interesting,' I said casually, trying not to sound interested at all.

'Mum's the word, though,' she said.

'What?'

'Stu is incredibly security-conscious about the whole Hassan connection. Something to do with avoiding bad publicity for the bank. You have to promise you won't tell anyone else what I just told you.'

She looked really nervous and vulnerable, as

though she wished the subject had not come up and regretted saying what she had said. Vulnerability made her look even more attractive and I could see a tiny moral hazard, an ethical dilemma looming on the horizon. Well, I would cross that bridge if and when I came to it.

'You can trust me,' I said, crossing my fingers behind my back.

Some more guests trickled in during the afternoon, and there were twelve of us round the dinner table.

It was a cheerful meal. I have to admit that Stu Goldberg was a good host, chatting genially with his guests. His tongue did seem to get louder and looser as the evening wore on, though, and I remembered what Freddie Parrott had said about him and alcohol.

Afterwards he buttonholed me. 'It's a warm night. How about a nightcap on the terrace?'

'Sure.'

We chatted about this and that for a while. After a couple more drinks, I noticed a definite slurring and wondered if I might have to help put him to bed.

I was quite conscious of the fact that I was here to work, not for recreation, and so far I had not made any progress with that. I needed to learn something that would get me closer to Hassan and his money.

'You're British, aren't you?' he asked.

'Guilty as charged.'

'Noticed the accent. What part?'

'London.'

He seemed to ponder this. Just when I thought he had fallen asleep, he recovered with a start.

'I have a cousin in St John's Wood. Do you know St John's Wood?'

'Of course. I have some good friends that live on Allitsen Road.'

'My cousin is a composer. One of the artistic Goldbergs. Did a weird thing. He was making good money as a stockbroker, then gave it all up to write music.'

'Sounds a truly saintly character.'

'Name of Henry. Ever hear of him?'

Henry Goldberg. Oddly enough I had. Before I left England, I used to attend the annual Thaxted Music Festival. I recalled some delightful piano pieces by the composer Henry Goldberg, so I made the connection immediately.

Goldberg seemed overwhelmed that I had heard of his cousin.

'He was well connected in London, he could have made millions.' He was so moved that a small tear formed and trickled down his cheek.

'Is that what it takes?'

He seemed surprised. 'What?'

'Being well connected?'

'Of course.'

He frowned at me as if noticing me for the first time. 'What's your line, anyway?'

'Accountant.'

'Bean counter, eh?'

'That's what they call us.'

'My cousin Henry was not a bean counter; he was a rainmaker. Know what that is?'

'Tell me.'

'It's the guy that brings in the business. You bloody accountants, all you do is keep score. Any fool can do that.'

I stared at him and he held up a hand in apology.

'Listen, no offence. Really! But I built up a major bank, a *major,* major bank; I know what it takes.'

'I'm sure you do,' I said.

'You have to know the right people.'

'The right people?'

He nodded sagely. 'Rich people.'

'You must know a lot of rich people.'

'Damn straight I do.' It came out 'shtraight'.

'Care to name a few?'

He turned to face me, a cynical grin on his slack face.

'I'm just interested,' I said. I contrived an embarrassed smile, a sort of 'You guessed my guilty secret' expression.

He slid the brandy bottle towards him and poured himself another shot.

'Do you handle any Middle Eastern money?' I asked.

'Sure! All those guys come and see us. Dubai, Kuwait, Abu Dhabi, you name 'em. Want to know why?'

'Why?'

'Because they know we can make money for them.'

'How about Libya?' I held my breath.

'Oh sure. Got to be careful there though, with all the bad press nowadays.'

This was a crucial moment. I sensed the best tactic was a sympathetic silence.

He peered owlishly at me. Did he suspect something? If he did, I would soon find out.

'Do you mean that you manage some of the Libyan national funds?' I asked.

'Well, not exactly. But it's Qaddafi money.'

'I thought Libya's assets were frozen. Isn't that a problem?'

He shrugged. 'Not for us. These particular funds are not frozen; they are a special case. We manage the funds actively and, for doing so, we earn substantial fees.'

'If they were to become frozen, you would lose control of them, right?'

'Possibly, or at least we would have to manage them very much more conservatively. If that happened we would make much less money.'

Another long pause, broken by me.

'You mentioned Qaddafi – I read somewhere that he had a whole bunch of children, eight wasn't it?'

Goldberg smiled. 'Nine.'

'Nine?'

'You forgot Hassan.'

'Hassan?'

'You didn't know about him?'

I stared. Silence is not the same as lying. Not exactly.

'Hassan is Qaddafi's biological son by one of his female bodyguards,' said Goldberg.

I whistled. 'Fancy that.'

He nodded and tried to top up my glass but I put my hand over it. He filled his own.

'We manage over a billion dollars of his money.'

'That much?'

'It's not his exactly, but you know what I mean.'

I nodded understandingly.

'Does he hang out with the rest of the Qaddafi family?'

Goldberg shook his head. 'No. He lives separately. The colonel prefers – or rather preferred – to keep his existence quiet although, of course, some people knew.'

'Where does Hassan live?'

'Right now? In Libya some place.'

'How did you meet him?'

He suddenly looked suspicious. 'Who wants to know?'

I held up my hands, innocently. 'Just curious.'

He seemed to relax again.

'There's a certain gentleman in the Libyan Ministry of Finance who is a lot richer because he introduced Hassan to Goldberg Freilich.'

'You mean you paid a middleman?

Goldberg shrugged. 'Of course. You have to in that part of the world.' He grinned slackly. 'And don't think about ratting us out to the Feds under FCPA, we've got that angle covered.'

'FCPA?'

He stared at me. 'The Foreign Corrupt Practices Act. I can't believe you've never heard of it.'

Actually I had heard of it, but I held my tongue.

'In a nutshell, it is illegal to bribe someone to steer foreign business your way. But we've taken legal advice and, if the payment is plausibly structured as something else, we can sidestep the law – sort of. In other words, the Feds can't touch us.'

My weekend was starting to pay dividends – I silently thanked Freddie Parrott. I had wondered all along if some other Libyan would be acting as a kind of conduit to Hassan.

But I needed to know more.

'Boy, you guys are smart,' I said admiringly.

'One has to know how to go about these things.'

Smirk is an over-used word, but the look of cunning self-congratulation that suffused his face definitely qualified.

'Did you meet Colonel Qaddafi?'

'No. A couple of my guys flew to Tripoli. They were taken to a luxury villa out by the beach.'

'And?'

'They met Hassan and this other guy I'm telling you about – he likes to call himself a Senior Treasury Official.'

'And Hassan is really Qaddafi's son?'

Goldberg nodded. 'An arrogant young tyke, apparently. Well spoken in a quiet way, excellent command of English, but acts like he's the centre of the universe.'

'Okay to work with?'

'Not bad. But that is more down to . . .' He paused, as if he had been about to mention a name but had thought better of it.

'Down to the man from the Treasury?'

'Yeah. Mr Five Percent, let's call him.'

'Five percent of a billion? That buys a lot of couscous.'

'It sure does.'

I felt like asking more questions, but it was

getting late. I had learned a lot, and hopefully preserved my cover. Better not push my luck.

I got up.

'Long day, I think I'll turn in.'

He reached for the bottle again. 'One for the road?'

'What road?'

He scowled. 'What's the matter, can't handle a drink or two?'

'I'm afraid you're right,' I said. 'It's not very manly, but I've always been that way. Just body chemistry, I guess.'

'Well you're a smart young fellow. You could have a future in the banking business.'

'You really think so?'

He nodded. 'Call me when you get back to town and we'll talk about it.'

Dispensing patronage seemed to put him in a good frame of mind. I could cheerfully have smacked him but I just smiled respectfully and took my leave.

I was cautiously optimistic. The day had started badly, with my tanking a game of squash, but it was ending better. My next step was coming into focus – if I wanted to come face to face with Hassan, I realised I would have to start by tracking down the mysterious Mr Five Percent.

Which meant a trip to Tripoli.

To get upstairs, I had to walk through the lounge. Hansi was there alone, watching late night television. I sat down beside her.

'How's he doing?' she asked.

'I think the technical term is smashed.'

'That's par for the course.'

On the screen, a stand-up comedian was poking fun at President Obama's inconsistent attitude towards countries affected by the Arab Spring.

'What do you make of Stu?' I asked.

'He's gone downhill lately.'

'How so?'

She shifted on the couch. Her hip touched mine. She didn't seem to notice, but I did.

'He seems to have lost momentum in his business life.'

'Why do you think that is?'

'Lacks a sense of purpose, perhaps. They won't let him do what he's good at.'

'Which is?'

'Wheeling and dealing. Buying companies. Nowadays, the emphasis at Goldberg's is on making the different divisions work together efficiently. Stu does deals; he doesn't do efficiency.'

That explained something. There was a curious inconsistency between the attempt to run me down on a Manhattan street, which I assumed came from Goldberg Freilich, and its chairman's pally attitude today. It only made sense if Stu Goldberg was out of touch with what was going on in his own organisation.

'When are you heading back to town?' I asked.

'Tomorrow morning.'

'Me too.'

We watched some more television.

'Want to go upstairs and fool around?' I asked. The words just slipped out.

It got a half smile out of her. 'I hardly know you,' she said.

'We could change that.'

'Tell you what,' she said. 'Why don't I give you my phone number? You can buy me dinner some time.'

I can tell a brush-off when I hear one, but she had been nice enough to put me off gracefully and I awarded her bonus points for that. We walked upstairs.

When we reached her bedroom door, she stood on tiptoe and kissed me on the mouth. It was a pretty good kiss. Not long, but good.

'Don't forget to call,' she said.

12

NOVEMBER 13TH, 2011

Hansi had not lied to Oliver, but she had not been completely frank either. After they parted, she waited a few minutes, then slipped out of her room and along the corridor to Stu Goldberg's huge master suite at the front of the house.

'How are the Columbia classes going?' he asked casually, as they sipped champagne after making love.

She had watched him go through the performance of selecting a bottle from the well-stocked bar in the corner of the room, scrutinising the label and so on. She wondered how often he had put on this little show and for how many women. It would have been more impressive but for the shortcomings in his middle-aged figure, the pale buttocks and incipient paunch. His amorous efforts seemed to have sobered him up a bit although, since he habitually set about the task in singleminded silence, she could not really be sure. The whole scene was unromantic, but his bank balance made up for a lot of negatives, she reminded herself.

'They're going well,' she said. 'According to my supervisor, I have a shot at graduating summa cum laude.'

He looked surprised. 'Not bad for a hot babe.'

She stroked his chest. 'You're pretty hot yourself.'

Goldberg could not resist a feeling of satisfaction. To someone who craved the best of everything, thinking of women as trophies was a given. Hansi had wits, looks, youth, oh, definitely youth. What was not to like? And of all the men around, she had chosen him. The fact that he might have purchased her affections, rather than charming her with his winning personality, had quickly been relegated to a distant corner of his mind.

'What do you make of Oliver Steele?' he asked idly.

She smiled. 'Intelligent, but doesn't have your sophistication. Bit of a straight arrow.'

'What does he want?'

'I'm not sure what you mean.'

'Come on. They all want something.'

'They?'

'The folk who come kissing up to me.'

She caught her breath; he was getting uncomfortably close to home. But he seemed not to notice.

'He seems to be looking for capital. Maybe he's starting a hedge fund, isn't everyone?' she joked.

'It's odd though,' he said.

'Why?'

'If he is, I'd have expected him to ask me for money, flat out. He knows I'm in banking. What makes you think he is into something like that?'

She blushed. 'I overheard him on the phone. The call was from someone he worked with. I think he or one of his colleagues was looking towards Libya in search of finance.'

She felt Goldberg tense. 'Say that again?'

'He was talking to someone called Carlton.'

'Carlton who?' Good-natured Stu suddenly sounded much more focused.

'I don't know. When he took the call, he said "Hi, Carlton, how's the sailing?" or something like that.'

Goldberg swore. 'It has to be that little rat Carlton Tisch!' He was speaking to himself, not to her.

'Someone you know?'

'Our paths have crossed.'

She shifted slightly away in the bed. She sensed

that the romantic mood had dissolved; it was becoming a business meeting. It was an uncomfortable feeling.

'What else did he say?' asked Goldberg. He sounded inquisitorial. She pulled the heavy silk bedspread up to cover her breasts.

'Something about a possible source of funds.'

'Did he mention Hassan?' he snapped.

'Of course not,' she lied.

13

AUGUST 14TH, 2011

I n fact, there was a whole recent chapter in her life that Hansi had not shared, and could not share, with Stu Goldberg.

A few months ago and 5,000 miles away in Johannesburg, South Africa, she had met someone – another banker – called Danie Kruger,. He and Hansi met when they sat next to each other at brunch at the Johannesburg Country Club.

Danie Kruger ran a hedge fund and, due to a series of poor decisions, he was in a spot of trouble. Thirty-five and unmarried, Danie was tall and solid, a former rugby player from Pretoria, conventionally handsome with a bluff, unsubtle manner. He had short ginger hair and a face and neck burned reddish from the sun, real Afrikaner colouring.

'Is anyone sitting here?' He stood, holding a plate of salmon.

'You are, now.' She pointed to the chair and smiled.

Sunday brunch at the Country Club was a social and culinary event. Pride of place at the enormous buffet was a whole marlin four feet long. Silver dishes of smoked salmon, caviar, ham, eggs and roast meat were ranged on either side. The finest South African wines flowed. To hold back was impossible.

And neither Danie nor Hansi were the type to refrain from taking something they wanted.

From the moment their eyes met, they realised that they understood one another. Both were Afrikaners, both were ambitious. Both had strong appetites and not just for food.

'I'm Hansi. These are my cousins Piet and Lisa,' she introduced them and they nodded.

'Danie.' He bowed slightly and sat down.

'What do you do, Danie?'

'I run a hedge fund.'

'My word, you must be very smart.'

He shrugged. 'I can leap tall buildings in a single bound when I'm on form, but not so much just now.'

Her looks – dark hair, pale skin and the kind of smile that made the receiver feel special – made it easy to confide. By the second bottle of Cape Riesling, his tongue was loosened.

'I was a rising star at Johannesburg Global Mining, you may have heard of them?'

She laughed. 'Who hasn't? The third biggest mining group in Africa.'

'Second biggest. I joined them after graduating in Economics from Wits.'

'Fancy that, I was there too. What was your position at JGM?'

He shrugged. 'I moved up the ladder pretty fast, but I was a bit of a maverick.'

'What happened?'

'I was in line for Finance Director. Long story short, they said that, with me being an Afrikaner, my appointment would send the wrong message – Mandela and his lot were elder statesmen now, not convicts, everything had changed.'

'Who got the job?'

'An Oxford-educated Zulu woman who had played her cards right. Not as capable as me but politics ruled the day. '

'So you quit?'

He nodded. 'I told them to go play marbles and I went and started a fund, managing the money of some rich friends. I did okay at first, but later I made a few risky bets. Some of them have not paid off yet.'

'Investing for high returns involves gambling,' commented Hansi.

Kruger stared at her. She did not look the type to carry a conversation on a financial topic, let alone show insight. Her cousins had already tuned out and were talking to each other about farming.

'The situation now is not great, quite honestly. We have some unrealised losses; if the fund were liquidated today, things would be tricky.'

'Then you must let me pay for brunch,' she said playfully.

'Luckily, there are rules limiting how soon my investors can withdraw their money. They must give plenty of notice before they can cash out. So I have some leeway. But, bottom line, I have a few months in which to raise 100 million dollars. If I don't do that, things could start to get tricky.'

'Oh, I'm sure you'll make it,' she smiled.

He shrugged. 'I've got a few ideas.'

'It's a pity you can't get your hands on some of that Qaddafi money,' she said.

'What Qaddafi money?'

'There is a lot of it slopping around. Including much that will never be found by the authorities, despite their best efforts.'

'What exactly do you do for a living?' he asked sharply.

'I'm a business studies student at Columbia. My dissertation is on potentate capital.'

'Nice phrase. That explains a few things.'

She nodded.

'So tell me about Qaddafi,' he said.

'Well, let's see. Colonel Qaddafi probably holds the world record for making money disappear. Some say he salted away as much as 200 billion dollars during his forty-year reign.'

'Where is it all now?'

'That's the big question! About half of it, 100 billion, we can account for.'

'And the rest?'

'The rest could be anywhere. Western governments are doing their best to track it down but they won't succeed, frankly.'

'How come?'

'It's not difficult to hide money, and nobody ever accused Qaddafi of being stupid. Finding it is a lot harder; the authorities face so many obstacles when it comes to following the trail.'

'Don't they use computers?'

'Of course they do. There are programmes to search for words like "Qaddafi" or "Libya". But they won't identify accounts with the sort of dry, anonymous names that lawyers are fond of – like 'Third Street Nominees' or 'Acceptance Holdings.'

'I wish that you would try and get me an introduction,' he said.

She was quiet for a minute, trying to decide whether she liked Kruger enough to want to help him.

'Did you ever hear of Hassan, who is the natural son of Qaddafi by one of his female bodyguards?'

He shook his head.

'He is rumoured to control a major tranche of Libya/Qaddafi funds.'

'And you know this how?'

'He was a year ahead of me in the MBA programme at Columbia. He graduated last year, so he is probably in Libya now, not in the United States, but as far as I know he still controls that money.'

That was how Danie Kruger got the word, over a chance meeting at lunch. At the time, Hansi thought nothing of it, having not yet met Stu Goldberg and come within the web of his paranoia. But now, it presented her with an awkward case of divided loyalty. After they met, Danie Kruger had tried to do some research into Hassan but found very little. She knew that, and also that, based on his meeting with her and feeling he had nothing to lose, he decided to travel to Tripoli, hoping to track Hassan down and borrow some of the money he needed. But she dared say none of this to Goldberg.

Hansi fidgeted and Goldberg put out a hand and grasped her wrist.

'That's it; I did not hear him say anything more.' She disengaged herself and got out of bed. 'I think I'll drive back to town, I have classes tomorrow.'

He seemed to catch himself. With an effort he modified his tone and forced a smile.

'Sorry to sound so serious, there is a lot of stuff going on.'

'That's okay,' she said more softly. This was the man that was financing her Manhattan apartment and a more-than-comfortable lifestyle, she reminded herself.

She rescued her panties from the floor and headed for the bathroom. Goldberg heard the hissing of the shower. When she emerged, fully dressed, he seemed lost in thought and barely acknowledged her presence.

'I guess I can see myself out,' she said drily. He waved a languid hand.

After she left, he donned a bathrobe and went downstairs, where he poured himself another brandy. He sat out on the patio for fully half an hour in the warm night, gazing into space.

Finally he looked at his watch; it was one o'clock

in the morning. He picked up the phone and dialled a number. The country and area codes were 011-218, the prefixes for Tripoli.

In Libya, it would be just before seven am.

14

NOVEMBER 14TH, 2011

I t was Monday morning and Stu Goldberg was feeling antsy. In a few minutes he would have his regular weekly meeting with Harry Hartmann, the CEO of Goldberg Freilich and, as usual, he was dreading it.

The problem was that they were polar opposites. Hartmann, known to the media as Hacksaw Harry for his ruthless approach to firing employees he considered redundant, was abrasive where Goldberg was polite, and brashly decisive where Goldberg was relaxed and philosophical. This would not have mattered much except that Hartmann's manner towards Goldberg, despite Stu's achievement in assembling a huge financial conglomerate, was one of thinly masked contempt.

A wiry forty year old with sandy hair and pale

blue eyes, Hartmann blew through the door of Stu's office talking loudly on his mobile phone, threw himself into a chair and flung a heavy briefcase on the tooled leather top of Stu's desk. Finishing his call, he muttered, 'Good Morning,' opened the brief-case and withdrew a half-inch wad of reports. He flipped it open at one of several yellow tabs.

'I presume you've read these?' he barked.

'And those are?'

'The monthly financials. You got your set last week.'

'I probably did, but we've been a bit swamped lately.' His secretary Jean was hovering and now advanced carrying Stu's copy of the reports, which she slid in front of him. He forced a smile at Hartmann.

'Why don't you remind me what they say?'

Hartmann sighed impatiently. 'Well, thanks to significant right-sizing in recent months, initiated by me, our company is firing on all cylinders.'

The emphasis on the 'our' was not lost on Stu. It was a not-so-subtle reminder that, next to himself, Hartmann was the group's largest individual share-holder. He had been President of the Freilich stock-broking firm that Goldberg Freilich had acquired early in the group's development. As part of the acquisition agreement, he had negotiated a generous service contract for himself including stock options that were now worth, on paper, over a hundred million dollars. Back in those days, Stu had been desperate to maintain the pace of his acquisition programme. He had surrendered to many demands that he would nowadays not even consider, but it was too late now to go back and change things; the die was cast and he was stuck with Hartmann.

He reluctantly picked up the report and studied it. His eye was caught by an entry in red ink, a rare exception among the string of black figures in the profit column.

'We're still losing money on Wills and Estates.' He had picked out the loss-maker just to annoy Hartmann. It was a small division that handled wills and their administration; the bank often acted as executor for wealthy clients who had died and who, for whatever reason, had not wanted a member of their own family to administer their estate.

Hartmann frowned. 'If you recall, we both agreed that a modest loss was acceptable because that division rounds out our product offering. It underlines the fact that we are a full-service bank.'

'And that matters why?'

'Because we make a lot of money churning the investments of high net worth individuals – far more than we lose by handling their estates when they die.'

'Why don't we just raise our prices for the executorship work?'

'We're already charging as much as the market will bear. We do have competitors, you know. Besides, such fees are very visible. Our brokerage profits, on the other hand, are hidden – the customer never sees them.'

'How come?'

Hartmann sighed again. 'We've discussed this before. Our profit is obscured because so much of it is buried in the spread, the difference between the buying and selling price we quote.'

Stu was starting to get a headache. 'I just think every division should be profitable.'

Hartmann said, 'And apple pie is good. Bravo!'

Stu flushed pink with annoyance. Controlling himself with an effort, he flipped through to the last page of the profit and loss summary.

'Our overall profit is up eight percent,' he said grudgingly. 'But the income from conventional business is flat. Where did the growth come from?'

'Investment income.'

'With Prop Funds?'

'Correct.'

The term was shorthand for Proprietary Funds, meaning that the group traded using its own funds rather than those of its customers. Politically, moves were under way to limit this kind of activity, on the grounds that the risks could undermine the strength of banks that should be concerned with preserving a rock-solid home for their investors.

'What else is profitable?'

Hartmann shrugged. 'Many things. Feel free to actually read the report,' he said sarcastically. 'We made some good money in commodity trading.'

To Stu, the mysteries of commodity trading were even more of a closed book than banking as a whole. He had a vague idea that it involved the price of pork bellies on the Commodities Exchange. Beyond that, he was happy to leave it to a few highly motivated traders in the dealing room, whose compensation included huge bonuses.

He fidgeted; he had done enough thinking for one morning. His gaze wandered and came to rest on the squash ball sitting in a marble ashtray on his desk. Seeing the little rubber object cheered him up. Just over an inch across, it was black except for the white Dunlop logo and two tiny yellow dots that tagged it as an 'extra slow' version. It was the type favoured at the Racquet Club where he would be in an hour's time, taking out his dislike of Hartmann by walloping the ball as hard as he could, imagining the sandy-haired executive whimpering with pain as he did so.

He stood up abruptly. 'Well, I appreciate your helpful inputs, as ever.'

Hartmann nodded curtly. He saw he had little option but to leave. That did not bother him – his schedule, like his life, was close-packed; he liked it that way. One day, he thought, he would force Goldberg out and take his job. It was just a matter of picking the right time.

15

Shortly after Hartmann left, Hansi van Rensburg noticed the sheaf of pages on Stu's desk and picked it up. 'What's this?'

Goldberg laughed. 'About the most boring reading you can imagine.'

She glanced at the title: 'Quarterly Operating Statements – Company Confidential.' She smiled. 'You don't enjoy this stuff much, do you?'

'I hate it,' he said vehemently.

'Do you consider yourself numerically challenged?' she asked playfully. He shook his head.

'I don't think so. I picked up an MBA at Harvard so I guess I know how to fake it. I can muddle through. But I care much more about the big picture, so these little numbers just annoy me.'

She read a few pages, then flipped to the end. 'Good results,' she observed.

'Keep them to yourself,' he warned. 'They won't be made public for another five days; they are the basis for the quarterly "Form 10Q" that we have to file as a public company.'

She turned to the detail pages. Her studies at Columbia included classes on how to read financial statements, but this was the first time she had seen a real live set prior to publication and it was oddly thrilling. She wanted to ask if she could take it home, but Goldberg would probably say no, so she waited until his back was turned and slid it into her handbag anyway.

When she got home she showered, slipped into pyjamas and poured herself a glass of Chardonnay before taking out the statements and curling up in bed for a good illicit read.

She noticed, just as Goldberg had in his meeting with Harry Hartmann, that while the overall profit was better than the previous year, it was the sum of some wide swings in the divisions. The statements were laid out so that the profit could be compared, line by line, with the same period a year ago and she could see clearly that the biggest improvement was in commodity trading. The line in question was footnoted to an appendix at the back of the document. Curious, she turned to it. The bank had invested its own funds in some very large contracts and it listed several brokerage firms that had handled the trades. The largest was a company called Mercury Metals, which, from the name, she assumed to be specialists in metal trading.

She yawned. It was dry stuff. She had classes in the morning, so she set the reports aside and put out the light. Within moments she was asleep.

16

NOVEMBER 15TH, 2011

Early the next day, on her way to class, she went in to Goldberg Freilich and slipped the reports back into Jean's in-basket before either Jean or Stu Goldberg arrived.

That afternoon, back at the office after her classes, she waited for an opportunity, when Goldberg seemed not to be too busy. Borrowing the reports from Jean again, she took them into his office.

'Mind if I ask a few questions about these? It's good for my studies.'

'Not at all, fire away,' he said genially.

'Well, it's interesting how commodities propped up our overall results for the quarter.'

'Yes, that was handy.'

'Do you know any of the details, which commodities were involved and so on?'

He shook his head. 'Not really. Hartmann deals with all that stuff.'

He saw the look of disappointment on her face and added, 'Why don't you call him if you want to learn more about it? I'm sure he would be happy to help you. He's a busy fellow but he can usually find time to talk to a pretty girl.'

She smiled. 'Flatterer.' But she wrote down Hartmann's phone number and, a little later on, called and arranged to go and see him that afternoon.

Hartmann's office was not on Wall Street but in the 300 block of Park Avenue. She set out in a cab, wondering if he had deliberately situated it there so as to emphasise his nuts-and-bolts image and his independence from the lofty financial mystique of down town but, when she arrived, she saw that, in fact, it was located in a palatial edifice that was the headquarters of the Freilich stockbrokerage, rubbing shoulders with the Waldorf Astoria. If anything, the neighbourhood looked richer than Wall Street itself.

But Hartmann's office was utilitarian, with dove grey walls and a plain, if expensive, glass and stainless steel desk. He was in shirtsleeves, his jacket draped ostentatiously over the back of his chair. He smiled, flashing a wolfish array of white teeth, and ushered her to an automated coffee machine which dispensed a passable liquid into paper cups, another contrast with the more gracious atmosphere surrounding Stu Goldberg, whose secretary brought your refreshments on Crown Derby china.

'So you're studying for an MBA? That's terrific,' he said as an opener.

Hansi was past being irritated at people who were surprised that a good-looking woman was also intelligent enough to study business at a major university. She had developed a special demure smile of agreement, which she now deployed for Hartmann's benefit. It had the desired effect. He relaxed visibly, leaning back in his chair and radiating goodwill.

'Well, I can see how valuable it must be for you to get out of the classroom and interact with the real world, so go ahead and ask me any questions, anything you like.'

She had deliberately not brought the financial statements with her, reasoning that if she brandished them and started questioning highlighted passages, it would sound too much like an interrogation. Instead, she had made notes about what questions to ask, and committed them to memory. She looked up at the ceiling, went pink, and stammered, 'Oh gee, I don't really know what to ask.'

His pale blue eyes appraised her coldly; then he smiled.

'MBAs are supposed to be analytical. So if in doubt, why not ask about the numbers?'

'Oh, right. Well, I see the group did pretty well in the first quarter. Who were the main contributors to that?'

He nodded. 'There were several. Let me show you.' He produced his own copy of the quarterly statements and handed it to her.

She feigned helplessness. 'Where do I look?'

With a trace of impatience he leaned over her shoulder, a few inches closer than necessary, and ran his finger down the column. 'Here, see the large numbers – the ones in black, of course.' He laughed.

She peered at the page. 'This line made quite a big difference. It says "Prop Trading"; what does that mean?'

'That's short for "Proprietary Trading". It's the term we use for trades where we use our own funds, rather than those of our customers.'

'Isn't that risky?'

'It is if you don't know what you are doing, but we *do* know what we're doing. And as you see, the proof is in the pudding; we made out extremely well.'

After half an hour of questions and answers, she looked at her watch. 'I must go. I have classes.' She handed the reports back. 'Thank you so much, that was really interesting, and fun too.'

His eyes flickered away, his gaze not meeting hers. 'I'm thinking we should keep in touch; there's a lot I could teach you.'

She didn't much like the sound of that, but she nodded. 'That would be very nice. Why not call me this evening?'

'Splendid, I will,' he said.

She had no wish to start a relationship with this man who she found crude and unattractive, but she was calculating her responses carefully; she wanted to preserve the relaxed mood for just a while longer. As he was walking her to the door, she said, as if reflecting, 'It must have been tough for whoever took the loss.'

'Excuse me?'

'That kind of trading is a zero sum game, isn't it?'

'In what sense?'

'Well, if Goldberg Freilich made a big profit, someone else must have made a big loss – or did I misunderstand how these things work?' She smiled innocently.

'No, you are more or less right. But that is their problem, not ours.' He grinned.

'Just out of curiosity, who was the other party, or parties?'

He blinked briefly, then laughed. 'That would be Mercury Metals; they are the outfit who took the biggest hit.'

'Does that mean their stock will go down when these results are released, just as Goldberg's will go up?'

He shook his head. 'They are a privately owned business, so their stock is not quoted.'

'One of those faceless Chicago entities?'

He laughed. 'Something like that, but more international. They are based offshore, in some tax haven somewhere.'

As they waited for the elevator, she smiled and touched his arm. 'I really appreciate the help, thank you so much.'

'You're welcome. I'll call you.'

'Do that.'

But when he called that evening he learned that a touch of flu had laid her low, so a date would have to be postponed. His reaction was grumpy but resigned.

17

NOVEMBER 15TH, 2011

That evening, Hansi googled Mercury Metals. She had no idea what to expect; she just had an odd feeling that something – she had no idea what – was out of kilter.

Nothing came up at first. Apparently the company did not have its own website, nor was there a dedicated Wikipedia entry for it, although she learned some useful stuff about the element mercury, apparently the only element apart from bromine that was liquid at room temperature. She filed this away under information unlikely-ever-to-be-needed and moved on.

She remembered what Hartmann had said lightly about Mercury being based in a tax haven and tried linking it with the names of several offshore islands in turn. She specified the Cayman

Islands, Belize and Bermuda, all without success and was starting to lose hope when she tried Tortola.

She had spent a sailing holiday there a couple of years before and someone had pointed out that there was something of the order of a million corporations registered in Road Town, the island's modest capital. In some cases, company assets might consist only of a single ship or building; others were much more complex.

The tax advantages of setting up a Tortola subsidiary were so great that the governments of Britain, the United States and other first world countries had targeted the island as a major centre of tax avoidance. In Britain, the Prime Minister, David Cameron had announced a 'Tax Evasion Summit' and had written to the BVI, among other overseas territories, warning them that he had made 'fighting the scourge of tax evasion and aggressive tax avoidance' a priority. In the United States, according to Government sources, 83 of the 100 largest publicly traded companies acknowledged owning subsidiaries in places that offered tax and secrecy advantages. By one estimate, more than half of all world trade passed through tax havens, at least on paper. This was all very interesting, but it did not get her any closer to learning something useful about Mercury Metals.

But she then got lucky. When she did another

round of googling, linking Mercury with the words 'Metal Trading', she came across an intriguing lawsuit. It concerned an aggrieved customer of Mercury Metals who felt he had been cheated by being overcharged commission on certain transactions. He was hell-bent on getting satisfaction through the courts, specifically the Eastern Caribbean Supreme Court.

What caught Hansi's eye was the strenuous attempt by the prosecution to find out who really owned Mercury – something the owners were clearly reluctant to reveal. The shareholder of record was a trust company in Tortola called 'Road Town Intermediators' – the name alone inspired her curiosity. Its main activity seemed to be the providing of nominee shareholders and directors to various Tortola-based corporations that, along with local attorneys, it had helped set up.

She went back to Stu Goldberg the next day and shared what she had found. He looked a bit perplexed.

'Why are you telling me all this?' he asked.

'Don't you think it's a bit odd?'

'What is?'

'Well, for one thing, that so much trade was done with such a little known entity.'

Goldberg shook his head. 'Not really. Little known to the public, perhaps, but you will probably find that the company is well known to professionals in its field. That is often the way in this business.'

'I think I'll do a bit more research,' she said.

He shrugged. 'Suit yourself.'

As soon as she had left his office, he picked up the phone and called Hartmann.

'We need to talk,' he said.

18

NOVEMBER 14TH, 2011

Driving back into town from Southampton, I pondered what to do next.

My choices were fairly limited.

The key to the money I was looking for probably lay either in the bowels of Goldberg Freilich, or else in the hands of Hassan al-Manwani, son of Qaddafi, the young man Stu Goldberg had described as an arrogant tyke.

I decided to follow the bank lead first, possibly by putting pressure on Jim Gelson. It would mean staying in New York.

This suited me quite well, as I had other business in the city. Carlton thinks he is my sole client and treats me accordingly – basically as a paid vassal – but I actually have several other accounts. One of them is a movie producer going through an incredibly messy divorce. When it comes to money, neither he nor his wife believes a word the other says and each has retained forensic accountants to comb through the other's financial affairs in search of hidden assets. New York bank and brokerage accounts were involved, so I was in the right part of the world.

Did the prospect of a romantic dinner with Hansi van Rensburg also influence my decision? Absolutely not – the idea was ridiculous.

I dropped my rental car off at Hertz and took a taxi back to the brownstone.

As it turned out, a couple of days of totally absorbing work was involved. Progress can be slow in hostile situations where each party is doing his or her level best to mislead the other, and it was Wednesday afternoon before I could turn my attention to tracing the Qaddafi/Kalestian money.

Just as I was reviewing my notes from Macau, the phone rang.

It was Hansi.

'Well this is nice,' I said.

'You didn't call,' she said.

'I was about to.'

'Honest?'

'Honest,' I said. She laughed.

In relationships with women, I am usually the one that takes the initiative. I suppose I am programmed by my British upbringing to believe that the man should make the first move. But now that I come to think about it, my few successful liaisons have usually started out the other way round. The woman has said or done something – quite out of the blue – to start the ball rolling. As was happening now. So I felt a surge of optimism; life suddenly looked a whole lot brighter than it had five minutes ago.

'What's new?' I asked.

'Nothing much. Classes this afternoon. Thing is, there's nothing in the fridge so I was considering eating out tonight.'

'I could help you with that,' I said.

'Great minds,' she said.

There was silence for a minute, but it was the right kind of silence.

'I don't know where you live,' I said.

She gave me an address on Horatio Street, in Greenwich Village. Then she paused again.

'Anything special on your mind?' I asked.

'No.' Then, 'Well yes. There's some rather heavy stuff going down.'

'I see you've picked up the vernacular,' I said. 'Care to elaborate?'

'It can wait till this evening.'

'What time?'

'Say seven? There's a guy bringing a new TV, a

present from Stu, at six-thirty but he should be done by then.'

'A present from Stu, eh? Lucky you.'

'Yes, well. We can talk about that.'

'Okay.'

At seven o'clock, I arrived at her building.

It had no elevator and was not staffed by a porter. Accommodation in the Village used to be plain and cheap but nowhere in Manhattan is cheap any more, so now it is plain and expensive. She had told me she lived on the fourth floor. I walked upstairs, passing a delivery guy in TV store overalls on his way down. We exchanged nods.

To my surprise, the door was ajar. I tapped on it and shouted 'Hello!'

No reply, so I walked in.

There were no signs of a struggle. No signs, that is, unless you count the body on the kitchen floor.

When you see something like that, your spine tingles. That may sound like a cliché but it's true. The senses heighten. I knelt down and felt her neck for a pulse but it was obviously pointless. Her throat had been cut. There was a large pool of blood on the tiled floor under her head. Her cheek was pressed against the cold tiles but the skin of her face and neck was still warm to the touch. Her eyes were open. Whatever Hansi had felt like chatting about over dinner would forever remain a mystery.

Using my mobile phone, I called emergency and asked for the police.

Waiting for them, I sat on an expensive leather sofa and looked around me. It was a two-bedroom apartment with an open-plan living-room-cum-kitchen that was probably a conversion from two smaller rooms. The furniture and décor were not student-type, definitely more affluent than that, and in good taste. In the middle of the living room, still in its box, was a 40-inch Samsung flat panel television – apparently the new toy she had mentioned, since it had not yet been unpacked.

On an impulse, I got up and looked around. In one of the drawers, I came across a yellow legal pad Hansi had apparently been using to make notes on.

There were pencil jottings, mostly of phone numbers and website addresses; they looked as if they had been made while she was telephoning or searching her computer. A few phrases in particular caught my eye: 'So Mercury Metals is owned by a woman! Someone called Viola Barry, whoever that is. Who knew?'

The name meant nothing to me. I tore off the page, folded it and put it in my pocket, then sat down and waited for the police.

I did not have long to wait. In a few minutes, I heard footsteps tramping up the stairs and in came two plain-clothes detectives. One introduced himself as Frank Silver; I did not get the name of the other.

Silver whistled. 'What happened here?' he asked quietly. His pale blue eyes took in the situation quickly and his first action, like mine, was to check Lori's body for signs of life. He stood up and turned to me.

'And you are?'

'Oliver Steele.'

'What brings you here, Mr Steele?'

'I came to take Hansi out to dinner. As soon as I saw what had happened, I called the police. This whole scene is exactly as I found it.'

'How did you get in?'

'The door was open.'

'What is your relationship with the deceased?'

'We had only just met, at the house of friends where we were both visiting over the weekend.'

'Nothing more intimate?'

'No.'

'And where was that?'

'The friends? In the Hamptons. We drove back independently today; we spoke by telephone during the morning and agreed to have dinner this evening. I had just arrived to take her out.'

He stared straight through me, neither believing nor disbelieving. Then he said, 'I shall ask my colleague to search you. It is just procedure.'

I submitted to being patted down. Apparently this made him feel better; after that, he was more relaxed.

'Do you have any identification?'

I thought about giving him my business card, the one describing me as a financial sleuth, but thought better of it. I showed him a Florida driver's licence and CPA card instead. There is something about being a Certified Public Accountant that makes people reluctant to think of you as a criminal, unless it be one of the white-collar, upper-class kind, and he mellowed even more.

He wrote a few lines in a pocket notebook. Then he looked round the apartment. He pointed to the television in its box.

'What do you make of that?'

'She mentioned over the phone that it was going to be delivered today.'

He made more notes. As he was writing, I remembered the man who had passed me on the stairs.

'I think I saw the man who brought it, the delivery guy.'

At that point, the evening became very drawn out indeed, involving a trip to the police station, a session with a police artist to whom I described the man in overalls as best I could, and the writing out and signing by me of a statement on a white police form.

One thing missing from my statement was the name of Stu Goldberg. Nobody asked me for the identity of our weekend host so I did not volunteer it. I am not sure why, except that I wanted to think, the sort of thinking that is best done in peace and quiet, not in a noisy place surrounded by officious detectives barking questions. If that was wrong, then I did wrong. Detective Silver, seeing from my licence that I lived in Florida, asked me not to leave town for a few days and I agreed.

Finally I was free to depart. I made my way back to the brownstone, getting in around midnight. I decided to wait until the morning to call Carlton. There was cold chicken and ham in the fridge so I ate some, washed it down with a beer, and went to bed.

19

NOVEMBER 17TH, 2011

Next morning, I took out the sheet of paper I had rescued from Hansi's apartment, and looked at it. What did it mean? Who was Viola Barry?

I wanted to talk it over with Carlton, so I decided to head for Tortola again. Was my journey really necessary? Probably not, but New York was starting to have seriously negative associations for me and the clean air and perfect climate of the islands were exerting a powerful attraction.

When I got there, Carlton was in the kitchen, talking to a local businessman named James Trelawney, known for reasons I never discovered, and did not like to ask, as Hangman.

Hangman was in the car hire business. He

owned, with a partner, a fleet of four-wheel drive vehicles – Jeeps and the like. If you were a first-time visitor to the island you might rent from Avis or Hertz but if you really knew Tortola, Hangman was your man.

I never met his partner but I suspect he must have been a pretty good low-key manager because Hangman himself did not seem the administrative type. Trelawneys were Tortola royalty – the island's main ferry terminal was called the Trelawney International Terminal – and he had the self-assurance to go with that. He was one of the more extroverted folk I've met, tall, thin, dark-skinned, wearing blindingly white, immaculately pressed shirt and shorts. He was energetic and very articulate. He and Carlton treated each other with respect because each saw in the other a shrewd toughness that had made them, in their different fields, highly successful.

Hangman had been out fishing on one of his own powerboats and had brought some wahoo steaks as a present for Mimi. She had fired up the barbecue and was grilling them. Wahoo is a large game fish with razor-sharp teeth that fights violently when hooked; its white-grey flesh has a surprisingly delicate flavour, betraying its membership of the mackerel family, and is much prized. Caught and grilled the same day, the steaks were delicious, the freshness jumping off the plate.

We sat round the outdoor dinner table.

'So what's new in New York?' asked Carlton after we had washed the steaks down with a brisk Chardonnay from the Riteway market at Sopers Hole.

'I don't want to talk shop and bore your guest.'

He shook his head. 'Hangman won't mind.'

So I explained about the note I had found in Hansi's apartment.

'But I don't know where it gets us,' I said.

'I can tell you one thing that may help,' Carlton said with a dry smile. 'Harry Hartmann's wife's name is Viola.'

'Nominee wife,' said Mimi immediately.

'Meaning?'

'Meaning that your man Hartmann probably owns Mercury Metals himself. I'll bet dollars to doughnuts that Barry is his wife's maiden name.' She smiled. 'It takes one to know one. Carlton sometimes uses me that way. You would be amazed at some of the weird stuff I own, but it's strictly on paper.'

I still could not put it all together. If Harry Hartmann owned Mercury and Mercury had lost huge amounts of money, I could understand Harry being embarrassed. Nobody likes to be exposed as a loser, especially if his public image is that of a hugely successful businessman. But would that be enough reason for him to kill the person who gave him away? Hardly, unless Hartmann was a raging sociopath and, although he might be brash and lacking in personal charm, the man had no history of violence, at least as far as I knew.

Hangman had been listening quietly. 'Can I ask a question?'

'Of course,' I said quickly. I suppose I was embarrassed because I had thought that, being just a local guy, he might feel excluded from the conversation.

'You said this fellow Hartmann joined the bank as a vice president when his company was taken over?'

'That is correct.'

'Did he have stock options, by any chance?'

'He certainly did, about a hundred million dollars' worth.'

'Then he has a strong interest in pushing the price of the stock as high as he can.'

'True.'

'So if he creates some major transactions between Goldberg Freilich and Mercury Metals, with Goldberg booking the profit and Mercury taking the loss, that will help Goldberg stock and thus the value of his own options, not to mention his reputation as a management wizard.'

'Oh now I get it,' I said. 'But there's the little matter of the billion-dollar loss for Mercury, which is just Hartmann in another form. That's an awful lot of money for an individual to have to find, even a rich guy like him.'

'Not if the debt owed by Mercury to Goldberg remains unpaid, which may well be the case.'

'It will have to be paid some time,' I said.

'Yes, but it can be hidden away somewhere in Goldberg Freilich's balance sheet for quite a while. Besides, Hartmann may be getting desperate, thinking very short term, just trying to get past today at the expense of tomorrow.'

'Pushing a bow wave of losses forward into the future?' I asked.

'Exactly. Which suggests that the house may be about to come tumbling down at Goldberg Freilich.'

'It's certainly possible,' I said. 'It happened at Enron.' I looked at Hangman sharply. It was the first time it crossed my mind that a successful local businessman might also be a student of investment matters. But this was Tortola, BVI, home of almost a million registered corporations. It might be time to rethink some of my assumptions.

Carlton lit a cigar and looked thoughtful. 'Talking of Enron, Goldberg Freilich has another problem, and this could be the smoking gun as far as Hartmann is concerned.'

We all looked at him.

'Consolidation,' he said.

There was silence for a minute, probably because nobody had the faintest idea what he was talking about. Then I got it.

'Special purpose entities?' I asked tentatively.

'Exactly!'

'What's he talking about?' asked Mimi, slightly irritated. She did not care for Carlton's habit of being smugly cryptic about financial matters that she was ignorant of. He seemed to enjoy doing it more and more as he got older.

I explained: 'If the two companies, Goldberg Freilich and Mercury Metals, are considered to be under common control, their results would have to be consolidated. In layman's terms, they must be added together. Mercury is apparently controlled by the management of Goldberg Freilich in the person of Mr Harry Hartmann, via his wife. Ergo their results must be consolidated. When that is done, the profit in Goldberg is cancelled out by the loss in Mercury and the net result is zero – neither profit nor loss. It makes the whole exercise pointless.'

Hangman laughed. 'By concealing the element of common control, Hartmann was cooking the books.'

'Hansi found that out,' I said.

'But she never told anyone.'

'Someone killed her first,' I said.

'What would have happened if she had made the information public?' asked Mimi.

'All hell would have broken loose,' I said. 'Goldberg Freilich's results would have to be restated, for starters. Hartmann would have been indicted and would probably go to prison, along with anyone else knowingly involved in the fraud.'

'Could still happen,' said Carlton quietly.

We all thought about that for a bit.

'What happens next?' asked Mimi.

'Better leave that to me,' said Carlton quickly.

My brain started churning immediately, because I know how Carlton's mind works. He had, just moments ago, come into possession of some very sensitive information, and to Carlton that only meant one thing – opportunity.

The candles in the middle of the varnished wood table top were burning low and beginning to flicker. Overhead lamps in the kitchen cast some light out onto the terrace but the main source of illumination was the full moon that hung in the sky above Jost Van Dyke, the island across the bay. I yawned and looked at my watch.

'It's been a lovely evening but I'm quite tired, it's odd how these warm tropical evenings get to me. I think I'll turn in. Thanks for the delicious fish, Hangman. Good night, everyone.'

Back in my room, before I went to bed, I made a brief but important phone call to my friend Freddie Parrott in New York.

Next morning I slept until nine, then stumbled out to the terrace and sat for a few minutes with both elbows on the breakfast table, my hands round a mug of strong black coffee brewed by the Tisches' maid Louise, gazing at the incredibly green islands across the bay. Only half conscious, I had barely taken my first sip when I was confronted by an angry Carlton.

The little man was jumping up and down, red in the face. Steam was coming out of his ears. Well, not literally, but you get the general idea. He was not happy.

'What did you do?' he snapped.

'Sorry?'

'Don't come the innocent with me.'

'Not sure what you mean.'

'You leaked the news.'

'What news is that?'

'Goldberg and the special purpose entities. It was in the *Journal* this morning. Goldberg stock cratered in after-hours trading, so someone must have put the word out last night.'

'Well, that's all very interesting but I don't understand why you are so upset.'

Actually, I knew exactly why he was upset, of course. I had judged correctly that he had planned to make a killing by shorting Goldberg stock and, for some obscure reason, I had been determined not to let him do that; hence my timely call to Freddie.

I suppose that shows a basic ambivalence in my attitude to Carlton.

I like the guy. His wife is charming and the fact that they have a great relationship tells me he isn't all bad. But his other side – the shark-like quality that compels him to sniff out every opportunity to make money and then go for it, full ahead and damn the torpedoes – irked me.

Was I jealous? Yes, of course. I would absolutely kill to have Carlton's clarity of vision when it comes to spotting opportunities, although I happen to believe I would exercise the gift in a more enlightened way. I had a sudden, implausible vision of myself as master investor, dazzling the financial community with my superb command of information and timing, a combination of Soros shorting sterling and Nathan Rothschild using his carrier pigeons to make a killing after Waterloo. I, of course, after making adequate provision for myself, would have dedicated the bulk of my fortune to charity – meet Oliver Steele, the great philanthropist.

Carlton has a disconcerting way of reading

minds. He sat down next to me and we enjoyed the spectacular view for a few moments. He had calmed down with surprising speed, as he always does.

'It's just a game, you know,' he said quietly.

'You think?'

'Nobody gets physically hurt. The only ones who may lose big are the pros, and they can afford it.'

To him, at least, this seemed sufficient justification; ten minutes later he was cheerfully explaining how he intended to win the next round-the-island race.

So we remained friends, at least according to our own, subtly tinted-(or tainted)-by-commerce brand of friendship.

I went home to Coconut Grove, wanting to get out of the pressure cooker environment that Carlton always seemed to generate around himself.

I had been planning to phone Carlton next morning just to keep the relationship smooth, but I never got the chance because he called me at eight am while I was still working on my first cup of coffee. His news was game-changing.

'Kathy has been kidnapped.'

It took me a moment to focus.

'What do you mean? Do you mean kidnapped as in for ransom?'

'We don't know.'

'How do you know she was kidnapped?'

'We had a call from the fellow she was with when it happened. She was in Tripoli.'

I rose three feet in the air. 'What the heck was she doing in Tripoli? Why did nobody tell me she was going there?'

'We only just found out. It's something she did on her own initiative.'

'I should have been told.'

'This is not about you; calm down.'

Carlton's manner was gruff even on a good day, but that was a definite rebuke. Which I guess I deserved. I took a deep breath.

'Was she with people there? Libyans?'

'No, a Swiss, an attorney called Berg. It happened yesterday. We had spoken to her by phone when she called Mimi. She was in a taxi, driving from the airport to her hotel.'

'What did she plan to do there?'

'We're not sure, but there are two possibilities. She told Mimi she thought that, if she could find Hassan's mother, she could find Hassan. Sounded iffy but you know Kathy, that's how she thinks.'

'What is the other possibility?'

'She may think she knows where his money is.'

'How so?'

'Well, it turns out this guy Berg is an attorney with the Swiss government. His department tries to trace stolen money, what the Swiss call "potentate capital". Apparently Kathy found that out. She called him out of the blue and told him she had a line on a large cache of Qaddafi's funds.'

'Is that true?'

'I don't know. If she did, she never told me. She's quite capable of making up a story just to get this lawyer's attention. She suggested that he come and meet her in Tripoli and she would share her information.'

'And did she?'

'Did she what?'

'Share information.'

'She never got the chance. According to Berg, they had barely shaken hands when a couple of Arabs in nightshirts, waving machine guns, grabbed her. In full view of a lobby full of hotel guests and staff, they dragged her out of the hotel and away into the night.'

'Unreal.'

'Yeah. Luckily she left her purse behind; they didn't get that. Berg found her phone. It took him a few hours to think of it, but eventually he pressed the redial button to call the last number she dialled, which was here.'

What I felt was unprintable, but I said nothing out loud.

Carlton said, 'You had better come here so we can make a plan.'

I don't often contradict Carlton point-blank, but this was different. Another meeting with him was the last thing I needed just now.

'Where can I reach this Swiss?'

'He's staying at the hotel. He speaks good English.'

'I wasn't planning to speak to him in Schweiz-erdeutsch,' I said testily. 'Now if you will excuse me, I have to go.'

'Go where?'

'Libya, of course.'

'You too?'

'You have a better idea?'

This was not the first time Kathy had been in trouble; she has quite a talent for it.

There was the time in Las Vegas when she got very close to the al Qaeda terrorist Saddiq, taping an electronic bug to his underpants so that we could overhear him talking to his associates – the trick worked well, I admit.

Or there was the time she charmed fugitive drug dealer Frankie Leon, wanted in the United States for murder and other misdeeds, and coaxed him onto US soil by promising to sell him a deserted Bahamian island as his private tax domicile. Sounds absurd, but Leon bought the idea and was promptly arrested in the Florida Keys. Not Kathy's fault that he jumped bail, helped by his sleazy attorney and escaped in a high-powered speedboat to offshore parts where, as far as I know, he remains to this day.

Her attitude to me is interesting. We met when I rescued her father, who had a $200,000 gambling problem, from the clutches of a sadistic debt collector. You might think that would count for something but apparently no good deed goes unpunished because sometimes she seems to resent rather than like me.

But that was all in the rear-view mirror now. I know I tend to grumble about Kathy and the way she occasionally upstages me in front of Carlton. I will even admit to being a bit thin-skinned about it. But the shocking news had caused a flash, a moment of clarity. Without question, our antagonism is professional, not personal and this sudden development reminded me how much I liked her; I could not possibly stand by and do nothing.

I was making hurried travel plans when Freddie Parrott called.

'I have to know,' he said. 'What was the score?'

'Goldberg beat me,' I said. 'I let him. But there's more.'

By the time I had brought him up to date, he had grown very quiet. Finally he said, 'I'll give you the number of someone to call in Tripoli. His name is Ian Calder.'

'What's the connection?'

'We played tennis and squash when I was doing my Rhodes scholarship at Oxford and he was at LSE. Now he runs the Tripoli office of one of the big accounting firms. He's one of the good guys.'

I noted the phone number carefully. The brotherhood of the racquet had stood me in good stead so far.

20

NOVEMBER 21ST, 2011

Two days and several airports later, I was having morning coffee with attorney Victor Berg in the lobby of the Corinthia Hotel.

He was a dapper individual in a suit. Not one of those tweedy English suits that look as if the wearer should have mud on his brogues; this was a smooth bright blue number in some material like gabardine, much more orderly – more, well, Swiss.

Anxious doesn't begin to describe the look on his pale face. He probably wasn't used to dealing with kidnappings, especially right under his nose. But, besides anxiety, there was something else: embarrassment.

'I'm so glad you are here,' he said.

'Okay,' I said.

'It's not my responsibility, you see.'

'I see.'

'I'll do what I can to help, naturally.'

'It has been two days since she was taken.' I said. 'Tell me what happened.'

'We were sitting here, in this very lounge, talking.'

He looked around nervously, as if afraid the same thing would happen again. Two large guards stood uncomfortably, one on each side of the main doors, their hands resting lightly on the machine guns slung over their shoulders. Their khakis had security company flashes – hired help. I guessed they had been posted there in the aftermath of the incident.

He saw the direction of my gaze.

'The hotel has increased its security.'

'Has anything been heard from her, or her captors?'

'No.'

'Did you call the police?'

'The hotel called them, of course. But I doubt if they will achieve anything. Life is chaotic here.'

'How did you both come to be in Tripoli?'

He brightened, as if relieved to talk about something he knew.

'Miss Smith telephoned me. I work for the Swiss Government in a department concerned with our banking system. Swiss banks are the most secure in the world, as you know, but recently they have been much criticised. The same features that make Switzerland a safe haven for honest money have also led to its abuse by some notorious despots.'

'Like Qaddafi?'

'Among others. We realise that this kind of thing has been going on for far too long. It gained global notoriety when Nazis stashed the wealth confiscated from Jewish families during the war there.'

'Which those families were often unable to recover.'

He bent his head in concession. 'Although we had earlier provided the same service to Jews who had the foresight to move their money in good time. The saying that "money has no taste" is just as true for the oppressed as it is for the oppressors.'

I had neither the time nor the inclination for a debate, so I moved on.

'And you are here looking for money?'

He nodded. 'Potentate capital.'

'Where does Kathy come in?'

'I am afraid I don't know. I did not have time to ask before she was abducted.'

'She told you nothing?'

'Not at our meeting. When we spoke a few days ago, she said she had information I would find useful.'

'Did she mention anything specific?'

'Only that it involved Qaddafi's family. I thought she might mean one of his children.'

I felt a twinge of alarm. Sometimes you suddenly realise you must choose your words carefully, or you could get into trouble. Like when you are pulled over for speeding. I had that feeling now.

I had nothing against Victor Berg. He seemed affable. Professionally, he and I had similar objectives; we could probably help each other.

But we were also rivals. The money I was seeking for Michael Kalestian, with a nice commission for myself, was also of keen interest to Victor. To the extent that it turned out to be in Swiss banks, it risked becoming entangled in the tentacles of the Swiss Government's system. Only later – much later – would it be returned to some so-called representative of the Libyan people.

Did he know about Hassan and his wealth? If not, I was not going to be the one to tell him. But if he did – if it was already common knowledge in Victor Berg's circle – what then? In that case, all I would achieve by silence would be to keep Kathy's life at risk for even longer.

Clearly her safety was paramount. It trumped Michael Kalestian's selfish need for capital, not to mention mine for a commission. But otherwise, how was I going to get anything out of Victor Berg?

'What do you know about the Qaddafi family's whereabouts?' I asked.

'I understand that a convoy of Mercedes cars carrying the mother and at least one son was seen driving towards the Algerian border.'

'When?'

'Last week. If they weren't caught, they must be across the border by now.'

He was starting to fidget. I had not learned much, but I could not think what else to ask.

'How do you plan to go about finding Qaddafi's money?' I asked.

'I have the names of some government officials.'

'In the Ministry of Finance?'

'Among others.'

A thought struck me. 'Including Mr Five Percent?'

He looked puzzled, as though not sure what I was talking about. I wasn't sure either.

Awkward silence.

Not much doing there.

We shook hands and promised to keep in touch.

I felt discouraged. Berg had been no help in explaining Kathy's disappearance. Neither had he provided any clue that might help me find Hassan. I had to find another avenue.

I called the phone number Freddie Parrott had given me for Ian Calder, the expatriate Briton who managed the local office of LevyTeagardenHooper, the curiously unpunctuated accounting giant. I explained that I had a problem.

'Come on round.'

The voice was educated English, with a smoker's rasp.

I took a taxi and in minutes we came face to face.

Ian Calder was short and compact, in his forties, with a permanent wry grin on his face. He wore a short-sleeved cotton shirt and khaki slacks. The shirt did not quite conceal a barrel chest and hairy arms.

'You're just in time for lunch,' were his first words.

'As you wish.'

'What's your pleasure, local food or international?'

'Local.'

'A man after my own heart. Let's go.'

He drove a dusty Peugeot SUV a bit too fast, making the tyres squeal by leaving his turns until the last minute.

'Aren't you concerned about the hostilities?' I asked.

'Yes and no. It *is* dangerous, because, even though Qaddafi is dead, there are still plenty of loyalists who don't seem to have got the message. They roam around independently and have plenty of ammunition. On the other hand, the ordinary people of Tripoli are generally friendly to foreigners.'

'Do you have a personal bodyguard?'

He shook his head. 'No, unlike some. Most of the diplomats and oil executives who have remained here spend their lives cocooned by security guards. They are shuttled between home and office in armed processions, seeing little of the real life of the country. In my book, life is too short for that.'

'It's a point of view,' I said doubtfully. 'How much farther?'

'Almost there,' he said.

'Where are we?'

'This is the old City. Over there' – he pointed – 'is the Roman Arch of Marcus Aurelius.'

He parked and we got out.

'This is Semiramis, one of my favourite restaurants. The food is good, and it's not a hotel. When I eat in hotels I don't feel I'm in Libya.'

'I know what you mean.'

The head waiter, an Arab in smart Western dress, approached us, smiling.

'Mr Calder, welcome, sir.'

'Hi, Kemal. Can we have a table outside?'

'For you, sure.'

Menus arrived. 'What's good?' I asked.

'What do you fancy? Fish, couscous, falafel?'

'Surprise me.'

He ordered in Arabic, then smiled at me. 'No booze, I'm afraid.'

We sipped mint tea.

'Now, how can I help you?' he asked.

'I am here to find a missing woman.'

I explained how Kathy had vanished into the night, and his eyes widened. When I had finished my story, he nodded soberly.

'I hate to say it, but she may have fallen prey to a "kidnap for ransom" scheme of the kind that has become all too common here in recent months.'

'What is the best response?'

'You may just have to wait until they get in touch, whoever "they" are. Then, tell them that you will pay for her release. And hope that all they want is money!'

'I don't have any money, not personally. I could raise some, though.'

I was less confident of that than I sounded. Privately, I was wondering how to broach the idea to the notoriously tight-fisted Carlton. But Calder shook his head.

'It doesn't matter, at least not for now. You are just trying to make contact.'

'How would I start? To make contact, I mean?'

'Spread the word.'

'How?'

He shrugged.

'Advertise. In the local paper, or on the radio.'

'Is it that easy?'

'For you as a stranger, no. But I can have my office do that, it's not rocket science.'

'Thank you.'

It was a start, at least.

'How long have you lived in Libya?' I asked.

'All my life. My grandfather founded the firm in Tripoli after the war. My father opened a branch in Benghazi. I was sent back to England to boarding school and to train in the City. When I qualified, I came back here. A few years ago, we were absorbed by LevyTeagardenHooper.'

'That name,' I interjected.

'What about it?'

'It sounds silly. Just my opinion.'

He smiled. 'No comment. I didn't choose it.'

'And are you the senior partner in Libya?'

'We don't use that term. The other partners are ethnic Libyans and we all have an equal voice. Like me, they trained in England. Like them, I have Libyan citizenship. But as a Brit, of course, things work best if I take care of the British and American clients.'

'There can't be many of those, if the oil industry is nationalised.'

'You would be surprised. The oil patch still depends heavily on foreigners.'

'Hasn't Libya trained its own experts?'

'Yes, but it's not that simple. Libyans are smart people, but they don't work much outside Libya, so their expertise is limited. Suppose a well catches fire. The world's best putter-out of fires is based in Texas, everyone knows that. The same goes for other specialities, like electronic logging or drilling mud.'

'Drilling mud?'

'Take too long to explain.'

'What sort of service does your office provide?'

'Auditing is our bread and butter. But we also provide something even more useful.'

'What's that?'

'Scuttlebut.'

I raised my eyebrows and he smiled.

'Doing business here is about *who* you know, not what you know. We know who to talk to, which strings to pull. The official term is "market intelligence" but mostly, it's high quality gossip.'

'Do you know any members of the Qaddafi family personally?'

He shook his head. 'That isn't necessary. There is a whole layer of civil servants at a level below the family; they are the bureaucrats who run the country.'

'I imagine most dictatorships are like that. Somebody has to convert the leader's big ideas into reality, or at least make him think that they are doing so.'

'Exactly.'

'Have you heard of Mr Five Percent?' I asked casually.

He laughed. 'Of course.'

Bingo!

The waiter arrived with our food. He set a reddish earthenware pot in front of me, and whipped off the lid with a flourish.

Inside were what looked like pieces of braised veal. The pottery shell had sealed in the juices and it was tender and delicious. I ate with enthusiasm.

Calder watched. 'What do you think?'

I nodded.

'I never thought of Libya as veal country, but this is good. Is it imported?'

'Not imported, and not veal. It's baby camel.'

By then I had tasted enough to press on regardless.

Over coffee, black and sweet, I asked him: 'Tell me about Mr Five Percent.'

He gave me an appraising look.

'Mind if I ask why you want to know? I'm happy to do a favour for a friend of Freddie's but some areas are sensitive and we are hovering close to one of them.'

I explained about the Macau Excelsior and its financing shortfall. He listened intently.

Finally he nodded. 'Well, okay. But be warned in

advance: the gentleman has gotten that nickname for a reason.'

'For taking a cut, presumably.'

Calder nodded.

'Exactly. He occupies a senior – but unspecified – position in the Ministry of Finance. Over the years, by putting Libyan money together with investment-oriented foreigners, he has earned what is rumoured to be a very large personal fortune.'

'By taking kick-backs?'

'By making introductions.'

'That makes it sound rather easy.'

'Believe me, it's not.'

'What's so hard about introducing one person to another?'

'The hard part is not getting your head chopped off for doing it.' He smiled. 'Leave some room for dessert.'

We nibbled on little sweet pastries.

Calder said, 'With Qaddafi gone, there is a power vacuum – nobody knows who is in charge. Things may stabilise one day, but the process could take years. Meanwhile, banks are in the spotlight, even innocent transactions are under intense scrutiny. Even honest businesses are having trouble moving cash around. Do you understand?'

'I think so.'

'So if you want Laith to find you some money, you may have left it too late.'

'Laith?'

'Laith Saad. Mr Five Percent.'

'Ah!'

We finished our meal and he stood up. 'Let's go.'

'Thanks for lunch.'

'You're welcome. I'll set up a meeting with Laith.'

'I see why you are so prized by your clients.'

Driving back, I felt I was getting to know him a little bit, so I said, 'Your car could do with a wash.'

He laughed.

'Maybe not. Nowadays, it's a good idea to be inconspicuous. Before the Arab Spring, I drove a brand new Mercedes. I had it washed daily. But protective colouring is the order of the day now. This is my ten-year-old runabout from home.'

'It's less likely to be stolen?'

'Or blown up, with me inside it.

Danie Kruger had tried to find out more about Hassan but found very little. So, based on his meeting with Hansi, somewhat desperate and feeling he had nothing to lose, he travelled to Tripoli, hoping to track him down and borrow some of the money he needed.

The first thing that happened when he got to Tripoli was that a young Arab called Mustafa tried to steal the hubcaps off his car.

The car was a full-size rented Cadillac. It was parked in a decent part of town and there was nobody around.

Mustafa and a pal had been cruising the neighbourhood in his truck, in hope of finding a lone pedestrian who looked affluent enough to be worth mugging. They had not had much luck and were about to call it a night.

Mustafa was a product of his times. He was a working-class youth who spoke unusually good English, the result of much listening to American popular music and an appetite for any English language magazines he could lay his hands on. A year ago he had been nobody, unemployed, the skipper of his local soccer club, the Tripoli Tigers. Thanks to a lively intelligence, he was acknowledged as their leader, but he and his football-playing friends were basically just a happy-go-lucky bunch of toughs in their early to mid twenties.

When Qaddafi's grip on power began to loosen, with law and order falling apart, many things changed. The Tigers broke into a police station and helped themselves to firearms. Growing bolder, they kidnapped a local merchant, a notorious Qaddafi suck-up. They ransomed him for $10,000. His family paid up promptly and Mustafa saw how compliant well-off citizens could be when faced with some good old-fashioned intimidation.

Today the football team had rebranded themselves as the 'Islamic Freedom Army,' with several dozen members. They were not religious, despite the name, but they had weapons and a growing reputation for being willing to use them.

Mustafa spotted the Cadillac, which was parked

round the corner from a restaurant near the Corinthia Hotel. The hubcaps bore the distinctive Cadillac badge and, capriciously, Mustafa decided he wanted them. The street was deserted. He grabbed a tyre iron, jumped out of his truck and started to lever them off the car's wheels.

His timing could not have been worse. Just as he began to work, the restaurant door opened and out came several people, including the car's owner.

Mustafa realised that this could be serious. Petty crime was severely punished in Libya. You could be publicly whipped for taking food from a snack bar without paying. That had happened to a friend of his and the young man still had the welts on his back to prove it.

He made to run but it was a cul-de-sac, and he was cornered by the group. Their leader was this big red-haired guy in a suit. He barred Mustafa's way with an angry look on his face. Mustafa was holding a stolen hubcap in one hand so he didn't have much of a case but he gave it a try.

'Greetings, sir, I am delighted that you are here. I was coming to look for you.'

'Oh, is that right?'

The man smiled but his eyes were cold. He stood well over six feet tall and looked fit and strong. Mustafa was thin and wiry, barely five foot eight. The man outweighed him by fifty pounds.

'Yes, sir, these are special hubcaps, very sought after here in Tripoli which you might not know, you being a distinguished visitor.'

'What I know is that those are valuable, and you are stealing them. I should have you arrested.'

He turned to his companions. 'How do I call the police?'

'Please do not, sir,' Mustafa said quickly.

In fact, law and order had effectively collapsed in Tripoli. The police – what was left of them, many having deserted – had their work cut out responding to murder and major disorder. The risk of their turning out to arrest a petty thief for stealing hubcaps was slight, but still, he could not be entirely sure.

'I will make it up to you,' he pleaded.

Kruger looked him up and down.

'You may be an enterprising young fellow, but I doubt if you can help with the kind of business I am doing here.'

'I have many connections,' Mustafa improvised.

Kruger smiled. 'You are not a member of the elite; you are a thief.'

'Isn't it the same thing?'

The words just slipped out. But they seemed to amuse Kruger and he laughed heartily.

He seemed to forget about the police. He made Mustafa put the hubcap back on. Then to Mustafa's amazement he tipped him thirty dinars – about twenty American dollars.

'Go on, get out of here,' he said.

Then he paused.

'But you speak good English, perhaps you could be useful. Come and see me at the Corinthia tomorrow morning. Ask for Mr Kruger.'

When Mustafa presented himself at the hotel reception desk next day, the staff treated him with suspicion. But he persuaded them to call Kruger's room. Mr Kruger's word was enough, apparently, because their attitude changed and a page led Mustafa upstairs.

Kruger ushered Mustafa into an imposing suite with views across the city's rooftops. There was another man there, too, a foreigner in his thirties. Mustafa recognised him as one of the group outside the restaurant the night before.

Kruger sat Mustafa down and grilled him about himself. Mustafa explained how the Tripoli Tigers FC had become the Islamic Freedom Army. Kruger spoke English with a guttural accent that Mustafa could not place, but he frequently turned and spoke to his colleague in what Mustafa later learned was Afrikaans.

Finally he looked Mustafa in the eye and said, 'Look, my boy, I told you last night that I am negotiating for some big business here, very big indeed. I am speaking to senior members of your country's government, or what was the government until very recently. Whether they have the authority they claim to have is not always clear. Sometimes I think they are not telling me the truth. That is where you come in.'

'Of course, sir,' Mustafa said enthusiastically. He had no idea what Kruger meant. 'What would you like me to do?'

'I need a back channel, a second source of information, especially when I am not here. You will be my eyes and ears, my seeing eye dog.'

'You can absolutely rely on me for that,' Mustafa said.

He wondered what sort of business Kruger was negotiating, but he did not really care. If Kruger wanted him to know, no doubt he would tell him.

'I shall have expenses,' he said.

Kruger smiled ironically. But he did not say anything so after a minute Mustafa said, 'How much would you pay me?'

'How much do you want?'

Then, before Mustafa could speak, 'I will give you five hundred a month, starting today.'

'Dollars?'

'Yes.'

Mustafa had not been expecting nearly so much.

He almost fell over in surprise, but recovered quickly.

'That is not enough,' he said. 'It is not just for me, you understand. I have to pay my associates. To do what you want, I would need a thousand dollars.'

Kruger's eyes narrowed. 'I'll pay you six hundred.'

'In cash, fifties?'

'Not a problem.'

Kruger held out a hand and Mustafa shook it.

A thought occurred to the young Arab.

'If you want us to kill anyone, that will be extra.'

Kruger's expression froze.

Then, slowly, he nodded.

Later the same day, Kruger called Mustafa's mobile number.

'Come round here, I have a job for you.'

Mustafa was there in twenty minutes.

In Kruger's hotel suite with its expensive carpet and furnishings, he stood out like the tough street kid he was. He intrigued Kruger. He looked, frankly, capable of violence. Well, Kruger had nothing against a spot of judiciously applied violence when you had to get stuff done.

Mustafa wandered round the room. He had clearly never been in a place like that before. He stared at the wood-panelled refrigerator and opened it. He took out a half bottle of scotch that Kruger had smuggled into Libya in his luggage and had placed there. He fingered it, staring at the label before replacing it and selecting a small can of orange juice which he opened and drank.

Kruger said, 'I want you to find somebody for me.'

'No problem.'

'I hope so,' said Kruger. He explained about Hassan.

'I heard that rumour,' Mustafa said.

'What exactly did you hear?'

'That he is Qaddafi's bastard.'

'Is it true?'

'Probably.'

'I want to meet him.'

'Like I said, no problem.'

'How would you set about finding him?'

'I have contacts.'

There was a thoughtful look in Mustafa's eyes. He fingered the brocade curtains as if trying to assess their value.

'What will you give me if I bring him to you?'

'I'll make it worth your while.'

Mustafa made full eye contact with Kruger. 'Yes you will,' he said and smiled.

For a moment, Kruger glimpsed the man hiding within the boy.

It was a bit scary, even to a hardened sinner like him.

22

NOVEMBER 17TH, 2011

To him, I'm just the young thug, thought Mustafa. He could tell that was how Kruger saw him. Well, if that was what the man wanted to think, so be it.

As he took the elevator down from Kruger's suite and strolled out into the street, there were a lot of contrasts but the most striking one was the stink. The air in the hotel was sanitised, hospital-like – God knows what they dosed it with in their air-conditioning system. Outside, the odour was of sewers and garbage, not overpowering but notice-able after the clean hotel.

Abu picked him up in his truck which was air conditioned and, after that, the thought of the odour vanished from his mind.

He set out to look for Hassan's mother.

It was not very difficult. Some things that are secret on an official level are widely known on the street and the sexual peccadilloes of the Brother Leader definitely fell into that category. The woman's existence was common knowledge; her name was Rhianna al-Manwani. It was a simple matter to find out where she lived.

He wasted no time. Taking Abu with him, he went to her house.

He left Abu lurking out of sight round the corner. There was one of those glass peepholes in her front door. He assumed an ingratiating smile and rang the bell

'What is it?'

'You left your credit card in the grocery store,' Mustafa said.

He waved a card at her, too far away to be readable.

'It can't be mine,' she said.

'That's odd, it has your name,' Mustafa said cheerfully.

Well, it might sound incredible, but it worked. She opened the door a crack.

Abu came round the corner to join Mustafa and they shoved their way inside. The surprise on her face was almost comical as she realised she had been tricked. She retreated before them.

'What do you want?'

Mustafa could tell she was afraid. It was the worst of times in the city, after all. He smiled to put her at her ease.

'A word with your son Hassan.'

'He doesn't live here.'

'Fair enough,' he said. 'Where does he live?'

'Why do you want to know? Who are you?'

Abu moved close and leered in her face. She stood her ground, although she was a full head shorter. He pushed her hard in the chest and she staggered back until she was pressed against the wall. Abu pressed his arm against her throat, pinning her back.

Mustafa strolled over to the desk. There were keys, a mobile phone, pencils and a leather-covered address book. All neatly arranged – a woman who liked to have her life in order. He opened the address book. The very first entry was the name of her son, with an address and phone number. He put it in his jeans pocket and nodded at Rhianna.

'I think we're done here.'

She saw what he had taken and her face went white.

'What do you want with him?' Her voice, previously disdainful, wavered.

'Just a chat,' he smiled. He beckoned to Abu. 'Let's go!'

Abu said, 'Take her cell phone.'

'Good idea.' Mustafa slipped it into his pocket. Another thought struck him. 'Let's have a look in her bedroom.'

Abu leered again. Mustafa brushed impatiently past him into the small room. There was a night-stand by the frilly bed. On it stood an old-fashioned Bakelite telephone. He traced the cable to the wall and ripped it out of its socket.

'Now we can go.'

They left her slumped on the sofa, the apartment door open.

It was baking hot outside. Abu's truck was noisy and spotted with rust but Mustafa had the exciting feeling that fortune was with him.

The address for Hassan in his mother's address book was in a respectable part of town. It was a modern apartment building, smart and clean with six floors and had 'expatriate' written all over it. Its tenants were probably in the oil industry, he thought. Such people seemed to require a standard of living that was as essential to them as compressed air to a diver. They needed their own food, their own cars, their own furniture in their own apartments that had to be air conditioned and of a good size, with uniformed guards to protect them from the natives outside.

One guard was standing in the lobby, just inside the entrance. The military effect was somewhat spoiled by the cigarette drooping from his lips. He looked at Mustafa, then scowled and touched the handle of his holstered pistol.

'We're looking for Hassan al-Manwani,' Mustafa smiled.

'Nobody of that name here,' said the guard. He obviously expected them to go away.

Mustafa moved a step closer. Abu came in from the other side. The guard took a step back.

'Are you for the revolution, Brother?' Mustafa asked politely.

The guard licked his lips. It was a scary question because, nowadays, you never knew quite how to reply; it depended who was asking. The right answer would earn you a nod of approval; the wrong one could get you a bullet in the face.

Abu stepped in and punched the man in the stomach. He gasped and doubled over. Abu disarmed him and handed the pistol to Mustafa, then kicked him in the side as he fell.

They approached the desk where another guard was seated. He wore dark glasses. Despite his crisply pressed uniform, he looked soft. He had watched the fracas but had not come to the aid of his colleague.

'Hassan al-Manwani?' Mustafa enquired.

The guard swallowed nervously.

'That name is not registered here. Truly I do not know who you mean.'

Something in his manner told Mustafa he was telling the truth, but it did not matter because Mustafa already knew the apartment number, 64. It was presumably on the sixth floor.

Leaving the cowed guard sitting in his chair, they took the elevator.

They arrived on the sixth floor.

For the second time that day, Mustafa assumed a smile for the benefit of anyone looking out through the glass peephole. He knocked.

The door swung open immediately. The speed at which it happened caused him brief alarm, which he suppressed.

Standing in the doorway was a man only a couple of years older than Mustafa, and similar in height and dress. He was smooth skinned, clean-shaven, his eyebrows dark and silky, with a supercilious smile as he looked Mustafa up and down.

Mustafa was aware of an obvious gulf between them, heightened by the man's neat, almost soft appearance. He felt uncomfortable and the feeling made him angry.

'Hassan Qaddafi?' he asked gruffly.

The smile flickered slightly.

'That is not my name.'

'Well, whatever you call yourself. You're the person I've come to see.'

Hassan cocked an eyebrow. 'You and your rough friend?'

Abu took a step forward but Mustafa restrained him. Violence might come later, but not now.

'If you like.'

'What do you want with me?'

'Personally nothing. But my boss would like a word with you.'

'And your boss is?'

'Someone important.'

Hassan's smile broadened. 'Important, eh?'

'More so than you, my friend,' Mustafa scowled.

'Please be specific! Who is this mystery gentleman?'

Mustafa motioned to Abu to shut the door. He moved close to Hassan.

'Well I suppose you'll find out soon enough.'

Hassan drew back and waved his hand before his face, as if to disperse an unpleasant odour. Mustafa flushed, but controlled himself.

'His name is Danie Kruger. Perhaps he will teach you some manners.'

Then, to Abu, 'Take him!'

Abu moved towards Hassan.

But as he did so, the door to the bedroom flew open. Two men emerged, moving quickly, machine pistols at the ready. They trained their weapons on Abu who stopped short.

Hassan smiled at Mustafa. 'So?'

In silence, the gunmen disarmed Abu. Mustafa, too, was searched and disarmed. Abu scowled helplessly at Mustafa.

'What do you think you are doing?' Mustafa asked angrily.

Hassan stood in front of Mustafa, looking thoughtfully at him.

'I don't know anything about you – or your politics, if you have any. But it doesn't matter because I know one thing for sure – you are not my friend. We are living in a war zone and I ought to kill you; it is the only way to be safe in these mad times.'

'Will you at least talk to the man who sent me?' Mustafa asked.

Hassan appeared to consider the request.

Finally he said, 'Do you have a mobile phone?'

Mustafa nodded. 'Shall I call him?'

Hassan shook his head. 'Just dial his number and hand me the phone.'

Mustafa pressed a few keys, then reluctantly handed the device to Hassan.

'Thank you.' Hassan examined the screen. Then, seeming to come to a decision, he nodded to one of his gunmen. The man raised his weapon and shot Abu in the chest.

The gunshot echoed round the interior of the apartment, but it was probably inaudible or at least muffled out in the street, so life went on as usual in the fractured world that was Tripoli in the Arab Spring. Mustafa watched, horrified as Abu collapsed, blood spreading over his robe.

'Keep the blood off the carpet,' said Hassan. 'Move him into the kitchen, it is tiled in there.' He watched as this was done.

Then he pointed to Mustafa. 'Now shoot this man through his left hand.'

The phone rang in Danie Kruger's suite at the Corinthia Hotel.

He answered. 'Hello?'

'This is Hassan.'

'Hassan who?'

'I'm the person you sent Mustafa to see.'

'Oh, you're the son of . . .'

The voice cut him off.

'Just leave it at that. Someone may be listening.'

'It's quite safe, there's nobody here,' said Kruger.

'In Tripoli, telephone conversations are public property,' said Hassan drily.

'You speak pretty good English,' said Kruger. 'That is your American education, eh? I hear you got your MBA in New York.'

Hassan laughed shortly. 'Four years at a

boarding school in Surrey are where I learned proper English.'

Kruger shrugged. 'Very well.'

'And you are from South Africa. An Afrikaner, from your thick accent.'

Kruger was taken aback. 'You are a bit of a smart aleck, young man.'

'Smart enough. What do you want?'

'We should talk.'

'Give me a reason.'

'I can help you.'

Hassan laughed. 'Oh really?'

'Yes.' It came out 'Yiss'. 'There are some good points and some bad points about your situation. I can help you build on the good points.'

'How so?'

'You have access to money. That is good.'

'And the bad?'

'As soon as you show up in person to claim any of that money, you will either be arrested or shot, depending whether the nearest authorities are pro- or anti-Qaddafi.'

'I can see you have thought this through.'

'Yes I have.'

'You're quite smart.'

Kruger laughed. 'For an Afrikaner?'

'Yes.'

'Well, I think I am.'

'What do you propose?' asked Hassan.

'We should work together.'

'Meaning?'

'I assume you can transfer funds electronically. You probably have passwords that protect your identity. The banks that hold your money may not even know who you are.'

Hassan said nothing. The South African might be crude, but he had a good understanding of the situation.

'I am not saying that is true, but what if it is?'

'I think you need help. Oh, that system may work for modest transactions. But for major amounts, I suspect you need a front man, a personal representative, someone who is at home in Western banking circles. Someone like me.'

'What would you want in exchange?' asked Hassan.

'An investment.'

'What sort of investment?'

Kruger laughed. 'For that we shall have to meet.'

'I'll think about it,' said Hassan.

'While you are thinking, put Mustafa on the line,' said Kruger

'Can't do that, I am afraid.'

'Why not?'

Hassan laughed shortly. 'My bodyguard shot him just before I called you.'

Kruger swore. 'Is he dead?'

'No. The other man is dead; I kept Mustafa alive. But I think he is in too much pain to talk.'

'Are you mad?'

'No. But this is Tripoli.'

Mustafa was back in Kruger's hotel suite.

His left arm was in a sling. Much of his cockiness was gone.

'Well, you did a good job with that,' said Kruger sarcastically.

Mustafa looked at him and shrugged.

'He was ready for us.'

Kruger shook his head. 'Well, you probably know what we are going to do next.'

'What?'

'It's quite simple. We are going to shadow that little jerk Hassan and then, at the right moment, we shall bring him into line.'

'It will be my pleasure,' gritted Mustafa, looking at his injured hand.

'The problem is I don't know where to look. He will probably have left his apartment. He won't stay there; he is no longer anonymous in that building.'

'I know who would know,' mused Kruger.

'His mother?'

'Exactly.'

'Want me to go back there and sweat her a bit?' asked Mustafa.

'Yes, why don't you do that?'

'Okay, boss.' Mustafa made for the door, but Kruger stopped him.

'Wait!'

'Yes?'

'On second thoughts, I'll come with you. I'd like to talk to her myself.'

23

NOVEMBER 18TH, 2011

As Kathy Smith was being dragged away from the Corinthia Hotel her brain froze and, for a few seconds, she was unable to process what was happening.

She winced as a gun barrel was jammed in the small of her back. She tried to wriggle out of the rough grip on her arms. She felt a violent tug as she was hoisted out of her chair.

As they dragged her across the floor, she could hear the clatter of her own shoes, medium heels, on the marble tile. She smelled rank breath in her face as one of her assailants leaned in and barked incomprehensibly at her. She tried to go limp, since she was clearly not strong enough to break free. She was hoping that they would be taken by surprise and lose their grip, but they just grasped her more firmly.

She tried to twist round and look at Victor Berg, but they were holding on to her by brute force. She did catch a glimpse of him before she was wrenched away; her last impression was of the shocked horror on his earnest Swiss face.

Then they were outside. She felt cool hotel air being replaced by the moist heat of Tripoli and then by more air conditioning, this time with accents of leather and sweat as she was bundled roughly into the back of a large car. She sat squeezed between her two guards, smelling their sour odour as the car pulled away from the kerb, engine roaring.

The driver barked over his shoulder in Arabic. One of her captors produced a grubby scarf, which he tied roughly over her eyes. Pretty pointless, she thought, if they were trying to stop her from seeing where they were taking her; they could have saved their energy because the whole scene was totally unfamiliar. One street looked just like another.

She felt oddly relieved that she had been blind-folded; perhaps it meant she was not going to be killed, but would be released at some point. She had read that terrorists in the Maghreb practised kidnap-ping for ransom. She had a moment of fearful amusement as she tried to imagine notoriously tight-fisted Carlton Tisch reacting to a ransom demand for one of his wife's girlfriends. Then she came down to earth and faced the dire truth: she was alone, helpless and far beyond the reach of anyone who, in the normal world, might come to her aid.

After a while, the engine note gave way to a lower, steadier hum with less frequent changes in direction. She guessed that they had left the city and were in open country. That went on for what seemed like hours; as time passed, she found she was slowly able to calm down and collect her thoughts.

'Where are you taking me?' she demanded loudly.

The only reply was in Arabic from the man on her right, followed by laughter from the others. So much for establishing a dialogue with your captors.

She wondered if there was a way she could contact Victor, the nearest thing she had to an ally in the whole of North Africa, but she could think of nothing. She had no purse, no phone, no money – what was the use of even dreaming?

Her reverie ended abruptly when she felt the crunch of gravel and the car turned for the last time and stopped.

She pulled the blindfold from her eyes, expecting resistance from her guards, but there was none. This was explained when she looked around and realised that they were indoors, offering no clue as to their whereabouts.

They were inside a large garage. The car that had brought her, she now saw, was a black Mercedes. It shared the garage with three other vehicles. One was a dark green Range Rover; next to it, a white Toyota Land Cruiser. The third vehicle, which she did not recognise, had the rakish lines of a powerful sports car. An enthusiast could have told her that it was a Bugatti Veyron, the sixteen-cylinder monster that is the fastest street car in the world and also the most expensive. Unlike the dusty Mercedes in which she had arrived, all three cars were polished to a mirror finish.

The overhead door was closing behind them but, as she peered out, she could just see a walled courtyard with high wooden gates being pushed shut by a white-robed figure with a rifle slung over his shoulder.

A fountain played in the middle of the courtyard, its jets splashing softly into a ceramic basin, white glazed tiles with blue figuring. Then she was hustled out of the garage through a connecting corridor, apparently leading to the main house.

They were walking along a passage with rough, whitewashed walls. Wrought iron sconces supported what at first sight looked like candles but the steadiness of their light betrayed them, however artful, as electric. The place was cool and spotlessly clean. In the background, a generator hummed.

She was hustled through a Moorish archway into a great formal room. Patterned wall tiles and Persian rugs, with damask sofas that matched the curtains over the windows, gave an air of luxury verging on opulence. Clearly no expense had been spared; its formal quality betrayed the hand of a professional decorator rather than the owner himself.

A slight figure was seated at a desk at the far end of the room. As they entered, he stood and approached Kathy, motioning the guards aside.

He held out a hand and smiled, self-satisfied rather than welcoming.

'Greetings. I hope your journey was not too stressful.'

She scowled and ignored the hand.

She saw a young man, maybe twenty-seven – slim and no taller than herself. He was good looking, almost effeminate, with a smooth face and soft brown eyes beneath dark lashes. He was not intimidating but, at the same time, he had the self-assurance of a person used to getting his own way and accustomed to being the centre of attention in his own surroundings.

He looked her up and down, mildly impertinent, taking in the tight blouse and the skirt hemline above the knees. She ran her hands involuntarily over her thighs, tugging the fabric down. Her palms were moist despite the air conditioning.

'Who the hell are you?' she said.

The smug smile broadened.

'I'm surprised you have to ask, since you have just flown several thousand miles to meet me.'

Hassan al-Manwani. She was completely blind-sided, although she realised immediately that she should not have been. The Western manners, the obvious affluence, the secrecy, all made sense. But how on earth had he known she was coming, or where she would be staying?

He saw her surprise, and laughed. 'You are wondering how I found you.'

She scowled acknowledgment.

'I have sources,' he said. Again the annoying smile. She was about to make a hostile reply but caught herself. It had never been her plan to antago-nise Hassan, after all. On the contrary, a good rapport was essential if she was to coax money from him for Michael Kalestian's hotel.

She looked around.

'What is this place? Where are we?'

He shook his head. 'I would rather not say. But you are quite safe. I am sorry I had to use a rather crude method to bring us face to face but the truth is I simply could not risk having you wandering round Tripoli creating noise and attention while you looked for me. There are many hostile parties about, including warlords thirsting for my blood, so I have to keep a very low profile.'

Kathy was rapidly recovering her poise.

'Do you know why I am in Libya?' she asked.

He shrugged. 'Not exactly. I am aware that a man from South Africa is here seeking capital for a hedge fund; perhaps you are associated with him.'

That was unexpected as well as untrue. She hesitated. She suddenly felt very tired, not surprisingly since she had endured a transatlantic journey, a kidnapping and an hour-long drive, blindfolded, to where she now was. She pulled herself together.

'We can discuss that,' she said.

Hassan Qaddafi spread his arms. 'I'm listening.'

She shook her head.

'Later. What I want now is to sleep.'

He frowned and she sensed annoyance but to heck with it, she was not going to budge.

'And a decent bathroom, if there is one.'

'The accommodation here is well up to American standards,' he said curtly.

He proved to be right. A maid, oriental in appearance, showed her to a bedroom that would not have disgraced a five-star hotel. She surveyed the room and the adjoining bathroom testily, trying to find fault, but could see none.

She turned to the maid and spoke slowly and loud, with gestures. 'My name is Kathy. What is your name?'

'Josefina.'

'Do you speak English?'

Josefina laughed. 'I am from the Philippines; it is one of our official languages.'

'Oh. Well, I have no clothes. Your employer did not see fit to let me pack a bag.'

Josefina looked her up and down. 'I am about the same size as you. I can lend you some pyjamas. Meanwhile I will have your clothes laundered; they will be ready in the morning.'

It was the first kind word Kathy had heard and for a moment she felt like crying. Thoughts of Stockholm syndrome flashed through her mind. Get a grip, she told herself crossly.

She took a long hot shower and headed for bed, in Josefina's pale blue pyjamas. Expensive sheets, she noted. The moment her head touched the pillow, she was asleep.

She awoke feeling much refreshed.

Sunlight streamed in through the window. She rolled over and checked her Casio digital wristwatch. It said ten past three am. If that was true, it should still be dark outside. Then she remembered the six hours difference in time zones between Libya and the Caribbean. Libyan time was ten past nine in the morning. She had not adjusted her watch after the journey.

Her clothes were waiting for her on the dresser in a neat pile, washed and ironed.

She dressed and walked tentatively out of her

room and down the hall, emerging in the courtyard. A male servant saw her and motioned her to sit down at a wrought iron table. Without saying a word, he brought a clean white cloth and set the table. Breakfast came, consisting of strong Turkish coffee, flat pitta bread and little dishes of hummus, black olives, a crumbly white cheese similar to feta and several kinds of jam. No eggs or waffles, not exactly the Hilton, she thought to herself, but the unfamiliar flavours combined appealingly and the meal went down surprisingly well.

Hassan Qaddafi appeared and sat down opposite her. After enquiring politely how she had slept, he came to the point. 'What exactly do you want from me?'

She took her time pouring more coffee.

His fingers tapped on the tabletop and she noticed the impatience. She told herself to make allowances, that this was someone on the run who dared not admit his existence in public lest he get assassinated. Not an easy situation.

This did not quite arouse her sympathy – he still seemed arrogant and she was not warming to him – but it was a factor to take into account.

'Here's the thing. I represent Michael Kalestian.'

Hassan's eyes widened. Clearly he was surprised. He looked thoughtful.

'Well I know what he wants,' he said.

Kathy nodded. 'He needs money to finish his casino.'

'I understand. Unfortunately there is a problem.'

'What sort of problem? A casino in Macau is still an excellent investment, just as it was when you put money into it before.'

'Oh, I am sure it will be profitable. That is not the issue.'

'What is, then?'

He sighed. 'Logistics, I suppose you could say.'

'I don't understand.'

'Well my funds are not here in Libya.'

'Where are they?'

'That is really none of your business. Suffice to say, they are in safe custody with a major bank.'

She nodded. 'I know, Goldberg Freilich. So what?'

He frowned. 'You are better informed than I expected. Anyway, since the Arab Spring the bank has grown very nervous and hyper-cautious.'

'Have your funds been frozen?'

'Not so far.'

He was clearly uncomfortable with the discussion, but she pressed on: 'If the US Government were to find out about them, I am sure they would be. So apparently, like a lot of missing money, your assets have not come to their attention.'

'And I want to keep it that way.'

'So what is the problem?'

'The bank is insisting that I appear and sign off personally before it will release major funds. It argues that, with the political chaos, there is a serious risk that someone masquerading as me could give it bogus instructions and, in effect, steal the money.'

'Meanwhile, you are hiding here in Libya!'

'Precisely.'

'How much money is there?'

'Over a billion dollars.'

She whistled. 'Where did it come from, if I may ask?'

He looked at her coldly. 'My father advanced me funds several times over the years. I increased them by good investment.'

It was only a partial answer. The real question was the source of his father's money, since it probably belonged to the people of Libya. But it was as good a reply as she was likely to get.

'Kalestian says he needs fifty million to get up and running,' she said.

'That sounds about right.'

'How can we get it to him?'

He thought for a few minutes before answering. 'I would need to leave Libya.'

'Why?'

'Because of Goldberg Freilich's insistence on having my instructions in person.'

'And does that mean face to face?'

He nodded. 'They are adamant.'

'That seems a bit unreasonable, in the circumstances'

He shrugged. 'I suppose it depends on your point of view. It is certainly making life difficult for me.'

'Here's a brilliant thought,' said Kathy. 'Why don't they just pop the papers in their briefcase, jump on a plane and come and meet you in Tripoli?'

He shook his head. 'I suggested that, but they categorically refuse to set foot in Libya. Frankly, they are afraid. Even though they are a major public company, they think they are perceived as a Jewish bank, with a Jewish name, and that their people would be mistreated here.'

'Is that true?'

'I don't know. My father could actually be quite flexible in private – when it came to money, he would talk to anybody – but today, in all this chaos with nobody in charge, who knows what could happen?'

She nodded. Most of the bankers she had met, although happy to take audacious risks with other people's money, were not noted for physical courage.

'So what is the answer?'

He said, 'If I could get to another country . . .'

'Algeria, perhaps?'

'Possibly. But access would be tricky. Some members of my family have just escaped that way and, as a result, the rebels will be watching those routes carefully now.'

'What about Chad?' she asked. She had a rough idea of North African geography, enough to know that Chad was on Libya's southern border. 'I guess there is a lot of desert between here and there?'

He smiled drily. 'With the right vehicle and some extra cans of petrol, I suppose it could be done. But Chad presents other problems.'

'Such as?'

'It is a failed state. Even more chaotic than Libya, if you can imagine that. It is overrun with Sudanese refugees, most of them starving. Apart from a few dedicated relief workers, no Westerner in his right mind would go there.'

'So where else is there?'

He thought. 'Niger is a possibility. It is on our southern border, to the west of Chad. That too would be a long, tough journey, what with zero rainfall and scorching desert temperatures up to 120 degrees.'

'Doesn't sound appealing.'

'On the other hand, the local inhabitants there are Touareg tribesmen, loyal to my father. If we could get across the border to Niger, I would feel much safer.'

Kathy nodded decisively. 'There's your answer. It is the best solution – for you, perhaps the only one. Go for it. I'll come with you. You will be physically safe and we can get our business done. We'll alert Goldberg Freilich to meet us in wherever the capital of Niger is.'

He smiled. 'Niamey.'

She stood up. 'Niamey, here we come.'

Hassan told Kathy that they should set out for Niger immediately. Kathy sent Josefina to find her some essentials while she and Hassan looked at the map.

It was no easy venture; Libya's southern desert was notoriously hot and arid. Once across the border, there was still more desert; they would have to drive another 100 miles to get to Agadez, the only significant town in Niger's barren northern province. There, they should be among Touareg sympathisers and could proceed safely to Niamey where, according to agreement reached in a rapid exchange of e-mail messages with New York, someone from Goldberg Freilich would be waiting.

'I guess we won't be taking the Bugatti?' said Kathy drily.

Hassan shook his head.

'Afraid not. In theory it can cruise at 160 miles an hour for hours on end, but for that you need perfect roads and the comfort of knowing that there is a Bugatti mechanic nearby with a supply of spare parts. The road is rough and sometimes strewn with rocks or debris. In some places, we may even have to use oilfield roads, which are just a thin layer of asphalt, dripped off a barrel on the back of a truck and allowed to dry in the sun.'

'So what should we do?'

'We'll take the Land Cruiser. You saw it in the garage. It has the best combination of off-road performance and reliability. It uses a lot of fuel, but we can carry some spare cans in the back. You don't smoke, do you?'

She wasn't sure if he was joking. She shook her head.

An hour later, the Toyota was loaded and ready; Kathy had borrowed a T-shirt and jeans from Josefina and a zip-up handbag with some essentials the maid had put together. She was starting to get excited about the trip; it was a bit like setting out on an adventurous holiday. She noticed that Hassan too was travelling light – a single suitcase. She commented on it.

He tapped the side of his head. 'The important stuff is in here.'

'Meaning?'

'It's all in my mind. Account numbers, contacts, passwords.'

That made sense. She recalled Kipling's wily horse trader in Kim, Mahbub Ali, who was plied with drink and searched while unconscious, but to no avail because the secrets he carried for his British masters were stowed securely away in his brain.

With preparations made, they were ready to set out.

But it was not to be.

Just as they were about to climb into the Toyota, there was a massive crash. The wooden doors of the courtyard burst open and a heavy truck rolled into the compound. Several Arabs leaped out with machine guns firing. The noise was deafening. None of the shots found a human target but they smashed into the compound's walls, dislodging flakes of masonry and etching ugly scars in the limestone.

A young Arab descended from the truck's cab, one arm in a sling, a pistol in his right hand. He grinned at Hassan but it was not a pleasant expression.

Kathy saw Hassan blench. Clearly the intruder was no stranger.

'You?' said Hassan softly.

Mustafa shrugged as if to say, 'Why ever would you be surprised?'

Hassan looked round; half a dozen guns were trained on him.

'What do you want?' he muttered.

'All in good time,' said Mustafa equably. He stalked round the Toyota, peering in at the baggage and the petrol cans.

'Where might you be going?'

Hassan shook his head but said nothing.

Mustafa approached Hassan.

'I've learned a lot about you in the past few days.'

'May your knowledge choke you,' said Hassan.

Mustafa laughed. 'I am in too good health for that. But as for you – it's not so easy being Qaddafi's bastard nowadays, is it?' The resentment in his voice was palpable.

He turned to Kathy and looked her up and down. 'Who the hell are you?'

'Who wants to know?' she said sweetly.

His eyes narrowed. 'You will find out very soon.'

He looked round the courtyard and seemed to come to a decision. On a signal, one of his men hustled Kathy and Josefina into a corner of the enclosed space where, weapon at the ready, he kept watch over them.

Mustafa turned back to Hassan. 'Here is the situation. They say you are worth a lot of money. My instructions are to find out how much, and where that money is!'

Hassan frowned. 'You are lucky I only wounded you before. You are also stupid; only a fool would expect me to tell you anything.'

Mustafa stepped forward and, with his good hand, struck Hassan across the face. A bulky ring on his second finger drew blood from Hassan's cheek.

Hassan flinched but uttered no sound. Mustafa hit him again, this time with the back of his hand on the other side of his face. Hassan staggered back. Two guards, afraid he might run, moved forward and gripped his arms. One of them jabbed a gun in the small of his back.

Mustafa smiled. 'You are right, you are much too stubborn to tell me what I need. I salute your courage.'

'So why not stop this nonsense and let us go?' said Hassan. He spoke loudly but there was a tremor in his voice.

Mustafa shook his head. 'Let's try another way.'

He motioned to an assistant. 'Bring her here, Tarek.'

Kathy assumed that Mustafa was referring to her and she braced herself, but Tarek walked past her to the truck. Opening the door, he dragged out a handsome but dishevelled middle-aged woman whose hands were tied behind her back. Visibly distressed, she gave Hassan a sad, apologetic look.

Hassan went pale and Kathy guessed immediately that this was his mother.

'Now perhaps we can have a reasonable conversation,' said Mustafa, as he and his men hustled Hassan and the woman into the house. Kathy watched appalled; she moved to follow but Tarek blocked her way, barring the door with a scowl on his pockmarked face.

Ten minutes later, Hassan and Mustafa emerged by themselves. Apparently they had reached some kind of agreement. Mustafa issued a stream of orders to his men, and they boarded the truck.

Hassan beckoned to Kathy to get into the Toyota. He climbed into the driver's seat himself.

'What's going on?' she asked.

Hassan said nothing.

'Was that your mother?' she asked. He nodded, jaw clenched.

'Where are we going?'

'To Niger, as before.'

'Is your mother coming with us?'

He shook his head.

Mustafa appeared and, grinning, swung himself up to sit in front beside Hassan.

'Okay, my friends, let's go.'

Two guards pushed open the wooden gates. At a signal from Mustafa, the truck drove out of the compound and turned south, followed by the Toyota with Hassan driving. Most of Mustafa's men were in the truck, but Kathy noticed that several stayed behind.

It finally dawned on her that Hassan's mother was a hostage for his cooperation. As the vehicles gathered speed, Mustafa's confidence and Hassan's bitter silence confirmed this.

It was a sunny morning as they drove south into the desert.

The road stretched straight towards the horizon across a vast expanse of sandy terrain, devoid of features. The sky was a bright eggshell blue that would normally have uplifted the spirits of all but the most troubled souls.

Mustafa was humming noisily in crude semi-tones that might have been musical in some Eastern key but more likely, Kathy suspected, were just tuneless.

'Must you do that?' Hassan snapped.

'Well, I confess I am enjoying myself. We are on our way to unlock such wealth as I have never seen in my life. It is fun.'

Hassan was restraining his anger with difficulty. He stamped savagely on the accelerator causing the vehicle to surge ahead and draw closer to the truck ahead, coming within inches of its rear fender.

'If you scratch my paint, I'll make you pay for it,' said Mustafa drily.

'Would someone tell me what is going on?' said Kathy.

Mustafa's smile vanished, giving way to a pensiveness at odds with his rough appearance.

'It's not complicated. Your rich friend here is going to go ahead with the plan to meet his bankers in the capital of Niger. However, there is an important change of plan. Instead of making a large loan to your client, he is going to make an even larger loan to *my* client.'

She turned to Hassan. 'Can he do that?'

Hassan said nothing.

'As long as his mother is in my care, I can do whatever I please,' said Mustafa quietly.

They drove on in silence.

'I suppose the terms of your loan will be favourable,' said Kathy acidly.

Mustafa nodded. 'Trust me, it will not be repaid soon, if at all.'

Kathy did not like to think about what had been said behind closed doors back at the villa. The body language of the two men told its own story – Hassan tense and frustrated, Mustafa relaxed and confident. Nothing Hassan might do could trump the fact that, with a single phone call, Mustafa could have the mother killed.

Two things were now depressingly clear to Kathy – not only was the finance for Kalestian's casino probably a lost cause, but her own survival was none too safe a bet either.

With that grim realisation, she sat and pondered her fate as the two vehicles sped on into the desert.

24

NOVEMBER 22ND, 2011

I an Calder had phoned me back after our lunch.

'We have a meeting tomorrow morning with Laith Saad, at his villa.'

'Excellent.'

'Eleven-thirty. Best bib and tucker!'

'Oh right.'

So I was wearing my bespoke linen suit by Airey and Wheeler and my Bunnington tie with the magenta, black and silver stripes. I felt quite the gentleman.

It was an oppressively humid day, already hotter than the day before. Calder picked me up in his Peugeot.

'I see that, despite your orders to me, you are wearing a tie but no jacket,' I said.

'That's different. I'm local; you are the big cheese from the States.' Again the wry grin.

'Where are we going?'

'Laith's villa, twenty minutes out of town, to the west of the city. Prime beachside property, by the way, not really consistent with his modest salary from the Finance Ministry, but we don't enquire too closely about that.'

We drove for a while. Shortly we were in an expensive looking area.

'Nice houses,' I said.

He nodded. 'This is known as the Regatta district. These beachfront villas used to teem with expatriate employees and their families.

'They look pretty quiet now,' I said. Some were guarded but many looked shut up and deserted.

He shrugged. 'A lot of my fellow expats have been scared off. Violence, car-jacking, rogue militias, attacks on diplomats.'

'But not you?'

He laughed. 'I suppose I'm philosophical, I always hope for the best. But life in Libya is not for the nervous, that's for sure.'

. . .

We arrived punctually. The villa looked new; it was a clean-lined, modern structure that owed nothing to Islamic influence. The white horizontal planes of the house itself were offset by the presence at the main gate of two guards in Arab dress carrying machine guns. Calder spoke to them in Arabic and they parted sullenly to let us through.

The door was opened by one of the largest men I have ever seen. He said nothing but his manner was as unfriendly as the guards outside. We were shown into a sitting room, where full-length windows faced the sea over a narrow strip of beach. I guessed this was where the Goldberg Freilich executives had come to proposition Hassan in less frenzied times.

After a minute, in strolled a dark-haired man of medium height with a heavy tan.

He smiled and shook hands with me. 'Laith,' he said. He wore a white open-necked shirt that looked handmade. 'Can I offer you something? Tea, coffee?'

He spoke perfect English. He would have been quite at home at a tea party in Cheltenham or Belgravia.

'Do you have any sherry?' Calder asked.

Fat chance, I thought, no booze here, but I was wrong.

'I think I have some Tio Pepe somewhere. Or how about a tot of Harvey's Bristol Cream if you fancy something sweeter?'

'I thought alcohol was banned in Libya,' I said.

Laith laughed. 'There are always sources. The penalties for use are stiff, though, so one has to be discreet.'

We sipped our drinks, looking at the ocean.

'It's good of you to see me,' I said.

'You are most welcome. But if you are here seeking an investment, I am afraid you will be disappointed. My usefulness in that area has been much curtailed lately.'

'You don't sound too upset,' I said.

He laughed easily. 'I've had a good run. I like to think of myself as a passive entrepreneur. I lie in wait, taking advantage of opportunities when they come along.'

'Not many of those at the moment,' I suggested.

He shrugged. 'Good times come and go. At the moment, I am living off my fat. I play the odd game of tennis with Ian here and wait for better times.'

'Are you physically safe, with all the troubles?'

'I think so. You saw my guards; they are here around the clock.'

He listened carefully as I explained about Kathy's disappearance.

I finished by saying, 'I have to find her but I am at my wits end as to how to go about it.'

He shook his head gravely. 'I am sorry to say it but, as Ian told you, the young lady is quite possibly being held for ransom by one of the undisciplined gangs that are roaming our streets.' He looked at me sadly, as if apologising for his city.

I mentioned that Calder was advertising for leads. He nodded in agreement.

'That can do no harm. I too will make enquiries. I have a few sources in areas where they do not read the newspapers.'

'Thank you,' I said. 'In the meanwhile, do you have an address for Hassan?'

'I do not,' said Laith. 'His mother, though, should not be hard to find.'

He walked over to a bookshelf and took down a heavy volume, which he leafed through.

'Here we are: Rhianna al-Manwani.'

He read out an address and looked enquiringly at Calder.

Calder nodded, 'I know where that is.'

Laith smiled and held up the book for me to see. It was the Tripoli phone directory.

'Helpful chap,' I said in the car. 'What was that about you playing tennis together?'

'Oh, we play about once a month. Just doubles. A bunch of us were at LSE together a few years ago.'

'LSE? The London School of Economics?'

'That's right. Libya has a long standing connection there, although the relationship has been under a cloud lately.'

'I read about that. Something about Qaddafi's son donating money in exchange for getting a PhD?'

He nodded. 'Saif al Islam was awarded a PhD in 2008. However, there was a question as to how much of his thesis he wrote himself. A few months later, LSE accepted a gift of £300,000 – about $480,000 – from a foundation that he headed.'

'At the very least, LSE was not heeding the famous admonition about Caesar's wife?'

'Exactly. There was an enquiry and a Director of LSE resigned, citing errors in judgment.'

'What do *you* think – did Saif write his dissertation himself?'

'Who knows? But according to a professor who had supervised him independently, Saif lacked the intellectual depth to study at that level and showed no willingness to read or do course work. '

Calder was driving, with his usual zest, in the general direction of downtown Tripoli.

'I'd like to call on Rhianna al-Manwani, mother of Hassan,' I said.

'I thought you might.'

'Is it far?'

'We're only a few minutes away.'

When we drew up outside Rhianna's house, the

front door was ajar. In lawless Tripoli that was not a good sign.

'Just a moment,' said Calder. He opened the glove compartment. Inside was a small pistol, a Beretta. 'Take this.'

'You hold onto it,' I said. 'Stay here for now; give me five minutes, then come in.'

I tiptoed across the threshold.

I could hear a voice in the living room – a man speaking on the telephone. A thick accent marked him as South African – quite probably, I guessed, an Afrikaner like Hansi van Rensburg.

I heard him say, 'Mustafa? It's me again. Where are you?'

Silence, as he listened to the reply, then he continued: 'You have him? At his place near Mizdah? Fantastic!'

I did not dare move any closer; it was more important to listen.

'Going where? Niamey? Where the heck is that?'

More silence, then: 'No, it makes sense. Sounds like the asshole of the world but it's probably the last safe way out of the country. Either that or get lynched, like his dad . . . Hey, if that's where you have to go, do it . . . When you get across the border, call me again and I'll tell you how to play it. Or put the Goldberg people on the line and I'll tell them myself. We'll take that young fellow for every cent he has, in exchange for his mum's life. Call me later.'

At this point, I was planning to melt quietly away. No reason why the South African should ever know I was ever there; it could be helpful to maintain the element of surprise.

But as I was about to leave I heard something that stopped me in my tracks.

'Which girl? I thought Hassan lived alone – I wondered if he was gay, actually. What's her name? Smith? Doesn't ring a bell. Find out what she is doing there. If those two are an item, that may give us some leverage. You can get rid of her when she's no more use.'

I turned back and, entering the room, came face to face with the owner of the voice.

He was a big slab of a man, six foot four and 250 pounds, his weight beginning to settle round the midriff – a rugby forward going to seed in his thirties. His ginger hair was cropped short and the freckled skin of his face and neck was burned deep red by the sun. His expression was somewhere between startled and bad tempered.

'Who the hell are you?'

'Oliver Steele,' I said pleasantly. 'I might ask you the same question.'

He smiled sourly. 'Kruger is my name. And this is a private house.'

'It is indeed. It belongs to Mrs Rhianna al-Manwani.'

His lip curled. 'So what?'

'Where is she?'

'Where you won't find her.'

My temper was starting to get the better of me but I held it in check. Our next exchange could be crucial.

'Keeping company with Kathy Smith, perhaps?'

A look of recognition slowly spread over his meaty face.

'I've heard of you. You are the fellow who calls himself a financial sleuth!'

'I have been so described.'

'In that case we have something in common, because we both have business with young Hassan Qaddafi.'

What happened next happened fast.

He produced a small pistol and pointed it in my direction.

I had expected he would seek an advantage, but I had not expected that. From my limited knowledge of guns, it looked like a Glock Parabellum – plain but reliable. It certainly got my undivided attention.

I was trying to read his thoughts – no doubt he was assessing mine at the same time. Clearly we were rivals and he probably realised that if he could eliminate one competitor he would improve the chances of the other; I didn't have to be a financial sleuth to figure that out. It would be murder of course, but in this city that did not entail anything much in the way of consequences.

He leered, not a pleasant sight, and took aim.

There was a slight noise behind me. Ian Calder to the rescue, or so I hoped. Kruger looked up, and for a moment the Glock wavered up and away from my midriff. By moving smartly to one side, I was almost able to wriggle out of the target area. Almost but not quite. A bullet would still smack into my left shoulder. Better than being killed outright but still not my idea of a best-case solution.

No time for thought, just action. I launched myself forward, flew through the air and cannoned into the bulky South African. He lurched backwards flinging his arms out wide and before he could recover I fell across his gun arm.

He was heavier and stronger than me, no question. But with my full weight on his arm, I was in a position where, if I really wanted to, I could have broken it. Which I almost did, putting all the pressure on it that I could muster. He cried out in a high, almost girlish register. His fingers loosened and the gun fell on the floor.

I stood up and kicked it over towards Calder, who picked it up. Kruger swung a fist at me but I backed away from him and for a minute we all just stood and glared at each other in silence.

It felt very strange. You have to understand that two chartered accountants and a banker, even an Afrikaner banker, don't often get involved in fisticuffs, no matter how great the provocation. It would have been more normal for us to smile politely, bid each other good day, then go away and do our best to bankrupt each other at long distance, behind one another's backs. So the situation was a decidedly odd one and I think we all realised it.

The silence was broken by a shot that rang out behind me. It shattered a large wall mirror, inches above the South African's head.

'Is this guy being a nuisance?' Calder asked. He looked quite comfortable holding the Glock in one hand and the Beretta from his car's glove compartment in the other. I assumed it was the Beretta that he had fired.

Kruger's reaction was immediate: apparently he was not as courageous as his physical bulk would suggest because the expression on his face changed rapidly from angry to ingratiating.

'I was never going to shoot,' he said.

I had to make a quick decision.

'Sit down,' I barked at the South African. He was quick to obey.

Ian Calder slowly lowered the gun and looked at me enquiringly. 'What next?'

'We go,' I said. 'We have a lot of travelling to do.' I explained briefly what I had just overheard.

'Hang on,' said Calder. 'Are we just going to leave this jerk to his own resources? The first thing he'll do will be to warn his friend Mustafa.'

'You're right, of course. How will they communicate?'

'Mobile phone.'

'Which is also where he stores Mustafa's number, I'm willing to bet.'

We were helped by the way Kruger's gaze instinctively swivelled towards a phone that lay on the table.

'Smash it,' said Calder.

'Seems a pity,' I said.

Calder shrugged. Before either Kruger or I knew what was happening, he reversed his gun and holding it by the barrel, smashed the butt down on the slim phone, splintering the glass and denting the instrument beyond repair.

'Can't afford to be squeamish,' he said.

The fury in Kruger's eyes told us we had guessed right, and that his record of phone numbers, including Mustafa's, had been destroyed.

Back in the car, we discussed in detail what I had learned. 'Where is Niamey?' I asked.

'It's the capital of Niger.'

'Niger?'

'A landlocked former French colony on Libya's southern border.'

'It sounds as if Hassan's plan was to leave Libya and head for Niger at full speed.'

'But he got caught,' said Calder.

'By Mustafa.'

'It would help if we knew just who Mustafa is.'

'But we don't,' I said. My head was swimming.

But one thing was clear: wherever Hassan and Mustafa were, Kathy was with them.

Calder had asked what the plan was. I had to admit I had no idea.

According to Calder, Mizdeh was 200 miles south of Tripoli. If Mustafa and party were about to leave there and head south, I could see no way of intercepting them. Apparently they intended to meet up with the bankers on the other side of the border and deprive Hassan of his money, using his mother as leverage. After that, Kathy would be of little value to them and could be killed and dumped somewhere in the Sahara, food for passing predators.

'It's too late to catch up with them, isn't it?' I asked.

Calder said nothing. After his recent heroics, he

seemed rather subdued. He started the car and we drove back to the hotel.

When we got there and I was getting out of the vehicle, he said, 'I have the germ of an idea. It's a long shot, but something might come of it.'

'At this point, anything is worth considering,' I said miserably.

'One of my clients, Paragon Exploration, is drilling for oil in the desert down in that general area. I can give them a call.'

The call was productive, apparently, because we drove straight to a warehouse on the outskirts of Tripoli.

It stood in a secure compound, surrounded by a ten-foot fence topped with razor wire. The yard was piled high with long sections of pipe, massive steel valves and strange shaped tools that I assumed were some kind of drilling equipment.

We had to identify ourselves at the gated entrance. The guard was a burly European in khaki shirt and shorts. He wore a heavy pistol in a holster attached to a webbing belt. I guessed it was loaded, a safe assumption in this part of the world.

'You seem to have adjusted well to the conditions,' I said.

He saw me eying the pistol and laughed. 'That is normal dress, nothing to do with the emergency.

The inventory in this yard is worth the thick end of a million dollars.' His accent was unmistakably British.

'And trespassers will be shot?'

He shrugged. 'Nothing leaves this yard without my permission.'

He waved us towards the office where a slim, compact man got up from his desk to meet us. He had obviously been in the sun; his face was burned pink and his forehead, beneath thinning fair hair, was peeling badly. He wore khaki shorts and a Houston Astros T-shirt, seriously faded.

He beamed at Calder, then turned and pumped my hand. Pale blue eyes bored into me.

'John Harton, Midland, Texas; good to meet you, sir.'

The Texas drawl was strong, the manner cheerful.

'Oliver Steele, Miami and sometime Los Angeles,' I said.

'My sympathies, I lived in Long Beach for five years.'

'Not drilling, surely?'

He shook his head. 'Maintenance. Remember all those little oil pumps sticking out of the ground in Southern California, with their heads rocking to and fro?'

'Sure.'

'I looked after 800 of those.'

'Not things of beauty,' I said.

He nodded. 'But profitable. Anyway, Ian says you have a problem. How can I help?'

I explained the situation, emphasising the danger to the kidnapped Kathy.

'She should never have come here in present conditions, of course,' I said.

He brushed my apology aside. 'You need to catch up with that group, and quickly.'

'I agree. But how?'

He laughed and put an arm round my shoulder. 'Men of good will must stick together in times like these. Come and meet my friend Perry.'

He ushered us through the warehouse and out by a back door. In a walled courtyard behind the property stood a shiny red helicopter.

Harton pointed to it with obvious pride.

'Not huge, but she seats a pilot and four passengers.'

'I'm impressed.'

'And this is Perry, our pilot.'

'Hi, Perry,' I said.

Perry waved. He was a dried out looking character with wispy brown hair and, apparently, few words. A cigarette hung from his fingers.

'Takeoff in ten minutes. Does that work for you?' asked Harton.

I experienced a huge feeling of hope. 'Does it ever?'

I turned to Calder. 'Are you coming?'

'Wouldn't miss it!'

25

NOVEMBER 22ND, 2011

We took off and climbed rapidly. In moments, Tripoli's streets shrank to a dwindling pattern of thin, dusty lines. The aircraft moved south immediately, leaving the city behind. We cruised noisily at 5,000 feet over endless grey-brown desert, following what we assumed to be the route Mustafa and his party had taken.

Once airborne, I tried to take stock; doubts were beginning to creep in. How were three passengers in a small helicopter going to get the better of what was probably a group of well-armed toughs? I asked Calder the same question. He looked enquiringly at Harton, who said, 'We may be able to help with that.'

'It's a lot to ask,' I said.

'Let me explain.' He pulled out a chart and

pointed. 'Right now, we are heading for Paragon's base camp. It is pretty much in the middle of nowhere'

I followed his finger on the map.

'It seems to be some way north of the Libya-Niger border.'

'Correct. And, luckily for you, it lies fairly close to the route your friends and their captors must take to get to Niger. My idea is to hop over them in the 'copter, land at our camp and pick up reinforcements – issued with firearms, of course.'

'How will your people feel about that?' I asked.

He grinned. 'They'll enjoy it, trust me. Life down there gets pretty monotonous. It will be a welcome break.'

'Life is not much fun there?'

'It's a hardship posting. The work is well paid but dull. They work three weeks on and one week off. For those three weeks, it's work, eat and sleep, then more of the same.'

'It must get pretty hot?'

He nodded. '104 degrees is commonplace. It can reach 120. It is desert heat and therefore dry, but even so. Basically, the guys live in air-conditioned containers. People who suffer from claustrophobia need not apply.'

We had been flying for about an hour when

Harton pointed to twin specks moving along the desert road, far below.

'Think those are the folks you are looking for?'

'Maybe. Can we fly lower?'

The helicopter swooped down to a few feet above ground level, then cruised along parallel to the vehicles, its rotors blowing clouds of sand into the air. Harton felt in a side pocket and handed me some binoculars. 'Try and see who is in the vehicles. But be quick; we can't stay down here for long. If sand gets in the rotors we'll be in serious trouble.'

I fiddled with the focus. There was a white Toyota Land Cruiser followed by a larger, somewhat battered van. Looking closely, I recognised Kathy in the Toyota. She seemed to be looking at us but I could not tell whether she recognised me. With her in the vehicle were two men who could be Hassan and Mustafa.

'Why don't we just land and fight it out?' said Calder.

Harton shook his head. 'I wouldn't fancy our chances. This kind of bus is not built to be shot at. One stray bullet in the rotor mechanism and we would be finished.'

'You're right,' I said. 'We need reinforcements.'

'There's our camp,' said Harton a while later, pointing down.

An extensive pattern of trails, surrounding several small buildings, was coming into view.

'It covers a big area,' I said.

He nodded. 'It does, and that can be an issue when it comes to security.'

'Do you worry about terrorism?'

'All the time. There was a huge terrorist attack on a refinery in Algeria last year. A group associated with Al Qaeda occupied the Amenas gas plant, out in the desert. They took 800 hostages, including British and Americans.'

'Presumably the Algerian Government responded?'

'Oh sure they did, in head-on force, with Russian helicopter gunships and without consulting the governments of the nations involved. When the Algerians say they do not negotiate with terrorists, they really mean it.'

'What was the outcome?'

'Twenty-nine terrorists and thirty-nine foreign hostages were killed.'

'And you are afraid something like that could happen to you?'

'Of course, although here it would be different. We are a much smaller operation, only a dozen people. So our strategy is to give all our guys weapons, and make sure they know how to use them.'

'Is that normal for an exploration outfit?'

'No. But these are not normal times. With a revolution in progress, you can never be sure what to expect.'

The helicopter began to descend.

Harton said, 'I've called ahead. Three men and a truck will be ready to pick us up and drive north to meet Mustafa and company, who should be about sixty miles north of the base.

'What if we miss them in the desert?'

'It won't happen. There is only one road.'

'Don't people drive across the sand?'

He shook his head. 'It is possible, but it's a very bad idea. What looks smooth from up here is actually pretty bumpy. Anything over thirty miles an hour and you bend an axle before too long; then you're done for.'

Moments later we were on the ground and I was being introduced to the staff of Camp Paragon.

'This is Roger,' said Harton. Roger was a dark, thickset Brit with a steady gaze and straight eyebrows that met above his nose.

'He's our tool pusher.'

I knew just enough about drilling to know that a tool pusher was the engineer in charge of a drilling rig, responsible for all operations. Out here, he would report directly to John Harton. Roger's smile was mild and his voice quiet but Harton had told me he was a heavyweight boxing champion in his college days.

'And this is Beef.'

Beef was fair haired and pink cheeked, more outgoing than Roger. He looked as if he might enjoy a drink or three. Harton introduced him as a roughneck.

'You don't look all that rough,' I said, and he laughed.

Harton explained. 'Roughneck doesn't mean some kind of ignoramus. A roughneck is the guy that assists the tool pusher on a platform. It's skilled work.'

A third man emerged from the air-conditioned trailer.

'Here's Connor, he'll come along too.'

Connor blinked amiably at me through thick-lensed spectacles. His pale face looked more studious than rugged but his handshake crushed my knuckles.

'What do you do around here?' I asked.

He grinned. 'The most important job in the place.'

'He's the chef,' said Harton.

All three looked in their early thirties. After meeting them, I felt somewhat reassured.

'I really appreciate your help,' I said fervently.

'Let's go get' em,' said Beef, blinking cheerfully in the sun.

The pilot Perry was standing nearby, smoking.

Harton said, 'Perry, can you get back up there and act as a spotter?'

He nodded. 'Will do.'

Harton led us into the trailer. Unlocking a wall cabinet, he handed machine pistols to Calder and me and showed us how to use them.

'Anything else?' he asked.

I shook my head.

'Then let's go.'

We crowded into Paragon's big truck and set off five minutes after the helicopter. We drove in convoy out of the oil camp along a narrow, baking hot track, its surface dark and tacky.

'Interesting road,' said Calder.

'It serves its purpose,' said Harton tersely. 'We pour unrefined crude oil directly onto the sand. It solidifies in the sun, and there's your road.'

When we reached the main road, we turned and drove north at a steady eighty miles per hour. It was just a two-lane metalled strip stretching into the distance.

Harton produced a device like a bulky mobile phone.

'I would have expected you to have the latest sleek iPhone, you being technically savvy,' I said.

He laughed. 'Forget about getting a mobile signal out here. This is short-wave radio.'

He pressed a pre-selector button. 'Perry, what do you see up there?'

Perry's voice crackled: 'They are fifty miles north of you and converging fast. Between your speed and theirs, you should come face to face in twenty minutes.'

'What's the plan?' I asked Harton.

He grinned. 'Any ideas?'

'I suppose we should park in the middle of the road, so that they can't get by.'

'What if they swerve off the road, drive a few yards on the sand, and leave us in the dust?' he asked.

'Good point,' I said. 'We need a barrier, some heavy object that we can place in the middle of the road while we wait off to one side.'

'There's a spare pump housing in the back. It's two feet long and weighs fifty pounds. That and a couple of spare tyres, judiciously spread around, should block the road pretty well.'

'Fine, but let's think this through. What do we want to achieve?'

'Ream out the bad guys?' asked Beef hopefully.

'That too,' I said, 'But primarily, rescue Kathy.'

'And Hassan?' asked Calder.

'And Hassan, I suppose.' My relative lack of enthusiasm for that may have shown.

The bespectacled Connor was listening closely.

'You say that both Mustafa and Hassan are in the Toyota with Kathy, and that the rest of Mustafa's men are in the van. Maybe we should separate the two vehicles? Divide and conquer.'

'Hit the Toyota first?'

'Probably.'

'Mustafa will be armed,' I pointed out.

'For sure he will be. But do you have a better plan?'

We were approaching a spot where several large sand dunes formed an elevated ridge not far from the road.

'Stop here,' I said.

We manhandled the pump housing and a couple of tyres onto the hot tarmac, where they made an effective makeshift barrier. Then we drove a few yards away from the road and parked behind a dune. The sand mass was tall enough to hide our vehicle from the highway completely.

I still had a nagging uneasy feeling about the whole setup. Harton saw my concern.

'This probably isn't going to fool them,' he said. 'They saw the helicopter. They know we are after them, so they will be expecting some kind of ambush.'

'Speed will be the key,' I said. 'We have to hustle out there the moment they slow down. Get between the two vehicles, and attack in both directions.'

'If I may suggest,' said Harton, 'You and I should tackle the Toyota, taking Connor with us. Roger, Beef and Ian can tackle the truck.'

I wondered why he would choose Connor in particular for our team, but he seemed pretty sure of himself.

The radio crackled and Perry came on the air. 'They will be coming into view in seconds.'

From our hiding place behind the dune, we could not see the road, but we could hear the sound of vehicles approaching. In seconds, we heard them slow to a stop before our makeshift barrier.

Harton gunned the motor and our truck shot into the open with sand kicking up in all directions. We veered towards the two stationary vehicles. They had stopped barely ten yards apart but there was just enough space. He drove between them, turned broadside on and stopped like the third piece in a game of dominos.

Roger and Beef, guns ready, pushed their doors halfway open. From behind this shelter, they fired instantly at the van's rear tyres. The vehicle's back end subsided immediately with a weary sigh. At this point they ceased fire and waited for heads to appear, that they could target. But the occupants of the truck seemed in no great hurry to expose themselves. To discourage them further, Roger sprayed another burst of fire, neatly shattering the truck's wing mirrors on both sides.

In the silence that followed, Calder let loose with a burst of Arabic. It must have been an order to the occupants to give up their weapons, because assorted firearms clattered out of the van's windows onto the road.

'Do you think that's it?' I asked Calder.

'I don't know, but I'm about to order them to come out with their hands up. If they try anything funny, they will be saying hi to their maker in a heartbeat.'

More Arabic from Calder. Three rough but very scared-looking young men, one of whom was Tarek, emerged. They were made to lie spreadeagled on the sand while Roger and Beef searched them thoroughly and fastened their hands behind their backs with sticky grey duct tape, the engineer's answer to every emergency.

Harton and I got down from the truck and turned our attention to the other vehicle. The cleaner of the two Arabs, who I took to be Hassan, was alone in the front seat; he had presumably been driving. Mustafa was in the back, holding a gun to Kathy's head.

He looked like a man who knew the gig was up, but who, if he had to go, was determined to take someone with him. And that looked like being Kathy. He looked angry, tormented and hopeless, as if what had once been a carefree game had just degenerated into something lethal.

I approached him, followed closely by Connor who stood behind me and to my right.

'It's all over, you know,' I said.

I spoke as casually as I could. No sudden moves – I even put my pistol away in my pocket to create, if possible, a calmer atmosphere.

Mustafa stared round at the armed men ranged against him. He tightened his grip on Kathy, smiling sadly.

'Sorry,' he said. The gun was still trained on Kathy.

'Wait!' I said. 'We can work something out.'

He shook his head. 'Too late,' he said. 'Kruger was my ticket out of Libya. He said he would take me to Johannesburg. I don't know if he meant it. Probably just lying. Now here I am, still in the desert, with nowhere to turn.'

'You do have one perfectly good option,' I said quickly. 'We can all walk away from this peacefully, including you, but you need to put down the gun and release Kathy. And Hassan, of course.'

He shook his head sadly. 'I don't believe you.'

His finger tightened.

There was a single gunshot.

I swear I felt the wind of the bullet whistling past my ear.

A black dot appeared on Mustafa's forehead and he slumped in his seat, as if falling asleep; his gun arm collapsed and the pistol fell from his hand. His body sank slowly out of sight below the level of the dash.

I turned round. Connor was tucking his pistol into the waistband of his jeans. He nodded politely. 'It was never going to end well,' he said.

'You took a big risk,' I said.

Calder and Harton had approached and were listening.

Harton put his hand on Connor's shoulder. 'Not that much of a risk. He's quite a sharpshooter.' Connor said nothing.

Kathy got out of the car, scrambling over Mustafa's dead body. She walked shakily towards us and past me to Connor. She shook his hand; then she turned and gave me a huge hug.

Calder said, 'What now?'

'Let's get back to the camp and regroup,' said Harton.

'What about the debris?' asked Calder. He indicated Mustafa's dead body.

Beef said, 'Let's just dump the body behind the dunes and let nature take its course.'

It sounded crude. My feelings must have shown on my face because Harton noticed.

'Beef's right. It sounds heartless but it's probably best. Between the heat and the animals, it won't take long. In a week he'll just be bleached bones.'

'What about the live ones?'

'Shoot them all, that's best,' said Beef.

Harton shook his head. 'Yes and no,' he said. 'In a perfect world they would be tried for kidnapping, convicted, and locked up for a long time. That would be justice.'

'There is no justice in Libya,' I pointed out. 'The system has broken down.'

Harton said, 'Exactly. So let's just truss them up, put them on a truck up to Tripoli, and turn them loose on a street corner somewhere up there.'

'Without their weapons,' I suggested.

Harton nodded. 'Of course.'

Nobody seemed to have a better idea, so the three young men were hauled to their feet and prodded into the back of the Paragon truck which, with Beef and Connor as armed guards and Roger at the wheel, headed back to camp.

Hassan had not said much during all this. He rode with us in the Toyota. We all arrived together. Mustafa's men were marched off to a storeroom and locked in. Roger and Beef went back to work on the rig.

Connor said, 'Come into the canteen and I'll fix you a meal.'

He set to work with the freezer, microwave and grill. Then he put in front of us a dish consisting, to my amazement, of grilled venison steaks, pink in the middle, with mushrooms and new potatoes in a sauce that tasted of orange with a hint of coriander. Sitting in the small air-conditioned canteen, I had to admit that, despite the cheap cutlery and formica tabletop, it was one of the best meals I had ever eaten.

'This is awesome,' I said licking my lips. 'I can't believe we're in the middle of the Sahara.'

Connor looked pleased despite himself.

Harton laughed. 'We have to find ways to make these hardship postings appealing. Now you see how important Connor is.'

Hassan ate with us. He didn't say much. I got the impression that, despite his American education and his perfect English, he considered himself somewhat apart. I put this down to a combination of things – his parentage, his unique political position and his wealth – but it made dealing with him a bit awkward. However, he still held the key to my mission.

He did seem to appreciate that we had probably saved his life. When I suggested that I would welcome a quid pro quo for that, he did not seem surprised.

'Just to be clear,' I said, 'you and Mustafa were on your way to meet the Goldberg Freilich people in Niamey. You would have been forced to sign away your fortune, under threat of your mother being murdered.'

'That's about it.'

'So here's what I suggest. Let's go there anyway. But, instead of that transaction, you can lend Michael Kalestian the money he needs to finish his casino in Macau.'

I knew he could hardly refuse. And he knew that I knew. But the negotiator in him required that he bargain.

'I've felt for some time that my ownership share in the casino was too small. I would need a bigger piece of the action,' he said.

'I can talk to Kalestian about that,' I said. 'But do you agree in principle?'

He nodded slowly.

I got up. 'Good. What are we waiting for?'

I turned to John Harton. 'Want to come along?'

The engineer laughed. 'Thanks, but I'll pass. I need to get back to work.'

I shook him firmly by the hand. 'You saved our bacon.'

'Glad to help.'

In the late afternoon, the desert heat was abating, if only slightly. John Harton took me for a tour of the camp. On a structure attached to the roof of an adjoining shed, some powerful-looking aerials and dishes were arrayed. He noticed the direction of my gaze and said, 'Do you want to catch up on the news?'

'Can you get a signal out here?'

'Sure, satellite feed.'

We went into his office and he fired up the computer on his desk.

'Let's try News.google.com.'

He pressed a few keys and the screen lit up with news headlines from around the world. One item caught my eye: 'Loyalist remnants pursued in Libya.'

I read on: 'Weeks after Qaddafi's death, a pro-Qaddafi convoy tried to cross the border into Niger and was intercepted by the Nigerien army. Thirteen loyalists and one Nigerien soldier were killed.'

Short and sweet. The group had apparently been doing what we were just about to attempt and thirteen of them were dead. Food for thought.

Hassan wandered up and looked over my shoulder at the screen. As he watched, his face fell.

Trying to put an optimistic slant on things, I said,

'But that was a pro-Qaddafi convoy. We're not really pro Qaddafi.'

'Speak for yourself,' he muttered. I bit my tongue; I had forgotten that it was his father we were discussing.

'I'm sorry,' I said.

He shrugged. 'It doesn't change anything. At this point, my range of options is shrinking rapidly.'

But he was pretty subdued for a while.

There was maybe an hour of daylight left; it was not a good time to set out across the desert, so we stayed at the camp that night. We hit the road early next morning, heading south. There were four of us, Hassan and me in the Toyota Land Cruiser and Ian Calder and Kathy in another, smaller truck loaned by Paragon.

Kathy watched us loading gas cans into the back of the Land Cruiser.

'We could all fit in there. Why are we taking two vehicles?' she asked.

'Safety,' I said. 'It's important to have some redundancy; what if one vehicle breaks down?'

'We call the breakdown service.'

'I don't think so. There are no Automobile Club trucks in the Sahara.'

'Oh. How far do we have to go?'

I showed her the map. 'We are here, 400 miles south of Tripoli. On the map it looks as if we do not exist, but that's because Paragon's camp is not marked. We have 1,200 miles to go to reach Niamey. That means twenty hours of driving, if we don't stop.'

'That's an absurdly long way.'

'Yes it is. So we may as well get started.'

26

NOVEMBER 23RD, 2011

When Danie Kruger was left alone in Rhianna al-Manwani's house, his rage knew no bounds. His attempt to corral Hassan al-Manwani had obviously failed.

He returned to the hotel and sought consolation in his smuggled bottle of scotch. He had no idea what was happening – in his mind he desperately willed Mustafa to telephone the hotel, as if sheer telepathic effort would get the young Arab to call, but no message came.

Fuelled by alcohol, fearful thoughts crept in, which he had so far managed to keep at bay through a whirlwind of activity. If he could not secure an injection of cash very soon, his fund would collapse in an avalanche of bad debt and bad publicity from which he would probably never recover. But what could he do?

Any act that involved leaving his luxury suite faced the bleak reality that he was in an alien place where he knew nobody. Repeated belts of scotch from a hotel tooth mug eventually exhausted the bottle and by nine o'clock he had passed out, fully dressed, on the expensive king-size bed.

When the phone finally rang next morning it was not Mustafa but Tarek, one of his men. The news was bad; Mustafa was dead.

Kruger listened blearily as the young tough spoke in barely understandable English. Tarek was back in Tripoli but Mustafa had been killed in a gun battle in the desert. Hassan was heading south towards Niger with Oliver Steele and the girl Kathy in a white Toyota Land Cruiser.

'Why are they going there?' snapped Kruger, now fully awake.

Tarek did not know, but he thought the accountant Ian Calder was with them.

That was ominous, thought Kruger. Oliver Steele would certainly be doing his best to side with the financial princeling and it sounded as though a deal was in the works. Since Steele had just rescued Hassan from Kruger's people, that could only be bad for Kruger.

By now, Kruger's demons were getting the better

of him. He had always had a vengeful streak and at this point it overwhelmed his more rational thoughts. The humiliation of the previous day was still fresh – Calder's gunshot and his own backing down. He must get even.

Oliver Steele and Kathy Smith were the twin targets of his simmering resentment. He should have killed Steele but, at the crucial moment, his nerve had failed. Next time would be different. There was insult to repay. Never mind that financial hope was dwindling; getting even would be its own reward.

A plan started to form in his mind. He telephoned a number in London, the office of a low-profile, very expensive firm of private investigators.

'I want you to trace two people for me. Find them, follow them and give me an hourly report of their movements.'

'Where are they now?' was the response.

'In Africa. But in a day or two I expect them to return either to London or to the United States via New York or Florida.'

For most investigators, this would have been such a broad remit that they could not even have made a start. But this firm, an unique alliance of former income tax inspectors, immigration officials and SAS members, possessed a rare combination of contacts in key places and the ability to hack into some highly confidential databases. As a result, their penetration exceeded that of most governments, the latter being famous for not knowing how many, or what kind of people were crossing their own borders. The legality of their methods, questionable at best, rested on some obscure wording in anti-terrorist laws that was never designed for such purely commercial purposes.

None of which bothered Danie Kruger. His fund, even while heading for a financial precipice, could still afford the best.

He *would* be avenged.

27

NOVEMBER 23RD, 2011

J ust as Oliver and his party were setting out along the road to Niger, Larry Franklin, a professional criminal and bitter enemy of Oliver Steele, was taking stock of his life 3,000 miles away in the Central American nation of Belize.

Two years ago, thanks to Oliver's efforts, he had been forced to go into hiding to escape prosecution in the United States for tax fraud, drug trafficking and running an illegal internet gambling site.

A few titbits about Larry:

He is, or was, a drug dealer. He started in college, selling nickel bags of marijuana to fellow students – who doesn't do that? – but graduated to chopping off the fingers of rival dealers in the intensely competitive South Florida cocaine market.

In those days his name was not Larry Franklin but Frankie Leon. He had been overweight and chubby-faced, with cheeks pitted from teenage acne but when he 'retired' to Belize he underwent some major plastic surgery after which, trim-waisted, with a newly Roman nose, hair dyed blond and some serious facial scrubbing, he was briefly almost handsome. The lard round his midriff returned fairly quickly, but he still remained unrecognisable.

He was perfectly safe hiding out in Belize but he was bored. He wanted more. He desperately longed to emerge from the shadows and lead a relatively normal life. With nothing to do, he spent his mornings sitting outside a café on Goldson Street near the Swing Bridge, sipping a latte and reading the *New York Times*. Now and then he would glance over at the Consolidated Bank of Canada building, where he kept his money.

He did a lot of reading and one day he read an article about a financier called Marc Rich who had received a presidential pardon from President Clinton, as the President was leaving office. That sounded pretty good to Larry; might a presidential pardon be the solution for him? It trumped all outstanding charges, and also, what with President Roger Lawson, the present incumbent of the White House, being due to leave office next year and he being a notoriously flexible character, so rumour went, it could be bought.

There was one slight problem: Larry suspected he would need a source of clean money. That could be tricky. He had made several fortunes but none of them was exactly legal. One was from selling drugs in Florida, another was from an internet gambling site that operated in violation of US law, and so on.

He had heard about a businessman called Sidney Skolnik, a big Republican supporter who had made a lot of money in casinos. And casinos – the physical kind – were legal. Apparently most of Skolnik's money came not from Las Vegas but from Macau. He was not sure where Macau was so he looked it up; it was a former Portuguese possession on the coast of China, halfway around the world from Belize. He had absolutely no idea how to break into the Chinese casino business but you had to start somewhere, so he decided to take a trip to Macau.

As he was researching flights, he ran into another problem. The flights from Belize to Macau on major carriers all involved a stopover in Miami or Atlanta, but to set foot in the United States was risky. In theory, his new identity would hold up on a brief visit, especially if he took care to set foot only in international transit lounges, but you could never be sure. He needed a safer route.

He saw that a small local airline called Tropic Air

flew to Cancun in Mexico. From there, Air France flew nonstop to Paris. He could catch that flight and then one from Paris to Macau on Thai Airways, via Bangkok. It meant a thirty-six hour journey, but Thai Airways sounded okay and in first class he could have his ego massaged by pretty stewardesses, so he bought a ticket, paying in cash, and set out for Macau.

Arriving in Macau, Larry took a taxi to the Macau Bahia Resort, the flagship of Sidney Skolnik's empire. He had read that it was the most profitable casino in the world.

It was enormous, besides being an amazingly clever piece of architecture. It was built round a huge indoor lagoon, complete with white sandy beach, sparking blue water and real palm trees swaying in an artificial breeze. Everything was climate controlled to an even 75 degrees.

He would have been even more impressed except that he had seen its close counterpart in Las Vegas, the Las Vegas Bahia. The place was a self-contained city. He would have liked to spend time wandering round its ornate gaming rooms, its seventeen restaurants, four swimming pools and massive shopping mall with 200 shops. But he had other things to do.

He ordered a taxi with an English-speaking driver called Li and had the man take him on a guided tour of Macau.

They drove past the MGM Grand, the Sands, and the Venetian, all of which Larry recognised as being somewhat based on Las Vegas originals. Most were on reclaimed land in the Cotai area.

'Very interesting,' said Larry.

'Not finished yet,' said Li. 'More to see.'

Li took Larry to old Macau where the streets were narrow and picturesque, evoking Macau's Portuguese colonial past. He paused outside the circular tower of the Lisboa Hotel, an older but still impressive place.

'What's this?' Larry asked.

'This is what started it all. Before China took Macau back from the Portuguese, this was the only significant casino. It was the flagship of the empire of Mr Stanley Ho.'

'Was?'

'It may have been upstaged now by the big American places, but it still has very fine restaurant.'

'Is Mr Ho still around?'

Li nodded. 'Yes, but he is old – over ninety. Not in best health. He is very shrewd man – also majority stockholder in hovercraft ferry between here and Hong Kong, and other businesses.'

'So he was not forced out when the Chinese took over?'

Li laughed. 'Mr Ho too smart for that. In English phrase, "he has finger in many pies." His daughter Pansy is partner with MGM in the MGM Grand.'

They drove slowly back towards the Bahia. On the way, they passed a massive new building – obviously a resort in course of construction. It looked almost complete but was evidently not yet open; orange cones blocked the drive leading up to the massive facade.

'What's that?'

'That is new casino, Excelsior. Is very big. But there is problem.'

'What kind of problem?'

Li laughed. 'Always same, finance.'

Larry snapped to attention. 'Tell me more.'

'Owner needs money to finish inside.'

'How much money?'

Li shrugged. He did not know.

But Larry had seen what he needed. His mind was working at full speed now. 'That's enough for today. You've been a big help.'

'So back to the Bahia?'

'You know what? I think I will eat dinner at the Lisboa.'

Studying the menu, he wavered between stir-fried crab, Macanese chilli shrimps or something called bacalhau. On enquiring, he learned that bacalhau was Portuguese for dried salted cod. That did not sound too appetising so he ordered the shrimp.

They were delicious. Things were looking up.

29

NOVEMBER 23RD, 2011

I t is hard not to talk about *something* on a long car journey, and here I was with Hassan, my captive so to speak. As I drove, keeping a steady eighty on the long straight road, a bunch of questions were running round in my mind.

Now that he had more or less agreed to continue supporting Michael Kalestian, I hoped he would relax and be willing to open up about his own feelings.

I was curious to know how he felt about the relentlessly negative way his father was portrayed by the Western media. Obviously it was a touchy subject, so I tried to edge into it sideways. 'Do all these rebel groups have any common philosophy, other than opposition to your father?'

'None,' emphatically.

I glanced at him out of the corner of my eye. He was smiling faintly. I was struck by how dapper he always looked; the air conditioning was turned down to save fuel but despite the heat he was not sweating and his black hair was parted down the middle, not a lock out of place – pretty self-possessed for a young man with a price on his head. He looked calm and self-satisfied.

'None at all?'

He shook his head. 'The Arab Spring has been a wonderful opportunity for all the malcontents in the region to rise up and have their say, aided and abetted by sanctimonious politicians in Europe and America.'

'Really?'

I must have looked sceptical, because he shrugged. 'It's the truth.'

His composure irritated me. 'How do you answer those who say that your father was a tyrant and an embezzler?'

'That is nonsense. It's just too easy to paint my father as the blackest of villains, a torturer who plundered his country. It suited his political opponents, and I must admit his colourful behaviour made him an easy target.'

'That's for sure.'

He frowned. 'Let me give you some background

– the truth, not the pap you are fed by the European media.'

'Please do.'

'My father took office in a bloodless coup while old King Idris – five times married, by the way – was in Turkey for medical treatment. Idris, whose health was failing, had been about to abdicate in favour of his nephew Hasan. People call my father a tyrant, but who can say that Idris' nephew would not have been just as bad?'

'Some call Qaddafi a thief.'

Hassan shrugged. 'He was no accountant, for sure; maybe he spent some of the money in the state's accounts rather freely, but he was not as extravagant as some – consider the President of the United States, who maintains a massive security retinue, a bullet-proof limousine and the two gigantic airliners known as "Air Force One". He cared for his subjects. He housed them and provided education. Libyan health care is among the best in the region. Literacy is the highest of any Arab country. Women are treated well – many occupy responsible government and management positions. Does that sound like the behaviour of a tyrant?'

Up to that point, I had been willing to sympathise with Hassan. But this easy dismissal of the Brother Leader's shortcomings sounded pretty biased. I could not help thinking of the hair-raising rumours of rape and degradation, both of women and young men, in the dark basements of Qaddafi's fortified compound at Bab al-Azizia, to say nothing of the blowing up of Pan Am Flight 103 over Scotland, when hundreds of souls perished.

'Do you think your father would still be in power if he had behaved in a more restrained way?'

He frowned, as if suspecting for the first time that I was not a sympathetic questioner.

'It's possible. Obviously he was unpopular in some quarters. In politics there are always dissidents and, with his flamboyant manner, he was an easy target.'

He lapsed into silence. Time to change the subject.

'What did you do when the troubles started?'

'Obviously I took steps to protect myself. When society degenerates into chaos, nobody is safe from the mob.'

'What did you do?'

'To start with, I moved house. I rented an apartment in a modern block in Tripoli, an expensive building popular with expatriates.'

'In your own name?'

He shook his head. 'Of course not. Actually I sublet from a Texas oil well logging outfit. Their manager was leaving Libya and he found it convenient – and profitable – to rent informally to me. My name is not on any lease and the concierge knows me simply as Mr Ahmed, a local gentleman who works with the Americans. That may sound paranoid, but a year later my father was dead and the country was in chaos. Anyone suspected of being a Qaddafi ally had a target on his back. So the steps I took probably saved my life. Meanwhile, my investments were doing well. One area that appealed to me was the emerging market of China.'

'Is that is how you came to be associated with Michael Kalestian?'

'Yes. He was building a new hotel in Macau. He had a temporary cash-flow crisis, but other Las Vegas magnates like Steve Wynn and Sheldon Adelson had been successful in Macau and I was confident that the Excelsior would do well.'

'And all the while, the rebellion was gathering strength?'

'Yes. There were demonstrations. My father had to airlift mercenaries in, to restore order. The United Nations declared Libya a no-fly zone. France and Britain bombed Libyan airfields, destroying our air force. The US and Britain froze billions in bank accounts in the United States and seized real estate in Britain. It was becoming clear that my father's downfall was just a matter of time.

'His family – his wife Safiya and his legitimate children – were being sought by the rebels. Confusion reigned. My half brother Moatassem, for example, was rumoured to have been captured. The next day, he turned up at the Corinthia Hotel and gave a press conference. A few weeks later, he was reported killed. Again, he was seen in public hours later. Then finally he was gunned down and his body was put on public display. My mother wanted me to leave the country. Instead, I moved to the apartment, shaved off my beard and became Mr Ahmed.'

'Is that when you had to stop servicing the Macau investment?'

'Yes. It was becoming increasingly difficult. My money was at Goldberg Freilich; in order to approve any substantial transfers, I had to physically appear and I could not take that risk. I had to let Kalestian down. I telephoned him on Skype and tried to explain. He was not very sympathetic, obviously more concerned with his own problems than mine. But I value my neck above any investment. That was when I became the object of the attentions of the South African, Danie Kruger.'

Hassan smiled and cracked open a can of soda. 'The best way I can describe Kruger is that he is an intensely aggressive, somewhat desperate entrepreneur. I think he is more than a little crazy. And, as you know, he was almost the death of me.'

30

NOVEMBER 23RD, 2011

Some time later, a knot of dusty buildings became visible in the distance.

'We should stop here,' said Hassan.

'Where are we?'

'This is the village of Al Katrun. It has a filling station, the only one for hundreds of miles. Maybe they will have some gasoline; supplies are much interrupted at present, but we should at least check.'

'I thought we had enough for the journey,' said Kathy.

'But Hassan is right.' I said. 'It makes sense to keep the tanks full.'

'A word of caution,' said Hassan. 'If anyone enquires, you are commercial people with business in Niger and I am your paid interpreter. Not a word about politics or Qaddafi, okay?'

I nodded. 'That makes sense.'

'It is also vital for my safety and, since we are travelling together, for yours too. Last month, Al Katrun was captured by the National Liberation Army, bitter enemies of my father, although Qaddafi forces recaptured it almost immediately.'

'Well, that means they are your friends again, doesn't it?' asked Kathy.

'It should mean that. But the loyalty of the residents may have been seriously strained. They could lean either way now. Trust nobody.'

We slowed down and turned off the main road.

Al Katrun consisted basically of a single street. There were a few commercial buildings and not much else. Vistas of dun-coloured desert stretched all the way to the horizon on all sides. There was nobody in sight; the sun beat down from directly overhead. A couple of skinny dogs lay in a thin strip of shade next to a warehouse wall, their tongues hanging out. Their eyes followed us as we passed but they did not get up.

At the dilapidated gas station, Hassan got out and hammered on the door. A man in a stained T-shirt came out and they exchanged words. The man waved his arms and pointed down the street. Hassan came back shaking his head.

'Guess we'll have to make do with what we've got.'

'No petrol?'

'No. They've been dry for three days; they are expecting a delivery next week but he doesn't sound too confident about that. If you want a cold drink, he says there's a café in the next block.'

We drove a few yards and found the place. To my surprise, it was clean and reasonably cool, at least compared to the 120-degree heat outside. There was a Formica-topped counter with stools. We sat down and a young man put cans of orange soda, labelled in Arabic, in front of us.

'Busy?' Kathy asked drily, suspecting they were his first customers of the day. He smiled politely.

'English won't help you here,' said Hassan. He interpreted, and the man laughed and said a few words.

'He says there is a lot of traffic heading south, mostly refugees. He does not seem political, he understands why people would want to leave a country that is degenerating into a war zone.' Hassan smiled grimly. 'There is a lot less traffic in the opposite direction.'

'How far away is the Niger border?' I asked.

'About 200 miles. We should reach Tumu, the crossing point, in three hours.'

'Do you anticipate any difficulty there?'

'It is possible, although sometimes the office there is not even open. In fact, Niger has a consular office right here in Al Katrun. When the Tumu checkpoint is closed, travellers are supposed to report in at the consulate here.'

'Maybe we should go round there now?' asked Kathy.

Hassan shook his well groomed head. 'Not wise. Simpler to take our chances at the border.'

He seemed very sure of himself as usual. I thought: well, he got us this far. But I had an uneasy feeling about the plan. I would be keeping my fingers crossed for a few more hours.

Kathy strolled off in the direction of the primitive toilet facilities. When she came back, she said, 'Can I ride with Hassan for a bit?'

When Kathy makes an innocent suggestion like that, it often means she is up to something. But I couldn't think what could go wrong so I just nodded and rode with Ian Calder for a while.

31

NOVEMBER 23RD, 2011

Kathy had got Josefina to provide her with a supply of chocolate bars for the trip, not realising that, thanks to successive exposures to desert heat followed by automobile air conditioning, the chocolate would melt and re-form several times. Rummaging in her handbag, she selected the least deformed Hershey bar and offered it to Hassan.

She was warming up to him a little, after a rocky start; not that he had said or done anything particularly friendly, but he had not done anything hostile either and now they were apparently going to be allies, so she was willing to give him a second chance.

'Explain something for me because I'm

confused. Do you call yourself Qaddafi or Manwani?'

Some Arabs might have found her directness off-putting but, having lived in New York, Hassan just shrugged.

'My name is al-Manwani. I am not entitled to use my father's name, since he never married my mother. You probably know that she was a member of his female bodyguard. I am the result of a brief indiscretion between the two of them during a visit to New York, when my father went there to address the United Nations General Assembly.'

'How did he behave towards you personally?'

'Very well, although he never publicly acknowledged me as his son. He took an interest in my education, which he paid for. When I was growing up, he would send for me periodically and listen with apparent interest to my childish opinions. He could be a good listener when he chose, although I would not credit him with much sense of humour.'

'It sounds as if he was fond of you.'

'I think he was. His interest was cursory when I was a child but it grew when I began to study investment matters. Perhaps he saw a quality in me that he wished he himself had. While I was studying business in America I became interested in stock market analysis and when I graduated I diffidently suggested that he make some funds available for me to manage.'

'And he agreed?'

'Yes. He turned me over to Laith Saad, a bureaucrat in the Libyan Ministry of Finance. He observed, probably sarcastically, that I should learn from Saad. Saad was a civil servant but also a wheeler-dealer. He had enriched himself over the years by steering Libya's funds into a wide range of investments, from an Italian football club to the British publishers of the *Financial Times*. He was not a very trustworthy man and I was never sure why my father let him prosper in that way – perhaps because his track record over the years was good.'

Hassan smiled faintly: 'He also behaved with such grovelling flattery that my father – not the least vain of men – could not bring himself to replace him. Anyway, following my father's instructions, Saad opened an account in the Caymans and 500 million dollars were transferred. The nominal owner was a new company, Tripoli Benghazi Holdings, TBH for short.'

'And you chose the investments?'

'Yes. It was a chance to show off my knowledge and I have to say that I performed very well. I increased the value of the portfolio substantially. After a year, I felt confident enough to ask my father for more funds and he authorised another 500 million.'

'Then the Arab Spring arrived?'

Hassan nodded. 'One thing led to another and, in October 2011, my father was assassinated. The details are painful. There is a grossly offensive museum in Benghazi in which a video plays endlessly, showing my father being beaten, dragged through the streets and stabbed to death by the very people he had devoted his life to helping. It is a revolting example of the mindless vengefulness of the rebels.'

Kathy looked thoughtful. 'What really interests me is how did you manage to keep these funds of yours from falling into the British and American net, and being frozen?'

He looked at her cynically. 'Why are you interested?'

'It's my field,' she said lightly. 'Masters in International Taxation from USC and all that.'

He looked surprised. 'I didn't know.'

'There's a lot you don't know about me.'

He shrugged. 'I guess so. Well, if you want to know, here's what I did. I created two new corporations, working through attorneys in Belize. I called the first one Tripoli Benghazi Holdings Limited, the same name as the original Cayman company. I did that deliberately, to cause some added confusion.

'The second corporation was called Hartford Electrical Services. Why Hartford? Why not? I have absolutely no association with that city but I wanted a name that sounded completely un-Arabic, that would not catch curious eyes.

'Next, I closed out TBH Cayman, moving its assets into TBH Belize. Since the company names were the same, nobody noticed except the bankers and the lawyers and they were well rewarded for their silence.'

Kathy nodded. 'In Belize, for a bank employee to breach customer confidentiality is a felony punishable by imprisonment.'

Hassan gave her another surprised look. 'You are correct. Anyway, I finally transferred the assets again, into Hartford Electrical Services. The attorneys were getting used to my style by now. After that, I liquidated TBH Belize, which by then had no assets.'

'I get it,' Kathy said. 'You were erasing the trail from Libya.'

'Exactly. TBH Belize was just a cut-out. Everything was now in Hartford Electrical under my sole control. If a researcher tried to follow the trail, he would hit a brick wall in the shape of an intermediate company that no longer existed.'

'Neat,' said Kathy. The young Libyan was a bit

too pleased with himself for her liking, but he had certainly been ingenious.

'You followed that pretty well,' smiled Hassan. He looked at her appraisingly, taking in her nice legs, trim figure and cheerful grin. 'When all this is over, we should keep in touch. We could work together on some projects.'

Their eyes met, then she looked down modestly. 'I'd like that,' she said.

32

NOVEMBER 23RD, 2011

After about three hours, we reached the border with Niger.

The crossing point at Tumu was open. It was a pretty basic affair with a few huts and a bunch of none-too-friendly ebony-skinned guards with rifles.

Ian Calder took me on one side. 'A word of advice. If they start questioning you, just act dumb.'

'Dumb?'

'I don't mean speechless; I mean dumb as in stupid. Don't act cool or clever as if you were smarter than the guards. That doesn't work; it is guaranteed to make them resentful. Just act slow witted, as if you didn't understand what was happening; then they will feel superior and not patronised.'

The heavily built guard wore a grubby dark

green uniform and no hat. His belly overhung the waistband of his unpressed pants and sweat beaded his pitted cheeks. He eyed me suspiciously, holding my passport at arm's length and comparing me with the photo.

'Pourquoi allez-vous au Niger?'

I had forgotten that Niger was a former French territory. The regional accent was so broad that I could barely understand his words although I spoke passable schoolboy French.

'Nous allons a Niamey,' I said slowly.

He scowled. 'Oui, mais pourquoi?'

'Niamey,' I repeated. 'Nous y allons.'

The scowl intensified. 'J'ai demandé pourquoi?'

I shrugged, looking bewildered and repeated the word, 'Niamey.'

He sighed, exasperated and broke into English. 'Why you go?'

I looked at him blankly, then turned to Calder. 'What must I say?'

Calder assumed a look of obsequious respect and addressed the guard. 'I am his assistant.' He smiled and waited.

The guard heaved a great sigh as if to say, what total idiots, and waved us through. Kathy flashed him a brilliant smile as she passed the desk, and he nodded reluctantly.

Once clear of the border post and on the road again, Calder said, 'You see?'

I had to admit that his approach had worked.

But we still had some way to go.

We finally drove into Niamey at three o'clock the next afternoon.

Although it was the capital of Niger and boasted almost a million souls, the town was not impressive. Most of the buildings were only one or two storeys high. There were few vehicles and no pedestrians on the streets, which was not surprising, as the temperature was above 100 degrees.

It did have a number of hotels, but none of them looked very inviting.

'Where are you supposed to meet the bankers?' I asked Hassan.

'At the Grand Hotel du Sahel.'

'Sounds decent.'

'It's the best of a mediocre bunch.'

'Will the Goldberg people be there already?' I asked.

'They should be.'

'Who are they sending?'

Hassan shrugged. 'I don't know. Does it matter?'

'I suppose not, so long as they have the necessary authority,' I said. 'But first things first. Let's go and check in, I need a shower really badly.'

The Grand Hotel would not have rated five stars

in London or Paris but it was okay for Niger, maybe even a bit better than that. The water in the shower was not hot, but it was warm. The wi-fi worked, to my surprise. The air conditioning sort of. The sofa and bedding were clean, if well worn. There was a mini-bar with beer, French wine and Vichy water, presumably since we were in a former French territory. A medium-sized bottle of water cost ten dollars, so the price at least was First World. I drank most of a bottle and used the rest to brush my teeth in.

When I went downstairs, who should be waiting in the lounge, clutching a briefcase and smiling nervously, but my old pal Jim Gelson from Goldberg, Freilich in New York.

His face was deathly pale, although apparently not from seeing us.

'How was your journey?' I asked.

'Dreadful.'

'What was your route?'

'Air Morocco overnight from Kennedy to Oran. Then a four-hour layover and a noon flight to here.'

'That's not so bad.'

'I tried to order a kosher meal on Air Morocco but they laughed at me.'

'You poor thing,' I said. 'You need a stiff drink.'

He shook his head. 'Spot of tummy trouble.' But he accepted a bottle of mineral water.

The rest of us were enjoying our first beers for

quite a while. That included Hassan who was not supposed to drink alcohol. His time in England and the United States had apparently taught him some bad habits, though. He saw me watching, and frowned.

'Got plenty of money in that briefcase?' I asked Gelson.

He smiled without humour, turning towards Hassan and away from me. That put me in my place, subtly reminding me that Hassan was the client, the man of means and the guy to be kissed up to. Well, fair enough.

'I have a general idea of what you need but you had better tell me yourself,' he said to Hassan.

'Fine,' said Hassan. He nodded towards me. 'I want to lend my friend here fifty million dollars.'

Gelson returned his attention to me, this time with more respect.

'It's not for me personally,' I said hastily.

'What's the name of the borrowing entity?' asked Gelson.

I dug out a slip of paper I had been carrying around ever since leaving Kalestian in Macau. I read from it: 'Excelsior Macau Holdings Limited.'

'Where is that incorporated?' Gelson asked.

'Grand Cayman.'

Gelson rummaged in his briefcase, and consulted some notes. He nodded. 'That's okay.'

'I know it is,' said Hassan. 'I've sent them plenty of money before; I should know their name by now.'

'I was only checking,' said Gelson, sounding a bit offended. 'What are the terms of the loan?'

I waved the same sheet of paper. It was crushed and grubby, having been in my back pocket for several days. I pushed it across the table.

'Here!'

'Is that all you have?' Gelson asked disapprovingly.

'Yes,' I said.

He looked doubtful.

Ian Calder leaned forward. 'Let me see.'

He scanned it. 'Looks like a perfectly valid loan note. Fifty million dollars at five percent, interest payable monthly, the principal due in three years with no amortisation.'

'What is my security for the loan?' asked Hassan.

'It is secured on the general assets of the corporation and its subsidiaries, so you have pretty decent protection.' He held out the sheet.

Hassan took it. He had put on gold-rimmed reading glasses, which made him look surprisingly Western. 'I see it is to be interpreted subject to the laws of the State of Delaware; good, that is my standard practice. I am satisfied.'

Gelson nodded. It may have been dawning on

him that this was not Hassan's first rodeo. But he seemed reluctant to leave at that.

'This is all very informal for a large company,' he grumbled. 'Maybe we should consult the shareholders.'

'There are no other shareholders,' I pointed out gently. 'It's a private group. Or rather, apart from Hassan there is only one shareholder, Michael Kalestian, and he's not going to object.'

After an hour discussing tedious points of detail raised by both sides, and much scribbling on yellow legal pads, we finally had a set of documents that satisfied everyone present. Calder went off to get them typed.

'One thing still bothers me,' I said.

Gelson frowned. 'Another complication?'

'Possibly, I don't know. What about the UN freeze?'

Gelson shook his head.

'That only applies to assets of the Qaddafi family.'

'Yes,' I said.

'His *legal* family,' said Gelson.

I understood what he meant. Hassan did not count as family. I might think of him as a Qaddafi, but technically he bore his mother's name, al-Manwani, not his father's.

'That's splitting hairs, isn't it?' I asked. 'Aren't you worried about the bank violating a federal order?'

Gelson shook his head. 'We've read the rules. In the opinion of our attorneys, they do not apply to illegitimate offspring.'

'But are your attorneys right?'

Gelson frowned. 'They bill at 1,000 dollars an hour; they are the most expensive firm in Manhattan.'

'Oh, then it must be okay.'

He gave me a look.

'Besides,' he said, 'the techniques that the authorities use to hunt for potentate capital are all computerised. They are programmed to look for the names of offenders.'

'So?'

'So, if they focus on the usual keywords – in this case "Qaddafi" and "Libya" – they are unlikely to spot Hassan's stuff.'

'In other words, you won't be guilty of the worst crime of all?'

'What is that?'

'Getting found out.'

'Precisely.'

'By the way, that stuff about keywords – is that why so little of the money stashed away by dictators is ever found?' I asked.

'Hush,' said Gelson.

The documents came back, adequately typed. We needed a witness, so we called in the hotel manager, a genial German who spoke good English. Everyone signed multiple copies of everything. In front of each person around the table, a small mountain of papers accumulated.

Finally we were finished.

'What happens now?' I asked.

Gelson paused in the act of shovelling documents into his briefcase.

'I get the heck out of here.'

'Back to New York?'

He nodded. 'Not a moment too soon, as far as I am concerned. I need to get back to a normal diet.'

'Just one question: when can Michael Kalestian expect his money?' I asked.

'Within a week,' said Gelson. 'I shall be travelling for the next few days, but then I'll go straight to the office. For an amount this big our treasurer has to have the original documents, so I can't handle it by e-mail.'

He disappeared in the direction of his room. He certainly looked desperate to get out of town. A few minutes later, we waved him goodbye as he climbed into a taxi for Niamey's Hamani Diori airport to catch the once-a-day plane to Paris, his Adam's apple bobbing as he wrestled with his briefcase and a big matching suitcase. God knows what he had in there.

Then we stood around for a bit. The four of us –
Hassan, Kathy, Ian Calder and I – looked at each
other.

'Where are you going next?' I asked Hassan.

'I'm thinking about that.'

'You could go back to Tripoli.' We had arranged
for a Nigerien garage to return Paragon's truck to
them and Hassan could have ridden along.

'You think? Only if I want to commit suicide by
mob.' He laughed bitterly.

'I guess that would not be very smart. What
about Egypt?'

'Things aren't much better there. Maybe I'll go to
London, I could use a bit of peace and quiet; I can be
inconspicuous there, stay out of the limelight.'

'We can all travel together, then,' said Calder. 'I
need to get back to work but I don't fancy driving
back across that bloody desert. I was planning to fly
to London, stay a few days and then go back to
Tripoli.'

'Will you have a problem with Immigration?' I
asked Hassan. 'I don't know if a Qaddafi would be all
that welcome in Britain at the moment.'

He shook his head, smiling.

He reached in a pocket and produced what
looked like an EEC passport. 'Meet Hilario Mancuso,
Italian citizen.' He held out the document. It bore a
photo of Hassan, looking dour and responsible. I

held it up to the light. It had the latest magnetic chip embedded in the back of the main page.

'Nice workmanship,' I said politely.

'It's not a forgery,' he said. 'It's the real thing.'

'How can you be an Italian citizen?' asked Calder. 'That's impossible.'

Hassan smiled. 'Nothing is impossible in Italy.'

'So, thanks to our wonderful European Community, you can travel to and from England as you please?' I asked.

'Exactly.'

'The name Hilario is not Italian, it is Spanish,' said Calder.

'It was the best I could do,' said Hassan defensively. 'You try finding an Italian name beginning with H.'

We all shared a taxi to the airport. Nobody seemed to want to spend any longer in Niamey than was necessary.

When we got there, we found Gelson, as jumpy as ever, perched on a bench in the departure lounge with his Samsung Galaxy smart phone glued to his ear, desperately trying to get a signal. It turned out that we were all on the same flight to Paris, so his hurried departure from the hotel had gained him nothing.

At Paris, we London-bound travellers were able to catch a flight on to Heathrow an hour later. But unfortunately for Gelson, the last New York flight had just left, so that he could not get out to New York until the next day. To make matters worse, all the hotels in Paris were full as it was the week of the Prêt-à-Porter fashion shows.

When last seen, the nervous banker was working his phone frantically, trying to find a bed for the night.

33

NOVEMBER 24TH, 2011

W hen we got to London I stood in line at Immigration, next to Hassan.

The authorities were phasing in a new automated system. If you had one of the newer passports, you just slid the page with the magnetic chip over an electronic reader and then posed in front of a camera. This greatly shortened the lines of people and the time they had to wait.

I was pleased about that, but a bit annoyed that Hassan, posing as Hilario Mancuso, was able to pass into the country equally easily because he too had a recent passport.

Oliver would have been even less happy if he had known what happened next.

In an air-conditioned computer centre somewhere in England where unemployment was high and wages low, electrons raced, matching the incoming passenger records against a short list of 'red flag' names placed there by such as the nameless security company with whom Danie Kruger had contracted. No human intervention occurred but, within minutes, a text message was sent to Kruger's mobile phone, notifying him that Oliver Steele had passed through Immigration at Heathrow. Minutes later, another message arrived with similar wording but this time in reference to an American female – Kathy Smith.

Kruger's heart leaped and he called the security company.

'Do you know where they are now?' he asked.

The operative consulted his screen.

'No, but I see that Steele stayed at the Hyde Park Hotel in London on several past occasions. Do you want us to send someone over there on the chance that that's where he'll be heading next?'

'Do it,' said Kruger.

Kathy and I checked into a suite at the Hyde Park Hotel, a favourite of mine, overlooking the park. At my suggestion, Ian Calder checked in there too.

After rattling around four continents in a state of barely-controlled panic, I suddenly realised that I was totally exhausted; it was a huge luxury to enjoy a solid ten hours of sleep for the first time in weeks.

Next morning, the plane trees in Hyde Park looked fresh and green, dappled with rare autumn sunshine.

I needed to call Carlton Tisch in Tortola but it was too early in the day, given the five-hour time difference. Kathy wanted to go shopping, so I strolled with her down Brompton Road to Harrods. I had worked there years ago as a student in the Christmas holidays, selling pork pies in the food hall so, for nostalgia's sake, we headed to that department.

A word to serious shoppers: if you think you are immune to sticker shock, go and look round Harrods. The produce section had giant cèpes, fragrant French fungi priced at $58 a pound. That's a lot to pay for mushrooms. There was no price tag on the caviar – best not to ask. Near the Food Halls was the wristwatch department where I spotted a Rolex for $123,000. Watch and bracelet were both gold and the watch face was so encrusted with diamonds that you could hardly tell what time it was, but it still seemed pricy for a trinket whose timekeeping, while excellent, was really not much better than a $50 Casio.

The contrast between this wealth and the wretched poverty I had seen in Central Africa got to me. I'm not quite sure what it was that I resented. I could not blame Qaddafi for the poverty in Niger.

Nor even in Libya, where the standard of living was really not bad. Maybe it was the uneven distribution of wealth and the sheer vulgarity of the elite in that part of the world. The elite strolling round Harrods were pretty vulgar, come to that.

At one pm I escaped back to the hotel and dialled Tisch on Tortola. In BVI it was eight am.

Mimi answered the phone.

Mimi and Carlton, the 25-year-old and the 60-year-old, have an unusual relationship to say the least.

Sometimes their banter is so brutal it makes me wince. One morning at breakfast, Carlton was being particularly grumpy. Mimi plonked a cup of coffee in front of him and said, 'Start the day with a smile, get it over with!' which I actually thought was quite amusing.

Carlton stared blearily at her and said, 'If you can't put up with a rich old Jew you shouldn't have married me.'

To which she replied, 'Better a rich old Jew than no Jew at all.' To me this would suggest that they were teetering on the edge of divorce but instead they both broke into broad grins and were unusually affectionate for the rest of the day.

She greeted me cheerfully. 'You've just missed him, Oliver. He's down at Soper's.'

Soper's Hole was the marina where Carlton kept his yacht, Guinevere.

'He must have left pretty early.'

'It's the Peg Leg regatta tomorrow; he's working on the boat.'

Then I remembered. November, like most months on Tortola, was a good month for sailing and tomorrow was the annual Round the Island regatta for sailors over forty or, as Carlton maintained, the cream of the crop. Carlton would be competing – he was a past winner of the event. He would be busy aboard Guinevere, testing equipment, checking supplies and talking strategy with his crew member, Charlie.

As a skipper, Carlton was not noted for his sweet nature, which was putting it mildly. Politically he voted Democrat – or said he did – but, on his yacht, he was a total dictator. He would harangue his crew, whenever he felt it necessary, with a stream of profane and violent language, reducing men twice his size to sullen silence.

As a result, not many adults would crew for him more than once. He had run through all the friends and neighbours who might conceivably be available. His wife, if invited, would smile and cite a tennis or squash game.

This left very few candidates, of whom Charlie Climpton was one. The scion of old Philadelphia money, Charlie was an expert sailor and not afraid of Carlton, so they made a good pair.

'Well, tell him I'm on my way,' I said.

'Good, he'll be pleased. He should be back in an hour.'

Pity he doesn't show it, I thought. 'Bye, Mimi.'

'Bye, love.'

I was feeling restless so I went downstairs for a stroll. I bumped into Ian Calder.

He said, 'I have to check in at my head office in the City. Want to tag along?'

'Sure,' I said.

We went out into Knightsbridge.

In the hotel's cocktail lounge, an inconspicuous man sat at the bar sipping a dry martini in a triangular glass with two olives impaled on a toothpick. He had fair hair and wore a dark grey suit, white shirt and plain red tie. He could have been an executive, a salesman or a lawyer but he was actually an employee of Danie Kruger's nameless security company. As Oliver Steele and Ian Calder left the hotel, he got up, tossed some money on the counter and followed them at a discreet distance. Once again, the information was passed on to Kruger with almost no delay.

In the street, Calder saw me looking round for a

taxi. 'Forget that,' he said, 'I don't have time to play traffic roulette. We could be stuck in a jam for hours.'

So we descended into Knightsbridge underground station.

I was about to buy a ticket but Calder stopped me. He produced a couple of Oyster Cards and waved us through the electronic turnstile. Two minutes later we were on a Piccadilly Line train travelling east. Six stops to Holborn, change to the Central line, three stops to Bank and an escalator up to the surface. There we stood, gazing at the City in all its grey glory. Elapsed time, twenty minutes.

'What's your firm like?' I asked.

'The long or the short version?'

'The short.'

'It's very big.'

'Try a bit longer.'

He grinned. 'There are only five really big accounting firms left, after numerous mergers. Levy-TeagardenHooper is one of them.'

'Is bigger better?'

'Not in my opinion. Things have changed a lot in the last fifty years. The profession has become very impersonal.'

'That doesn't sound good.'

'It isn't. In the old days before megabanks and the compensation culture, most companies were audited by firms of just ten or fifteen partners – partners in the true sense, sharing profits and losses. Partners had unlimited liability so that, if their firm screwed up badly and was sued, they could go broke.

'As a result, accountants kept a sharp eye on their clients' behaviour. When an outsider studied a company's balance sheet, he could usually believe what he was reading. But as companies got bigger, accounting firms grew also. Many reorganised themselves as Limited Liability Partnerships. It became easier for partners to place profit above ethics.

'Today an accounting firm may have hundreds of so-called partners, although only the inner circle, the so-called "equity partners" make the big decisions.'

'Are you an equity partner?'

He grinned. 'Yes and no.'

'What does *that* mean?'

'I'm a bit of a special case.'

'How so?'

'I'm one of the guys who, thanks in my case to heredity, run offices in "special" locations.'

'Such as Libya?'

'Exactly. The powers that be aren't quite sure what goes on out there. They give me plenty of rope, because I know where the bodies are buried. They also grant me a decent share of the profit from my region.'

'Nice work if you can get it,' I said. I knew that

the average salary of partners in the biggest firms was well north of half a million a year. Pounds, that is.

'Yes it is.'

He was pretty shrewd in a low-key sort of way.

While Calder visited his office, I made an espresso last in Costa and read the *Evening Standard*. Afterwards, we joined up and strolled for a while, passing the Shard, the tallest of the new London skyscrapers.

It looked like a monstrous sliver of broken glass standing upright, hence the nickname – it was famous for its jagged design as well as for nose-bleed-high rents, which had left a number of floors empty. However, its tenants did include some major prestige businesses including Teague Industries, the group headed by Quentin Teague, Lord Teague of Tangleden and a partner in crime – I use the expression humorously – of my boss Carlton Tisch.

At that moment, before our very eyes, out of the Shard walked Hassan.

'What the devil is he doing here?' I said.

'Beats me,' said Calder. 'Let's ask him.'

'No, better not,' I said. I drew Calder aside so as not to confront the young Libyan.

Moments later, he had disappeared. But it got me thinking.

I was back at the hotel an hour later when my laptop buzzed. It was Carlton calling on Skype.

'Everything shipshape?' I asked.

'Of course.'

That was a relief. Hopefully I wouldn't have to listen to a litany of excuses next day about how the wind betrayed him, the sail maker screwed up or the other guys cheated.

'I'm in London,' I said, wondering where to start. Funny how the little man always made me feel slow-witted.

'So you got it done?' he rasped.

'I guess we did, after chasing Hassan around North Africa, saving his life and not getting much thanks for it.'

'You want gratitude, get a dog. From whom did you save him?'

'Some renegade banker from South Africa who thinks he can get his grubby fingers on the same stash we are after.'

'Danie Kruger,' said Tisch.

'You know him?'

'By repute. He was a senior manager at Johannesburg Global Mining. They fired him last year – there was some kind of scandal. Now he's based in London, trying to prop up a dodgy hedge fund.'

'You think it's the same guy?'

'It has to be. He's just the sort of cowboy who would be sniffing round that pot.'

'If you say so. I didn't take to him, I must say. Although it does raise the question: if he's a cowboy, what does that make us?'

Tisch ignored the remark.

'He is a player, for all his flaws. He succeeds by fair means or foul, mostly foul, and he's always hungry for more.'

'What exactly happened at Johannesburg?'

He shrugged. 'One hears stories. Something about buying stock in companies personally and then talking Jo'burg into taking them over.'

'Is that wrong?'

'It is if you get found out. Otherwise it's just smart.'

'Do I detect a touch of envy – or at least respect?'

He frowned. 'My point is if Danie Kruger is after your money, the death of some low-level minion like this Mustafa won't stop him. He'll continue to mess with you, big time.'

'Thanks,' I said. Kruger was obviously a dangerous spoiler. I wondered if I should have got Ian Calder to shoot him in Tripoli when I had the chance. The last thing we needed was someone like that gunning for us.

'What should we do?'

'Let me see what I can find out. Hold on, I'll Skype Teague in London.'

Carlton fiddled with the controls on his laptop. He had only discovered Skype recently and delighted in setting up complicated conference calls, it was a new toy.

Finally, 'I've got it,' he said triumphantly. The screen split in half down the middle; on the right-hand side, a moonlike face grinned at me, wearing thick-lensed glasses and smoking a cigar.

Quentin Teague was a genial English peer of the realm whose occasional collaborations with Carlton rested on the shared premise that each of them liked to make a lot of money quickly. Seeing him reminded me that I had spotted Hassan emerging from the Shard where, as I knew, Teague had offices.

'Hi, Quentin,' I said.

'How are you, young man?' he boomed.

I had to smile. He was thirty – the same age as me – although rich meals and old brandy had aged him faster. We had been trainees at the same accounting firm. He was a poor student but he muddled through. Then, unexpectedly, he bought a moribund company making rubber tyres just as demand surged and the price of rubber plunged, making him look prescient rather than lucky.

The media love a lord and they latched on to him. He went on buying businesses and today he is a superstar. His friendly mug and talent for one-liners keep him constantly in the headlines. He is no analyst, but excellent contacts and a gambler's luck keep his empire growing steadily. As the tenth Baron Teague, his connections in the City rivalled Tisch's on Wall Street. The aristocrat and the self-made son of immigrants somehow work well together, despite being polar opposites in style.

'What can I do you for?' he asked jovially.

'Do you know someone called Danie Kruger?'

'Of course. Saw him at Whites the other day. Not a member of course; probably the guest of some dotty earl.'

'What do you make of him?'

'Bit of a bounder.'

Coming from Teague this was severe criticism, given his own elastic standards.

'Is he in London?' I asked, surprised.

Teague nodded. 'Are you doing business with him?'

'It's complicated,' I said.

'Zip up your pockets.'

'So I heard. Thanks for the tip.'

'You're welcome. Anything else?'

'Well . . .' I hesitated.

'Yes?'

'We were outside the Shard today. Nice digs by the way.'

He laughed. 'Costing me a fortune.'

'Out walked someone we have an interest in.'

'Who was that?'

I looked at Carlton. He spread his hands as if to say 'Why not?'

'Chap called Hassan al-Manwani.'

'Oho!' A smile spread across Teague's bland face.

'You know about him?' I asked, surprised. 'I thought he was pretty low key.'

'Not much goes on around here that I don't get wind of.'

'Odd, though,' I said. 'We thought he was more active on Wall Street.'

'Maybe, but he has a finger in a few pies over here. Most of them do.'

'Them?'

'Qaddafis. Libyans. Whoever.'

'But Hassan is different. He's, er . . .' I paused.

'Illegitimate.'

'Yes.'

Teague guffawed. 'Makes no difference, why should it?'

'I don't know. He wasn't visiting you by any chance?'

'Nope.'

'Wonder what he was up to, then.'

'Maybe he was visiting his lawyers,' said Teague.

'Lawyers?'

'Culling and March are in the building, not the biggest of law firms, but seriously exclusive. They cater to elite clients who crave confidentiality. They sport a special cohort of lawyers who dole out advice like panthers licking their paws and bill their clients megabucks.'

'Do you use them yourself?'

'Are you kidding? Far too expensive. And I couldn't push them around; I prefer a good but menial firm that give me the advice I tell them to give me.'

'Do you think that's where Hassan was going?'

'Possibly. Culling and March are heavily into the offshore stuff. You can bet your bottom dollar that Hassan has a few quid tucked away on some tropical island. Might even be Tortola, eh Carlton?'

He laughed heartily. Tisch frowned. He did not like having his personal affairs discussed, even in jest.

Kathy had reached the coffee stage after lunch in the restaurant at the Tate Gallery. She was admiring the Rex Whistler murals and thinking vaguely about going back to the hotel and booking a flight to Florida, when her mobile gave the weird semi-throttled squeak that meant it wanted her to read an incoming text message. She was half expecting to hear from

Mimi – they usually exchanged texts once or twice a week, just to chat. But it was from Oliver.

'Urgent we meet. Am at Shard at 3 Joiner Street. Be in the lobby on 20th floor at 3 pm. Will explain later. Oliver.'

That's odd, she thought. She looked at her watch – 2.05 pm. Well, she had nothing better to do so, tossing her phone in her purse, she set out.

The traffic did not look bad so she flagged down a black London taxi. The driver, an East End cockney with Mediterranean features, was chatty.

'Do you know a place called the Shard?' she asked.

'Sure. Who doesn't? Bit of an eyesore, but they're doing a lot of that nowadays, slinging up high-rise monstrosities all over the shop, ruining the skyline.' He reset the meter and the roomy cab rumbled eastwards past Hyde Park Corner and down Piccadilly.

'Last time I took a taxi, I was kidnapped,' she said cheerfully.

He laughed uncertainly. 'Not in London I hope!'

'It was in Libya.'

'You don't look any the worse for it, darling.'

That was true, she thought, but only thanks to some amazing luck. All things considered, she had a lot to be grateful for. In that spirit, she tipped him ten pounds on a twenty-pound fare and got an appreciative smile and a 'God bless!'

She mounted shallow steps to the Shard, recognising instantly how it had got its name. It was an immensely tall, thin wedge of glass and steel. To a pedestrian at ground level looking up, its slab-like sides were sharp and menacing.

'Which lift goes to the twentieth floor?' she enquired of the woman at the reception desk.

'Shouldn't think you want to go there, miss,' said a blue-uniformed porter, overhearing.

'Why not?'

He grinned. 'Because it's vacant.'

'I have an appointment there.'

'Maybe it was the twenty-second floor, not the twentieth?'

She pulled out her phone and consulted the message. 'No, it's the twentieth. See?'

She waved the little device at the porter. He shrugged good-naturedly. 'Sorry love, it's not possible. Maybe your friend meant to say twenty-two and his finger slipped.'

'Unlikely. He's an accountant. What happens on the twenty-second floor?'

'Rice and Rice; it's a consulting firm, they're in financial public relations.'

The name meant nothing to Kathy.

'Tell you what,' the porter suggested. 'Why not just pop up to level twenty-two and see if your friend is there? It won't take a moment and you can ride our super-high-speed lift; there's no charge.'

So she did.

But, as the porter had predicted, there was no sign of Oliver on the twenty-second floor. The lifts had their own small waiting area separated from the PR firm by glass doors; it had creamy leather armchairs so she sat down to wait. She checked her watch; it was exactly three o'clock.

Five minutes went by before her natural impatience got the better of her. She looked round for inspiration. In the corner was a door that presumably led to the fire staircase; it was marked 'EMERGENCY' in red.

To most people, that would have been enough discouragement, but Kathy was not most people. She slipped past the door and descended the stairs, her footsteps echoing hollowly on the iron treads. She would get to the twentieth floor or die.

Which she nearly did.

The first person she saw as she stepped off the metal staircase onto the twentieth-floor landing was Oliver. To say that he looked surprised is an understatement.

'I got your message,' he said.

'What message? I got *your* message,' she said.

He frowned. 'I sent no message.'

'Neither did I!'

They stared at each other.

'This is not good,' said Oliver quietly.

At that moment, round the corner came the massive figure of Danie Kruger. 'No, for you it's not good, my friend.'

They stared at Kruger in astonishment.

There was something off about him. His voice sounded strong and resonant but his face was haggard. There were inconsistencies, too, in his dress. He was clad appropriately for the City; the jacket of his pinstripe navy suit hung in well cut folds from his broad shoulders. His shoes were polished – they gleamed with a shine worthy of a Guards officer on parade. But his white cotton shirt was grubby round the collar in a way that only white shirts worn five days in a row can be grubby. The narrow end of his silk tie was longer than the broad end, an elementary mistake. His eyes were blood-shot and he appeared not to have shaved for several days – the growth on his cheeks and chin was not designer stubble, it was just a mess.

But there was nothing dirty or uncared for about the sleek Glock Parabellum in his right hand. It was a twin of the weapon he had aimed at Oliver in Tripoli before Oliver and Calder had humiliated and disarmed him several days ago. And this time, it looked as if he was intent on a different outcome.

They were in a temporary lobby next to the lift

shafts. They could hear the lifts swooshing up and down past their floor but not stopping. The floor had not been decorated to a tenant's specification, so the walls were simply plasterboard painted white. Smells of new paint and sawdust hung in the air. There was no air conditioning and it was sunny outside, so the atmosphere was warm and humid. Apart from the exit to the stairs, there was only one door in the plasterboard, presumably opening onto the rest of the floor.

Kruger tried the handle of the door; it was locked. He aimed his gun at the latch and fired one shot into the mechanism, then tried again. This time the door swung open easily. Using his gun like a pointer, he motioned Oliver and Kathy through, and then followed them out onto the uncarpeted expanse of the vacant floor.

The all-round view through the building's huge windows was spectacular. They were high enough up that they had a detailed panorama in an arc from Tooley Street and the south side of the Thames, from Tower Bridge to London Bridge, then the Bank of England, St Paul's, high rise additions including the Gherkin, Nelson's Column in Trafalgar Square, then Big Ben and the Houses of Parliament.

'Very impressive, but why are we here?' asked Oliver.

'To be held to account,' said Kruger. He smiled but the tendons in his neck were taut.

'Well, that's nice,' said Oliver. 'Accountability can be good. For what, may I ask?'

Kruger breathed in, nostrils quivering.

'For Tripoli.'

Oliver raised his eyebrows. 'That's an interesting way of looking at things, because I thought it was your conduct that overstepped the mark.'

Kruger waved Oliver's words aside, using his gun arm like a fly-swatter. Oliver watched the weapon intently as it swung through the air. Kruger shepherded them across the floor towards the building's western wall. Through the huge glass panels, Oliver could see Guys Hospital and the George Inn, the old galleried coaching inn where Charles Dickens had trod during his days as a clerk in the gloomy wharves of the Pool of London.

Kruger swallowed and wiped a small drop of spit off his chin. 'Hassan Qaddafi or al-Manwani or whatever he likes to call himself was my last chance of saving my fund from bankruptcy. As it is, we have just defaulted on a major credit line; the world will hear about it tomorrow and that will be the end.'

He smiled tautly. 'I am broke.'

As he spoke, he was opening a window. Most of the panels were fixed but every so often there was a full-length window that opened. A wave of sound flooded up from the street far below and he had to raise his voice to be heard.

'If that's true, why make things even worse?' asked Oliver.

Kruger waved an arm. 'You don't understand. I've staked my name and my reputation on this. How could things get any worse?'

'Whatever you're thinking of doing with that gun, it won't help,' said Oliver gently.

Kruger's shoulders slumped. 'I feel awful,' he muttered unexpectedly.

Kathy had been quiet, watching the two men. She moved instinctively towards the big South African, raising a hand in sympathy. Immediately, he snapped to attention and trained the gun on her.

'Stand still,' he barked. 'Get out there on the balcony!' Another herding gesture with the gun.

Change the subject, thought Oliver desperately. They were all standing out on the narrow balcony now. Get him talking. Do anything to interrupt his momentum.

'Ever heard of the Skyscraper Index?' he asked brightly.

'What?'

'It's an index suggested by a banking analyst a few years ago. It linked the building of very tall skyscrapers with the onset of financial disaster.'

'I don't have time for nonsense.'

'Oh, it's not nonsense,' said Oliver quickly. 'There's a sound economic principle behind it. Investing in skyscrapers tends to reach its peak when the business cycle is close to exhausting itself and a recession is imminent. For example, in New York, the Empire State Building and the Chrysler Building were launched shortly before the great crash of 1929.'

'What of it?'

'Well, there's a parallel with your own case, wouldn't you say? I mean, here we are in a tall skyscraper, and now we hear that your hedge fund has collapsed. It's a nice comparison.'

'Shut up, do you hear?' Kruger gritted the words.

Oliver ignored him. 'Some members of the Wall Street community – bankers, brokers or whatever – supposedly climbed out on a ledge and jumped off.'

'I said be quiet.' Kruger was shouting now, but his anger seemed to have drained his energy. His manner had gone from bullying to self-pitying; his shoulders slumped with what looked like resignation.

'I often wondered about those stories,' said Oliver. 'You know, how much truth there was in them. Had the jumpers really nothing left to live for, stuff like that?'

Kruger stared silently at him.

'What do you think, Danie? Did things get that bad?'

'I don't know, I haven't read up on it.'

'You know what?' said Oliver. 'I think they were right. There comes a time when the best thing you can do is just go ahead and jump. It solves everything.'

Kruger shook his head but said nothing. The gun was pointed at Oliver's chest but the hand holding it wavered slightly.

'Go ahead, Danie. Last year you were fired. This year you're broke. You won't get a third chance. Go ahead and do it,' Oliver said quietly. The humorous tone of voice had gone, replaced by a low, almost hypnotic monotone that Kathy, although she knew him well enough, had not heard before.

Kruger gave Oliver a long, silent look. Then he leaned slowly back. He was a big man and the rail was only waist-high to him. Raising the pistol he pressed it against his temple and pulled the trigger.

His body toppled slowly backwards over the rail and disappeared. Kathy made to move forward and look down but Oliver pulled her away.

'Time to leave. And remember this clearly: we were never here,' he said.

They took the stairs down. Twenty storeys is a lot of stairs and it was ten minutes before they slipped unobtrusively out of the back entrance to the building. Round the corner there was a commotion involving ambulances and police that were arriving to deal with the body in a pinstripe suit that had just materialised, spattering blood on the pavement.

Walking fast, they reached Borough High Street, several blocks away, and then paused.

'Taxi,' shouted Kathy as they stood on the corner.

Oliver restrained her again. 'We must be anonymous. *Really* anonymous,' he said.

They walked across London Bridge and up King William Street to Bank station where they caught a train back to their hotel.

'I need a stiff drink,' said Kathy up in the suite.

'Good idea,' said Oliver. He ordered from Room Service.

A few minutes later, feeling stronger, Kathy confronted Oliver. 'You talked that wretched man into killing himself.'

'Yes, I did.'

'Doesn't that make you feel a little bit bad?'

He nodded. 'Yes, but not nearly as bad as the alternative.

34

NOVEMBER 25TH, 2011

It was all over bar the shouting, or so it seemed. My mission to finance Kalestian's casino was accomplished. The bad guys were dead. I should have been happy.

But I was not; I had a leaden feeling behind the eyes. It was like when you wake up in the morning and the sun is shining and you should be raring to leap out of bed and greet the day, but all you really want to do is roll over and go back to sleep again, because life sucks.

I know it wasn't anything physical, because I swallowed twice the recommended number of headache pills and that didn't help. And it wasn't depression, because I never get depressed.

Okay, it was depression.

And I knew why: too many deaths. And for what? To help some businessman open a casino.

Mustafa's death was sad but in a way predictable. He had operated in a violent arena, fought and lost, and paid the price. Connor had shot him because he had to. Not my fault.

Kruger's suicide, though, was down to me. Again it had been a choice between him or me, but it had tapped into a side of my character that I would rather not have had to confront. It had been disconcertingly easy to find and use the weapon – a few carefully chosen words – that pushed him, literally, over the edge.

And his toppling into space had been a dreadful way to exit.

But I couldn't afford to be fastidious. It was a role I had chosen – a hired hand doing what I had to do for money. Not what I had in mind when I graduated with distinction from Oxford and went into accountancy, but life tosses you curves and, as long as I stayed in the game, stuff would happen. My only choice was whether to quit or suck it up. And I wasn't ready to quit.

So now all that remained was to report back to Carlton and collect my cheque.

35

NOVEMBER 26TH, 2011

Next morning, I took a taxi to Victoria, caught the shuttle to Gatwick and boarded a British Airways Boeing 777 for the long flight to Antigua, nine hours of serious boredom.

In Antigua I had to cool my heels for several hours before boarding a small propellor-driven aircraft operated by LIAT, Leeward Island Air Transport, known locally, and not affectionately, as 'Leave Island Any Time'. After intermediate stops at St Kitts and St Maarten, I reached Tortola's Beef Island Airport well behind schedule.

There I rented a Jeep and drove for forty minutes from one end of Tortola to the other, swinging through vertiginous corkscrew and hairpin bends in the pitch dark. As I bumped along the final potholed track to Spring Point, I caught myself wondering how much longer I wanted to go on doing this stuff.

It was close to midnight when I finally reached the wrought iron gate to Carlton's driveway and punched in the combination. It swung open slowly and I had arrived.

Nobody was up. As usual, all the full-length windows were open and the doors unlocked – this was Tortola, not London or New York. A yellow Post-it Note on the fridge said, 'You are in the Camellia bedroom. Tread quietly. Mimi.'

The weather next morning was gorgeous as usual, 84 degrees with low humidity. A light breeze rustled the palms and a few puffy clouds framed the blue sky.

But the bad news was quick in coming.

Every morning, Carlton reads the *Wall Street Journal* on his computer. He called me in, looking grim.

'Read that,' he said, pointing to the screen.

The Goldberg Freilich investment fund containing Hassan's money had gone belly-up. Broke.

I read on in a state of shock.

It had something to do with interest rates. They

had suddenly moved the wrong way. As a result, Hassan and his fellow investors in the same fund had been wiped out. The confident line that Jim Gelson had fed me in a Wall Street coffee shop about Goldberg Freilich's brilliant investment skills now looked pretty threadbare. His claim that they had doubled Hassan's money may have been true temporarily, but only on paper, and now it had been stood on its head.

I tried to process that.

'Did you find out anything else?' I asked.

'About what you would expect. Goldberg Freilich are frantically downplaying the fact that they screwed up.'

'Wow,' I said intelligently.

Carlton looked thoughtful. 'Something like this has happened before, to Goldman Sachs in 2007. According to the *Wall Street Journal*, they were appointed to manage 1.3 billion dollars by Libya's sovereign wealth fund. They invested it in trades that lost 98 percent of their value; in other words they pretty much lost the lot.'

'The Libyans must have been delighted,' I said.

He laughed.

'Two senior executives of the bank had to fly to Tripoli to explain. They faced an inquisition led by the deputy chairman of the fund, one Mustafa Zarti, an associate of Saif al-Islam, the Colonel's son and then heir-apparent. According to a witness, Zarti went ballistic, cursing and threatening. The executives were so scared that Goldman Sachs hired special security to protect them until they could get safely out of Libya.'

'How did it all turn out?'

'Inconclusive. Talks went to and fro and then fell apart. At one point, Goldman Sachs is rumoured to have offered Libya new preference shares to the value of 5 billion dollars in exchange for 3.7 billion dollars in cash. It would have got the Libyans their 1.3 billion dollars back – sort of – and incidentally provided the bank with some useful liquidity. Talk about chutzpah. It would also have made Libya the largest single investor in Goldman Sachs at the time.'

'But the Arab Spring intervened?'

'Correct. Everything stalled.'

I was still pondering what I had heard.

'About Hassan – do you think he has other money?' I asked Carlton.

The blue eyes narrowed in his thin face. He stared at me.

'Outside the fund? Perhaps. You occasionally show flashes of intelligence.'

'I try.'

'Well, it's possible. Hassan is said to be pretty

shrewd with his investing, the Goldberg debacle aside.'

'So?'

'So he may have other reserves.'

'I guess I'd better talk to him,' I said.

'Do you know how to get in touch with him?'

I sighed heavily. 'I haven't the faintest idea.'

36

NOVEMBER 29TH, 2011

As soon as he got home from his trip to Macau, Larry Franklin phoned his attorney, Max Guberman in Miami.

Max was a pale, fleshy-faced man in a black silk suit, white shirt and dark tie. He looked a bit like a high-class undertaker. He wore gold-rimmed glasses, had very little facial expression and never took a moral point of view about anything. He took the call, sitting behind a big desk in a twentieth-storey office on Brickell Avenue with a panoramic view of the Rickenbacker Causeway, Key Biscayne and the blue Atlantic beyond.

'I have a job for you,' Larry said.

'Any travel involved?' Max asked warily. He knew Larry of old.

'Some.'

'Ah.' Max did not like to leave Miami.

He led a comfortable bachelor existence there, as a tax and immigration lawyer. He had a very nice lifestyle, derived from a stable of wealthy, living-on-the-edge clients. Or even over the edge – Max did not look too hard as long as they paid their bills. And non-payment was never a problem with Larry Franklin. Larry had always been good for it, ever since the old days when he had still been plain Frankie Leon.

Max had helped bail Leon out of jail down in the Keys, when he had been arrested on suspicion of murder. An hour later, Leon had boarded a high-powered speedboat and disappeared from view. Some people said Max should have realised that, the minute Leon made bail, he would skip the country, seeing that a lot of Max's income came from defending drug dealers subject to extradition proceedings. But it was the sort of thing nobody could prove for sure, and it never bothered Max – one of his strengths was the ability to sleep like a baby when he had just done something outrageous.

So Larry's credit was good with Max and when he said, 'I want you to go to Macau for me, there's a flight this evening,' Max swallowed his reluctance and went and packed a bag.

'This is all very mysterious,' said Michael Kalestian as they shook hands in Macau.

'Sorry my telephone call was a bit vague,' said Max, shooting his cuffs. The black suit worked in Miami but in the world of casinos, he realised, he looked a bit formal.

To compensate, he assumed an ingratiating smile. Then, since he didn't want to be away from home any longer than he had to, he came straight to the point.

'I represent an individual who wishes to invest in the gaming business. However, he has no previous experience in the industry.'

This was not strictly true. As Frankie Leon, Larry had run a major internet gaming website. But that did not count, Max reasoned, because it was a website, not a casino.

'He wishes to associate with a partner who has proven expertise in the field. And, of course, exemplary character.'

'Of course.' Michael nodded. He could hardly believe his luck. Was this real? 'I'm curious, how did you hear about me?'

Max nodded. 'A fair question. All I can tell you is that my client did his due diligence and has prepared a list of exceptionally well qualified partners. You are on that list.'

The more he lied the easier it got, and the more sincere his demeanour.

That's not good, thought Kalestian, there was competition.

He assumed his best nonchalant manner.

'Well, I'm flattered to be on your client's list. And it's true there have been a few minor cost over-runs. But I'm talking to various people. We're very close to finalising with one party in particular.'

Max nodded. He could bluff as well as the next man. He snapped his briefcase shut, and stood up. 'That's too bad then. Guess I've had a wasted visit.'

Even walking slowly, he had almost reached the door before Kalestian said, 'Wait!'

Max turned enquiringly.

'No reason why I shouldn't hear what your client has to say,' Kalestian allowed.

Max just happened to have a contract in his briefcase.

Michael read a couple of pages, then looked up. 'I'll have my attorney give this the once-over,' he said encouragingly.

Max's face fell. 'Oh, that's too bad. See, I'm on my way to meet with the other folks on the list. I would really have loved to hold things open for you, but unfortunately . . .'

And so on in the same vein. In the end, desperate for money, Michael signed the contract without showing it to his lawyer, truly a rookie mistake. Max Guberman grabbed the signed document and hurried back to Florida before Michael could change his mind.

Which is how Michael Kalestian and Larry Franklin became partners.

37

The Macau Excelsior was finally ready to open, and I was in Macau having a celebratory lunch with Michael Kalestian in Chateau Chop Chop, an outrageously expensive 'Oriental Steakhouse' on the second floor of the new hotel.

'How do you feel?' I asked Michael. 'You must be pretty pleased.'

'I feel like this is really it,' Michael said.

We were well into a second bottle of expensive claret. I had managed to keep pace with him over the first bottle but he had established a clear lead now, and was looking pretty mellow.

Later that day, 700 Chinese visitors, assembled by a tour group consolidator called the Precious Pearl Junket Company, would swarm into the ornate gaming rooms in a massive influx of eager humanity and their money. The dealers would smile warmly and start handing out blackjack and pai gow chips in denominations from ten dollars all the way up to 1,000.

The warm smile was important. In some casinos, the dealers are impassive and devoid of conversation but Michael did not run his business like that, he set great store by the personal touch. In those other grimly efficient places, dealers were trained to deal the cards as fast as possible so that the house could win as fast as possible, but that was not Michael's way.

He breathed deeply and beamed at me.

'People say the Chinese are inscrutable but that is nonsense, they get just as excited as anyone else by a big win, and just as downhearted when the luck drains out of the bottom of the horseshoe. A friendly smile is the least they deserve.'

He really wasn't a bad guy, I thought to myself. A bit crude, not the ice-cold investor his father had been but almost as successful in his own bumbling, good-natured way.

He grinned sympathetically. 'Sorry you weren't able to earn a commission, what with Qaddafi's money falling through and so on.'

'That's okay,' I said, gritting my teeth. I could really have used that money.

'That's business. Win some, lose some. The business of life,' he said.

'You're so right.' I tried to sound as if I really meant it.

But there was something I really wanted to ask him.

'You were very reticent about where you got the funds to finish this place.'

He shook his head silently.

'Can I have one guess?' I asked.

'That depends.'

'On what?'

'On who you think it is. I may or may not comment.'

'Is it Stanley Ho?'

'No.'

'Is it his daughter, Pansy?'

'That would be two guesses. You're only allowed one.'

I looked at my watch. 'Fair enough. Well, I have a plane to catch. Thanks for an excellent steak.'

He waved generously. 'Have a really great trip home.'

There was no way that twenty-four hours on a series of aeroplanes would be really great, even with the flat beds in Cathay Pacific's business class, but I smiled. It was hard not to share his euphoria.

I was on the point of leaving when a shadow fell across the table. We had company.

It was a strange looking man.

Yellow-blond hair, artificial suntan, chiselled Roman nose. An athlete's face, but not an athlete's body. There was an unappealing softness about the chest and belly, under the sporty polo shirt and khaki slacks.

I did not recognise him, but he stared as if he knew me. And there was more than just recognition, a flash of antagonism perhaps, followed by some kind of amusement.

The look was gone in a second; obviously it was not me that he had come to see. He gave Kalestian a big smile and held out a hand.

'Michael, sir?'

'Yes?'

'Larry Franklin.'

Kalestian looked surprised and not too pleased.

'I thought you said you were not going to be here?'

'Well, we say things sometimes, don't we? Then we change our mind.'

'What do you want?'

Franklin produced a thin sheaf of papers tied together with pink ribbon. It looked like some kind of legal document.

'Well, I thought it was about time we had a little

chat. It looks as though things here will be profitable right off the bat, so we need to discuss how to handle the cash flow from our casino.'

'My casino.'

'Excuse me?'

'You said "our casino". It's my casino.'

'Of course it is.' Franklin smiled.

'Well then?'

'You have invested much more than me, of course. But our contract does give me an equal say in how surplus cash is distributed. And it just so happens that a need has cropped up.'

'What sort of need?'

Franklin's smile froze. It was as if a shutter came down over his face. Being questioned aggressively was clearly not something he appreciated.

'Something of a personal nature. Not that you need to know, my friend. According to our agreement, either partner can withdraw funds as long as he approves an equal withdrawal to be made by the other party.'

'I don't need a withdrawal.'

'But I do.'

'I did not agree to anything like that!'

'I think you did.' Franklin made a big show of leafing through the contract. 'Page eleven. Near the bottom.'

'Let me see that.'

Kalestian snatched the document. He pored over it, paging through to the end, then looked up.

'This is not signed!'

'Of course not, it's a copy. The original is with my attorney in Miami and that *is* signed, very much so.'

It seemed tactless to hang around, so I left them going at it hammer and tongs.

On my way to the airport I reflected that I was well out of the affair. It was weird to be feeling sorry for someone as wealthy as Michael but, just then, I felt for him. It must be like getting married and then finding out on the honeymoon that your bride just wanted to get her hands on your money.

On the long flight home, I recalled what Carlton had said when I showed disappointment about Hassan's lack of thanks for our helping him in the desert. Along the lines of 'If you want gratitude, get a dog'. Michael, having chosen to lie down with a dog, was now discovering the fleas.

I was surprised how at ease I felt. I might not have made any money, but I had avoided the fleas.

EPILOGUE

NEW YORK

When Hacksaw Harry Hartmann's shenanigans with Mercury Metals were exposed, what happened next was predictable:

Harry and his wife were arrested and indicted for fraud. Bail was set at a million dollars each, which they paid in cash immediately. Stu Goldberg, too, was caught in the net although there was some muttering in Wall Street watering holes that an ambitious Attorney General had only included him to grab more headlines. Also indicted was one Lou Brass, Financial Controller for the group's stock-broking division.

Some interesting transactions between Mercury and Goldberg Freilich were uncovered. They had started in a small way and then got bigger and bigger. No cash settlement between the companies ever occurred, so a major account receivable had built up in the Goldberg balance sheet.

Controller Brass, who always did what Hartmann told him, had split each transaction into several smaller parts, assigning each part to a separate area of the balance sheet in a half-hearted attempt at concealing them from the company's auditors. The ruse worked for a while, but the truth was bound to come out sooner or later. Hacksaw Harry, like Mr Micawber, always believed that something would turn up but nothing did and finally the bad news, leaked by me to Freddie Parrott and from Freddie to a journalist friend, hit the fan.

The Attorney General struck a deal with Brass – immunity in exchange for his testimony against Hartmann. It was the icing on the cake, making Hartmann's conviction a virtual certainty.

Meanwhile, the wheels were turning in another case – the prosecution of Hartmann for the murder of Hansi van Rensburg. Here, although to me he was obviously as guilty as hell, the case was weaker. There was no weapon, and no eyewitness except for me, who had never consciously met Hartmann. I had only glimpsed a man of his height and build on the stairs. Still, it was enough for a grand jury to indict him.

At that point the media really hit their stride –

money *and* a glamorous dead girl, what could be better? The Hartmann mansion in Scarsdale was besieged by journalists. Viola Hartmann coped surprisingly well – she found being a celebrity rather exciting – but for Hacksaw Harry the shame was too much. He had been so in love with his own hard-charging image that, after it evaporated, life had little meaning. He had a heart attack and died a week before the fraud trial was due to begin.

At that point, much of the wind went out of the sails of the prosecution. They had fairly weak cases against naive Viola and slippery Stu and little interest in hounding Lou Brass, so they more or less called it a day.

Goldberg Freilich's audit firm was a major loser; it was flooded with lawsuits from resentful fund managers who had suffered when the stock tanked. The firm was fired by many of its audit clients and then disintegrated, so the Big Five became the Big Four. Many of the same accountants are back working for their former competitors now though, earning nice salaries for similar work, so their mortgages are okay.

LIBYA (in real life)

Once Qaddafi had been defeated, the boot in Libya was on the other foot. Disturbing stories surfaced about the torture and ill treatment of suspected pro-Qaddafi loyalists by the rebels.

The humanitarian aid organisation, *Doctors Without Borders* announced that it was suspending its work in prisoner detention centres. Its Director stated: 'Patients were brought to us in the middle of interrogation for medical care, in order to make them fit for more interrogation. This is unacceptable. Our role is to provide medical care to war casualties and sick detainees, not to repeatedly treat the same patients between torture sessions.'

In March 2014, twenty eight months after the death of Muammar Qaddafi, the Libyan Government announced that al-Saadi, the colonel's football-playing son, had been extradited from Niger where the forty-year-old playboy had been living in a state guesthouse after fleeing across the Sahara, possibly along the same road as his fictional half-brother. He was accused of shooting protesters and various other crimes. Internet pictures showed him in custody, having his head shaved.

The disposition of the Qaddafi family at that point was as follows:

Moatassem and **Saif al-Arab** (sons): Killed
Saif al-Islam and **al-Saadi** (sons): In prison

Khamis (son): Several reports of death but none confirmed

Safiya (wife), **Ayesha** (daughter), **Muhammad** and **Hannibal** (sons): In Oman after being granted political asylum.

Libya continued to seek the return of Qaddafi family members and officials from neighbouring countries, using money as leverage. They persuaded Mauritania to extradite Qaddafi's intelligence chief; soon afterwards, Libya donated $200 million 'to help the Mauritanian economy'.

What became of the women of Qaddafi's Amazonian Guard? Lurid tales abound, contradictory and mostly unverifiable. Some fought loyally for Qaddafi; others turned against him. Some were tortured, raped and shot by rebel forces whose brutality easily matched that attributed to the late Brother Leader. Most of them swiftly exchanged their smart uniforms for the anonymous robes of traditional Muslim women, often with the badge of the NTC, the National Transitional Council, attached.

The fictional Rhianna al-Manwani escaped to England, helped by her son.

MACAU

Michael Kalestian does not enjoy dealing with

his creepy partner Larry, but the casino makes a lot of money so he is learning to live with it.

LONDON

Hassan is living quietly in South Kensington as Hilario Mancuso, the name on his Italian passport. He's spotted now and then at the Ivy, or driving out to Oxfordshire for lunch at Le Manoir with one blonde or another. The source of his funds is a bit of a mystery but he's clearly not short of a buck.

THE END

You can find more *Oliver Steele and Kon Feaver* thrillers at the store or sales page where you bought this book, or at www.grahamtempest.com

Graham Tempest is a British-American author who divides his time between Oxfordshire and Florida.

GrahamTempest.com